D0395038

INVINCIBLE

ALSO BY AMY REED

Beautiful

Clean

Crazy

Over You

Damaged

INVINCIBLE

Amy Reed

Katherine Tegen Books is an imprint of HarperCollins Publishers.

Invincible

www.epicreads.com

Library of Congress Control Number: 2014949411
ISBN 978-0-06-229957-4

Typography by Michelle Gengaro-Kokmen
15 16 17 18 19 CG/RRDH 10 9 8 7 6 5 4 3 2 1
❖
First Edition

For Elouise and Brian, who make me whole

THEN.

one.

"LET'S GO TO THE CAFETERIA," STELLA SAYS. SHE IS RESTless. She is always restless.

Unlike everyone else in here, she is not in pajamas. Every day, without fail, she puts on her black skinny jeans, big black boots, a thick coat of red lipstick, and her signature black fedora with the peacock feather sticking out the side. Even though all we ever do is sit in each other's rooms. Even though we're not allowed to leave hospital grounds. Even though the only people she talks to voluntarily are me and Caleb and Dan, the Child Life Specialist, and none of us could care less what she looks like.

"Are you hungry?" Caleb asks. His pajamas have soccer balls on them. Mine are pink with white hearts. The left leg is cut off to make room for my white plaster cast, decorated with Sick Kid autographs.

"No, I'm not hungry." Stella groans. "I just need to get out of here. Aren't you guys going crazy? How can you not be going crazy?" She's like a caged animal. Pretty soon, she's going to start gnawing on the metal bars of my bed. She was like this even in Outpatient, even when she knew she was going to get to leave in a few hours.

"My parents are going to be here any minute," I say. "I should stay."

"Have you asked them yet about adopting me?"

"But you have parents, Stella," Caleb says. He has a hard time with sarcasm. Stella has diagnosed him with mild Asperger's in addition to the brain cancer we already know about.

"I'm going to get legally emancipated," she says. "Just as soon as we get this whole cancer thing figured out. I'm only still their daughter because I'm using them for their health insurance. God, Evie, I am so sick of your room."

We've been spending a lot of time in my room. And by "my room," I mean this particular room during this particular stay, which is going on two weeks now, my longest yet. There have been countless identical rooms over the past year, some in this part of the cancer floor, some in the super-duper sterile prison part of the floor when my white blood cell count was zero. It's a little hard for me to get around right now because I just got surgery and my leg is in a cast, so I can't just hop out of bed whenever I feel like it. Not that many kids on the cancer floor do much hopping.

I may seem lucky for getting one of the few single rooms, but everyone here knows they're reserved for the hopeless cases so some other poor kid doesn't have to deal with a dead roommate.

This one is pretty much the same as every other room I've had, so many by now that I've lost count, but half as big. I wasn't even here a night before Mom put up the same sad decorations as my last long stay, to make it "feel more like home." No number of family photos or teddy bears or bouquets of flowers will ever make this feel like home. All they do is confirm that I'm going to be here for too long.

"We could go to the teen lounge," Caleb says. "We could play a game."

"The teen lounge doesn't have any windows," Stella says.

"Turn the TV to the Discovery Channel," I say. "It'll be just like looking out the window, except you'll be in Africa or underwater or something."

"Or it'll be some reality show about Amish prostitutes or morbidly obese dwarfs who talk in tongues."

"That's TLC," I say. "The morbidly obese dwarves."

"You two are no help. Plus Dan might be lurking in the teen lounge and he'll just try to get me to talk about my feelings."

"It's good to talk about your feelings," Caleb says. "Dan says it'll make you sicker if you keep things bottled up inside."

"When have you known me to keep things bottled up inside?"

"Good point."

"You guys don't have to stay here," I say. "You can go do something without me. I'm fine by myself."

"Oh, Evie," Stella says. "Don't go acting all heroic. We're not going to leave you in here all by yourself."

"Really, it's okay."

"Can you stop thinking about everyone else for once and just admit that you can't live without me?"

"I want to watch the football game," Caleb says, grabbing my remote and turning on the TV.

"I hate you," Stella says, but she doesn't move. There aren't a whole lot of other options for us as far as activities go. Watching football in a cramped hospital room may not be everybody's idea of a good time, but it could be worse. It could always be worse.

I first met Stella eight months ago, when I was going in for my third round of chemo. It was her first and she wasn't happy about it, which I could tell because she was climbing the eight-foot-tall stuffed giraffe outside the outpatient oncology center while her mother and a security guard were trying to talk her down. Her mom was actually more like trying to scream her down in Mandarin, but neither approach was working.

She held on to that poor giraffe's head, screaming bloody murder until her mom finally managed to pull her down, and as she fell to the floor she made one last dramatic proclamation, calling everyone "heartless bloody dickholes." Parents covered their kids' ears; her mom swiped her on the side of her face with the back of her hand, and I decided Stella was both the most beautiful and bravest person I had ever seen in my life. She was showing all the fear and fury I felt but could never let out. She wasn't pretending to be anything she wasn't.

I walked up to her as she sat under the giraffe, sobbing. I

sat down next to her and said, "Hi, I'm Evie." Her makeup was smeared but that somehow made her even more glamorous. "Are you getting chemo?" I said.

"Yeah."

"Me too. It's not that bad."

"I'm going to lose my hair," she whimpered. "I can't lose my hair." She had beautiful hair. It was long and straight and perfect. She had thick bangs that came all the way down to her eyes. It was rock-star hair.

"You could get a wig," I said. My hair had already started thinning. Everyone assured me I was still beautiful, as if that was the most important thing for me to worry about.

"Wigs are for old ladies."

"What about a hat?"

She thought about that for a minute. "A hat could work," she said. "I could totally rock a hat."

We walked into the clinic together, our mothers following close behind.

My mom tried valiantly to befriend Stella's mom, but Mrs. Hsu was cold and suspicious right away. She still is, even after all this time. Families get to know each other well when their kids are in and out of the hospital all the time, when they're sitting together for hours on end in the injection clinic. They hug; they bake each other things and buy each other Christmas presents; they cry for each other's children. But not Stella's parents. They are always off to the side, silent, miserable, judging, and alone.

Stella and I got chemo that first time in adjacent rooms. After a few minutes of lying there while the poison pulsed through the portacath tube drilled in my chest, I heard a knock on my wall. I knocked back. She started a series of steady, measured taps. I thought maybe it was Morse code. I didn't know Morse code. Then I started counting and noticed a pattern that repeated itself after seven clusters of taps. You have a lot of time to kill when you're getting chemo for eight to ten hours.

I pulled out my phone and dialed what I counted. She picked up on the first ring.

From that moment forward, Stella was my secret best friend. By secret, I mean only in the cancer world, the hospital world, the world of Sick Kids. Stella and I never see each other outside this world. In the other world, the world of the well, we are other people. We are people who would not mix. In the other world, she's in an all-girl punk band and I'm a cheerleader. I mean *was*. Past tense. I'm not really sure what I am now.

In the other world, I already have a best friend. Kasey Wexler-Beene has had that title since she walked up to me on the first day of kindergarten with her bouncing blond pigtails and said, "Do you want to be friends?" We've been inseparable ever since. Until the cancer, that is. How can friends be anything but separable when one has cancer and spends most of her time either in the hospital or at home recovering from being in the hospital? How could a relationship not change when one is dying and the other is not, when one is halfway in another world that no amount of love or history or devotion will ever help the other understand?

But she tries, and I love her for that. At first, a lot of my friends joined her when she'd visit, either piling into the living room while I recuperated on the couch, or even coming to the hospital when I was too sick to go home. I could be hurt by their absence now, but I understand, and I don't blame them. They have their lives to live, and they shouldn't waste them sitting around watching me get sicker, and honestly it's a relief to have fewer people to smile and pretend for. But Kasey is forever loyal. She still comes to visit with my parents or my boyfriend, Will. But over the past few months, especially since I've gotten sicker and stopped going to school entirely, it's gotten harder and harder to find things to talk about, harder to find things we have in common. What do you talk about when one person's life has stopped and the other's has kept moving forward?

In some ways, I've already said good-bye to Kasey. I've already said good-bye to my family. They may not know it yet, they may think I'm still with them, but I've been drifting away for a long time now. The world of the sick has been claiming me a little more each day, with each round of blood work, with every CT scan and PET scan and bone scan, every biopsy and bone marrow aspiration, every surgery, every chemo injection, every radiation treatment, every blood transfusion, every pain med, every hospitalization. After a year of this, it's a miracle I still know how to speak to people outside the hospital. It has been so long since I belonged in their world, no matter how hard they try to keep me in it, no matter how hard I try to stay.

But I haven't said good-bye to Will yet. I can't. Even though

I know it's selfish, I can't let him go. I can't release him. Some part of me still believes we can make it through this together, that our love is strong enough to work miracles. I can't imagine going anywhere without him, even death, wherever or whatever that is. I have no idea what's going to happen to me after I die. I don't even know how to begin imagining it. People keep telling me it's going to be quiet and peaceful, that it will be a place I can be forever happy, but I don't believe them. The only thing I know for sure is it will be a place without Will. Wherever I go, I have to leave him behind. And how can that be paradise? What's the point of heaven if the person you love most in the world isn't there?

two.

"ARE YOU SURE YOU'RE OKAY?" MOM SAYS FOR THE MILlionth time, her eyebrows furrowed in her now permanent Worry Face. "We don't have to do this."

"Of course I'm okay," I say with as big a smile as I can squeeze out of my face.

Of course I'm not okay. I'm seventeen and I've been sitting in Oakland Children's Hospital for the past two weeks with a broken leg, and now I'm waiting for test results that will tell me how close I am to death. I just watched my parents beg the evil Nurse Moskowitz for permission to take me outside so I can breathe real air instead of the toxic stuff that circulates around the hospital. "It's not the smartest idea," Moskowitz said with her signature squint and pursed lips. "But I suppose it's safe as long as she's bundled up."

That was today's little victory. Hooray! Now my parents and my sister, Jenica, get to wheel me around the hospital's sad excuse for a courtyard, which isn't much more than a few picnic tables and paved circle around a tuft of grass next to the helicopter landing pad. I made my face placid as a medical assistant moved me from my bed to a wheelchair, an arduous process of disconnecting my IV and fluids, transferring and hiding my catheter and pee bag, and trying to not drop the giant broken log that used to be my leg. So yeah, I am the exact opposite of okay. But no one needs to know that. They have enough to deal with already.

I didn't really want to go for this "walk" in the first place, but I played along because we have to do something other than sit in my depressing room while we wait for Dr. Jacobs to show up with my test results. So now here we are, huddling beneath a gray blanket of winter drizzle, breathing the "real air" of a city with one of the worst rates of pediatric asthma in the country. Mom is trying hard to keep her smile, so I am too, and so is Dad. Smiling to keep each other smiling. That's what we do. It's our special family talent. Jenica taps away at her phone, too preoccupied to play this game as devotedly as us. We have become experts at ignoring the elephant in the room, even when he follows us outside, even when he's clomping around us and blowing his trunk for attention, even though he's been with us for so long he's practically part of our family, our loyal pet.

"Look at those daffodils," I say.

"They really do a nice job with the landscaping here," Dad says. "It really brightens the place up."

"I was thinking I could bring in ice cream tomorrow," Mom

chirps. "Maybe get some of those weird flavors you like at Tara's? What was that last one you tried? Curry?"

"Saffron," I say.

"Do you think Caleb and Stella would like some too? I'll get a bunch. We can have a little ice-cream party."

"It's freezing," Jenica says. "Nobody wants ice cream."

I don't tell them that even this pale winter light is too bright for me, that even with the buffer of my pain pills, it feels like a million tiny screws are boring through my eyes into my brain. I can feel the wet air seeping through my clothes. I try not to shiver. I don't want to tell anyone I'm cold. I don't want to make anyone worry more than they already are.

Someone has to make conversation. Someone has to help my poor mother out. "Did you hear from Stanford?" I say to Jenica.

"Not yet," she says, finally looking up from her phone. "Probably have a few weeks until they send out their letters. I feel good about it, though."

"And if you don't get in, there's always Berkeley, right?" Mom says. "Or even UC Davis?"

Jenica snorts. "I am *not* going to Davis. You can't be serious, Mom." Oh yeah, this is why we don't talk.

I can't help myself: "Don't forget, some of us aren't even going to get to go to college."

"Oh god!" Mom exhales.

"Girls!" Dad says, and wraps his arm protectively around Mom. She leans into him with all her weight, shoving her face into his chest, as if blocking out the world will make it stop hurting.

"I'm sorry, Mom." I am sorry. I didn't mean to hurt her, just Jenica. But even Jenica didn't deserve that. They're already hurting so much.

Mom returns to us, the brave smile plastered back on her face. "It's okay, honey." She takes my hand. "Oh, Evie, you're so cold!"

"I'm okay."

"Let's go back in," Jenica says. At least we can agree on something.

Neither Mom nor Dad seems to want to move. As miserable as this is, they don't want it to be over. These small moments outside my hospital room are some of the few things still connecting me to their world. No one talks about it, but there's always the possibility that any of these could be my last trip outside. My last chance breathing air outside the hospital. Forever.

I think I'm going to puke.

"Are you okay?" Dad says.

"I'm fine," I say again. Again and again and again and again, even though it will never be true. I don't mention the headache that has morphed into a full-blown migraine strong enough to tear through my painkiller haze.

The rain starts in earnest. The sky darkens. Jenica is the only one brave enough to turn around and start walking back to the hospital.

Nurse Moskowitz meets us at the elevator, all frowns and cold, efficient hands. "I should never have agreed to this," she says, shaking her head as she pushes my mom out of the way to take control of the wheelchair. "Evie's in no condition to be out in the rain."

Mom helps me get into dry pajamas while the others wait in the hall. Moskowitz takes my temperature, and it's barely above ninety-six. "Too low," she scolds Mom, and turns the heat up in my room. All I want to do is sleep, but that's when Dr. Jacobs arrives.

"Doctor," my dad says, shaking his hand. Everyone's sitting up a little straighter. Even Jenica has put her phone down and is paying attention.

"I think I have a migraine," I say.

"It's a little early for your pain pills," Moskowitz says.

"It's all right," Dr. Jacobs says. "She can have them now." He's usually such a stickler about meds. The news he's here to deliver must be bad.

Moskowitz gives me my pills and watches me swallow them before she'll leave the room. In the stillness before Dr. Jacobs starts talking, I gather myself up, close my eyes, take a deep breath, and then I'm gone. It is one of the things I do best. Jenica's good at school; I used to be good at cheerleading, and now I'm good at this. I zone out. I go away. I fly out of my body and up to the ceiling to watch the scene unfold. It is just information now. It is just facts. There is nothing for me to feel.

Metastasis.

I hear the word in Dr. Jacob's voice. I am vaguely aware of my mother crying. My father groans. Jenica whimpers. But I am above it all. I am keeping a clear head. Someone in this family has to.

Metastasis.

The dirty word. The forbidden word. The word that separates the merely sick from the almost-dead. The word "terminal" has gone out of style, but that's basically what it means. Metastasis means "spreading." It means the cancer is everywhere. It's what I expected. I know it's what we all expected, though no one had the guts to say it out loud.

A year ago, when I was first diagnosed, the cancer was just a tidy little tumor on my left hip bone. Ewing's sarcoma, a rare form of cancer that is almost exclusively reserved for teenagers, found its way into my body, got comfortable, and made a little home. But then it became ambitious. That's the nature of cancer; it's the overachiever of the disease world. It gets angry when you try to remove it. Sometimes the microscopic remnants left over after excision vow revenge and come back even stronger.

Of course, this is not how Dr. Jacobs describes it. His version of cancer doesn't have a personality. He's all monotone medical jargon behind the safety of his clipboard. "It's in your bone marrow now," he says with his practiced kindness. "We haven't been able to contain it." He continues explaining over my mother's breathy sobs, describing how the cancer had spread down my side and into my femur, then jumped ship into my marrow, weakening the bone enough to make it useless, which is why I ended up breaking my leg two weeks ago while just walking. All this despite surgery, radiation, and a week of all-day chemo every month for the past year. All this despite everything in my life coming to a halt.

The cancer had been there for a while, hiding, dancing its invisible dance that tests missed until it was too late. The disease had been twirling itself into a frenzy during the months after my original diagnosis and the surgery to remove the tumor. I got into a rhythm during those months of outpatient treatment, during those three short weeks between rounds of chemo. My hair would start growing back, my body remembered how to eat and make a little muscle, and I could walk for more than a minute without getting exhausted. I started going to school again. I gave myself permission to get used to the feeling of my own bed. Will and I would resume our standing Friday-night date as if nothing happened, and I could fall back into his arms where I belonged and pretend I could stay there forever. I would start feeling good again just as it became time to do it all over.

No one ever told me I was cured. No one even said "remission." But it's like we all collectively agreed to pretend there was a chance the tumor was gone. It was only natural that I become the ringleader—I was a cheerleader, after all. I saw those heartbroken eyes looking at me—my parents, Kasey, Will, everyone at school who was used to me being so fun and positive and full of life—all of them wanting me to assure them everything was okay, and I knew it was my responsibility to keep their hope alive. Every time I got home from another round of chemo, I forced a smile and said I felt great. I learned how to puke quietly. We all believed in miracles then. We had to.

My hip was always a little sore after the surgery that removed the tumor, but I knew deep down this new pain was different.

I knew the dull soreness of healing had turned into something sharper. Two months ago, when they discovered it had spread from my hip to my femur, I was not surprised. Even after radiation, while they were still waiting to do the tests that would tell them if the treatment worked, I knew it had gone even farther, deeper, and my whole body had started to betray me. Before their tests could confirm anything, I knew that everything inside me had somehow been infected. I knew all of this two weeks ago, walking with Will around Lake Merritt. I knew this new pain was never going to go away. But I wanted to give Will a good day, and even though it hurt, I knew it was my job to keep smiling. So that's what I did. I kept smiling until I couldn't.

It was one of those magical Bay Area winter days—the sun was out, the sky clear and blue, the temperature in the low sixties. Even the resident killer geese were on their best behavior. Moms were pushing strollers, pretty girls were jogging, handsome men were walking dogs, and Will was holding my hand in that perfect way he does—not so strong that he crushes me, but just firm enough that I know he's not letting go. He was telling me about how someone saw a stingray in the lake the other day, and I wanted so badly to talk about this small thing with him. I wanted to be in that moment in that place and have it be the only thing that mattered, but the pain in my leg was unbearable. In the midst of all that beauty, I could feel my grip on it slipping away. I tried to keep walking, even after the pain got so bad I couldn't see. I thought if I kept walking, if I kept pretending nothing was wrong, then I could be that almost-normal girl forever—a girl who just happened to be skinny and pale with a very short haircut, walking with a limp while leaning on a cane, holding the hand of her sweet and adorable boyfriend, taking a walk the way normal couples do.

But then I fell. I cannot describe the feeling of my leg breaking, the sound of the brittle bone cracking into shards inside me. I blacked out from the pain, but for some reason I clearly remember the squawking of the geese, as if they were angry with me for ruining their nice sunny day. I remember the jumble of spectators' voices, all those other people's dates made suddenly awkward. I remember Will's touch, his fingertips cool and gentle on my skin, and it was the only thing that felt right on my body; it was the only thing in the world that was solid and unmoving. As I listened to Will explaining my medical history to the paramedics, I remember thinking there is no good reason a seventeen-year-old kid should know anything close to what he knows about cancer. His voice was calm and low, in control like always, but the words were gibberish, just sounds, more like music than meaningful things.

My left femur broke into five pieces. They should have just left the cruel puzzle and never bothered to put it back together. But here I am with a titanium rod and five screws in my leg. I have a brand-new bionic leg that will most likely never even know what it feels like to walk. What am I going to do with all that fancy metal when I'm in the ground? The pieces will just be there, buried and unused, while the rest of me disintegrates and crumbles back into the earth.

Will would tell me to keep hoping. I don't have the heart to tell him that sometimes hope can be frivolous. It can be a big waste of time and love, not to mention money. People don't say that kind of thing out loud in a place like this, but it's true. What if I don't get stronger? What if I'm too tired to keep hoping, to keep pretending everything's going to be okay?

"Evie," Dad says. "Are you listening?"

I come back down from my faraway place, back to this strange world where the land of the living meets the land of the dead.

"So we should start talking about next steps," Dr. Jacobs says.

"Yes," says Mom.

"Yes," says Dad.

Just keep moving forward. Just keep doing something. As long as something's happening, we can hold on to the illusion that something's being fixed.

"As soon as Evie recovers from the surgery on her leg, we can start her on an even more aggressive series of chemo and radiation. She'll need a bone marrow transplant, of course. Stem cell therapy. Blood transfusions."

"Oh my," Mom gasps. She puts her hand over her trembling lips, as if hiding her fear will make this any less real.

"There's a clinical trial we may want to talk about. It's still in the early stages, so there aren't really any statistics available yet."

"What's the survival rate?" I say. "If I do all these treatments?"

Dr. Jacobs blinks, and for a split second, I see a crack in his armor of confidence.

"Four to seven percent," he says, with the kind of straight

face only very good doctors and very good actors are capable of. "And that's just a five-year prognosis. As you know, this particular cancer has a reputation for recurring."

Mom cries even harder. Dad sighs and puts his face in his hands. Tears are running down Jenica's face. The doctor and I are the only ones with dry eyes.

"When can we start?" Mom says.

"Well, there's the question of Evie's leg, of course. And her white blood cell counts aren't great yet. And—"

"No," I say.

"What?" says Dad.

"No. I don't want to do it."

"The clinical trial?" Mom says. "We haven't even heard the details yet."

"Not just the clinical trial. I mean all of it."

"Evie, you're not feeling well," Dad says. "You can't be expected to make a decision right now."

"Dad, I'm never feeling well. He said I have a four percent chance. I don't want to go through all that again for four percent. It's not worth it."

"Of course it's worth it," he growls. When feelings get too much, his sadness turns to anger.

"Four to seven percent," Mom pleads. "It could be seven." Her sadness turns to desperation. Her sadness turns to the absurd.

"Oh my god," Jenica says from the corner. Her whole body shakes. Somebody please go comfort her. Mom, Dad, she needs you too.

"Dr. Jacobs," Dad says, his face getting red, his jaw getting tight. "Will you please talk some sense into her?"

Dr. Jacobs looks at them both, then at me. He holds my gaze for a while, and I know he is on my side. "As a doctor, I'm almost always for trying anything possible. But that's not always the right decision for a family. You have to weigh your options very carefully. Treatment is really, really hard. Physically and emotionally. Evie knows that better than any of us."

Mom's mouth is open in disbelief. I think Dad may actually hit him.

After an excruciatingly long pause, Dr. Jacobs finally says, "I think you should listen to your daughter."

Yes. Finally. Somebody cares what I think. Feelings flood my body, but they leave so quickly I can't name any of them. What if I don't know what I think?

"I want a second opinion," Dad says immediately.

"That's absolutely your right," Dr. Jacobs says. "But I should remind you that I am the head of oncology, and diagnoses and prognoses are made by an entire team of doctors. Everybody's been a part of Evie's treatment. I'm afraid there isn't a doctor here who will tell you anything different."

"We'll go to a different hospital, then."

"Dad, no," I say. "You can't make me. I can't do this anymore. I can't make you do this anymore."

"Don't worry about us, Evie. We'll do whatever it takes."

"I know. That's the problem. Sometimes you have to know when to stop."

Silence. Too much silence. It's heavy. Crushing. It will flatten us all.

Then Jenica's phone rings and wipes the air clean.

"Dammit, Jenica!" Dad shouts. "Will you turn that damn thing off?"

"Sorry." She fumbles for her phone, hands shaking. I silently thank whoever called her.

"Can you give us some time alone, Doctor?" Mom says softly. "This is a lot to process."

"Of course. Let one of the nurses know if you want me paged, okay?" He puts his hand on my shoulder. "You too, kiddo. If you have any questions. You have me and Dan and the nurses and counselors all here to help you."

"I know," I say. "Okay."

"I'm going to work on putting together a palliative care team for Evie. It'll be me, Dan, a social worker and counselor, a chaplain if you want, and a nurse, probably Nurse Moskowitz."

"Ugh," I say.

Dr. Jacobs chuckles, and the sound of it is shocking. "Whatever you decide to do, we're going to do this together, and we're going to make you as comfortable as possible."

"Thank you, Dr. Jacobs," Mom says. Dad shakes his hand reluctantly, then the doctor walks out the door and we're left to fend for ourselves.

I speak before anyone has a chance to say anything: "I don't want to talk about this any more tonight."

"But Evie—"

"Please, Dad. I have a migraine. I'm really tired."

"Let's let her rest," Mom says, though I know it pains her. I know that what she really want is to be by my side all day and all night, holding my hand, keeping me talking. Especially now that she knows for sure that her time with me is almost over. I think this is what I should want too, but what I want more than anything right now is to be alone.

"You might as well go home," I say. "All I'm going to do is sleep."

"Are you sure?" Mom says. "I could stay with you. Are you sure you don't want to talk? This is a lot to deal with. It doesn't feel right to just leave you here all alone."

"Mom," Jenica says. "She said she wants us to leave. We should respect her wishes." Thank you, Jenica.

They take turns kissing me good-bye, and it strikes me how my family has become so efficient with our love. It takes all my strength to hold on to my neutral face as they file out the door. As soon as it closes behind them, my lips can finally rest in their usual grimace. I press the button to call the nurse so I can ask for a sleeping pill.

I lie in bed, alone, in darkness, waiting for yet another pill to soften the pain, hoping it'll happen before the feelings I've managed to avoid catch up with me. If there's one consolation of dying, it's that it won't be too long until I can stop pretending I'm not.

And so I guess this means it is time to die. It's time to let everyone off the hook, let Mom and Dad get on with their lives and stop wasting all their energy on the wrong daughter. Kasey shouldn't have to spend her precious free time at my bedside. And Will—my sweet, loyal, perfect Will—it's time to let him have something besides this dead-end love, let him find someone he can actually have a future with, let him become someone besides the guy with the dying girlfriend. It's time to let them all go. It's time to stop dragging them down with me.

The thing they don't understand is, this is not life. This is a vague, cruel shadow of life. I am ready even if they aren't. I'm ready to say good-bye.

three.

THERE'S NOTHING MORE DEPRESSING THAN VALENTINE'S Day in a children's hospital. Nothing.

I'll give them credit, though—they're valiant in their efforts to make it not suck. All the nurses are wearing pink scrubs, with various heart-shaped and glittery accessories. There are a million art supplies in the kids' playroom to make valentines. We woke up this morning to pink bags hanging off of everyone's door, filled with candy and fancy pencils and other random little toys. Someone's mom arrived with several Tupperware containers full of fresh-baked cookies, enough for every Cancer Kid to have at least two.

The little kids are falling for it, and I'm glad. It's good to see them smiling and busy, doing something besides sitting in bed watching TV with their exhausted families. I wish I could join them like I used to, but every attempt at re-creating normal life in here, every special event or activity, just makes me sad. I should have been down there with them like Caleb, nostalgic for his days as an assistant Sunday school teacher, distributing scissors and glitter and helping them laugh. But instead, I'm in the empty teen lounge, watching Stella deface the new issue of *Seventeen* magazine. This destruction seems more in line with what I'm feeling. I can't deal with sick kids right now.

My parents have finally accepted my decision. I get to go home in a couple of days. It took Dr. Jacobs and Dan describing in great detail how much pain and suffering I would experience if we went ahead with treatment. Did my parents really want to trade the slight possibility of my living a few extra months if the time I had left was going to be so miserable? Did they really think I was going to make it, or were they afraid of accepting the inevitable fact that they were going to have to let me go? Dan held my mom while she sobbed, and she looked so small in his long arms.

When she finally came up for air, she could not look at me. "Okay," she finally said. I looked out the window. My mother had just given permission for me to die.

We've found a new peace since then. Mom still breaks down in tears sometimes and I still float away, but mostly we're keeping our shit together as a family. Telling Stella and Caleb wasn't as hard as I thought it'd be, maybe because we already sort of accepted that a condition of our friendship is that one of us could die at any second. We hugged and shed a few tears, then we vowed not to talk about it anymore.

Telling Kasey was the hardest because, unlike Stella and

Caleb, she did not have the courtesy to save her strong feelings for later, so I had to comfort her through her meltdown. I was the one telling her everything is going to be okay, that life will go on just fine without me. That's a strange position to be in, comforting someone else about your own death.

But none of this comes close to what will be the most terrible part of all. I don't know how I'm going to tell Will that I'm giving up on the promise we made that we'd get through this together, that I'm leaving him to get through this alone, without me.

"Can you believe this shit?" Stella says, showing me a page featuring a scantily clad teen holding a math textbook with a confused look on her face. She has written in a thought bubble above the model's head: *Keep me stupid so I don't ask questions.* "I can't believe this is legal. It's like child porn."

"I'm sure she's eighteen," I say, grateful for the interruption of the depressing mess inside my head. Stella rolls her eyes.

"Hey, guys," Caleb says as he walks through the door with two construction-paper hearts. He hands one to each of us with a big dopey grin on his face.

It's still shocking to see him sometimes, so unlike the rest of us. We are all so obviously sick, but Caleb still seems healthy. He walks around the halls unassisted most of the time. He goes around cheering up little kids. Most of the time, he doesn't seem sick at all, definitely not sick enough to be an inpatient. But then he'll disappear for a day or two with a migraine that makes him unable to move, or he'll get really confused all of a sudden and forget how to talk and we have to get a nurse to take him away. But he always comes back cheerful and full of hope, even with double vision, even with sores in his mouth from the radiation. Brain cancer can be weird like that. One day you're doing your math homework, then all of a sudden you forget your name. Then you have a seizure and end up here, where doctors find a tumor the size of a Ping-Pong ball in your head.

Caleb's brain cancer was "cured" at age six, so he had a whole nine years of believing he was done with it, nine years to forget what being sick felt like, to forget the fear, nine years to create a normal life. He had nine years to feel grateful, to believe every day was a miracle. But at fifteen, just a semester into his first year of high school, just a week after getting cast in the school musical, he found out God made a mistake. He took back the cure. And yet Caleb still believes in Him, now more than ever.

The heart Caleb made me has a white doily stuck to it and several sparkly heart stickers. He appears to have had a little difficulty with a clump of sequins. It says in careful purple cursive: *For Evie. Love, Caleb.*

"Glitter," Stella says gravely. "The herpes of the crafting world." She leans over and looks at my valentine, then back at hers. "Wait a minute," she says. "Why does Evie's say 'Love, Caleb' and mine just says 'From Caleb?'"

Caleb blushes and looks away. He hurries over to the TV and busies himself with setting up a video game. I expect Stella to keep talking, to embarrass him further. But she just looks at me, smiles sadly, and looks back at her magazine.

"You three too cool to hang out with everyone else?" Dan says as he walks into the room. He has to duck his head slightly as he comes through the doorway, nearly dislodging some hanging pink hearts. He looks like he should be playing basketball for the NBA instead of hanging out in here with us. He won't tell us exactly how tall he is, but I know it's close to seven feet.

"Hi, Danimal," Stella coos, and gives a silly little wave with her fingers. Dan rolls his eyes.

"Evie, my friend," he says, sitting in the chair next to me. "How are you?"

"I'm okay."

"I've been meaning to come by and see you all day, but a couple of little kids were getting ready to go into surgery this morning and needed me."

"It's okay."

"You know it's okay for things to not be okay, right?" he says softly, as if lowering his voice a little could give us privacy in this tiny room. "You could tell me."

"I know." Does he really have to do this in front of Caleb and Stella?

"All right," he says, but I can tell he doesn't believe me. "I'm about to leave for the day. I'll come by and see you tomorrow, I promise. Is there anything you guys need? Caleb? You okay over there?"

Caleb is staring at the controller in his hand, as if he's wondering how it got there. After a few seconds, he looks up and smiles. "Hi, Dan," he says, like he just noticed he was here.

"My shoulders are sore, Big Dan," Stella says. "Can I have a massage?"

"Good night, Miss Hsu," he says. Stella cracks up, and I laugh a little too. The only reason she can get away with this is because she's Stella.

"He is so fun to flirt with," she says after he's gone.

"You should give my sister some pointers," I say. "She *loves* him."

"Your sister," Stella says, then pauses for dramatic effect, "has a big fat stick up her ass. And not the fun kind."

I love how raunchy Stella can be, how she'll say anything to get a reaction from people. Being with her and Caleb is the only thing that's making my new death sentence tolerable. They're the only ones who don't need to talk about it.

Caleb gives up on the video game and puts the controller down. "I don't understand," he says, scratching the flaky skin behind his ear. "Why do you want to flirt with Dan if you're a lesbian?"

"Oh my god!" Stella exclaims in mock horror. "I am so not a lesbian. Lesbians knit and have ten cats and drink herbal tea. Just because I've made out with a few girls doesn't mean we need to label it. And in case you forgot, I have a boyfriend."

"Yeah, but wasn't he—?" Caleb doesn't finish his sentence. Stella shoots him a look that makes it clear she has no interest in hearing the rest of his question.

"So you're bisexual?" I say.

"I'm just Stella." She grins, tipping her hat to us. And that's the end of that.

Only on pediatric cancer wards do you get friendships like ours. When you're sick like we are, how you present yourself to the world seems to lose its importance. No one cares about your hobbies or how you dress when you're sitting side by side for hours getting blood transfusions. No one cares about being cool when you're rubbing your friend's back while they puke into a bedpan.

It hits me that I'm going to have to say good-bye to them, too. Not just the world of the well. This one. I'm leaving my sick world too.

"I'm tired," I say. "I'm going to take a nap before my parents and Jenica get here."

"Want me to wheel you back to your room?" Caleb says.

"Sure. Thanks."

"I'll come up too," Stella says. "Maybe my roommate will be asleep and I can have phone sex with Cole."

"Gross," Caleb and I say in unison.

I just want to fall asleep before I start crying. If I start, I'm afraid I'll never be able to stop.

The second saddest thing, after Valentine's Day in a children's hospital, is a Valentine's Day present from your parents. The white stuffed dog mine brought me holds a heart in its mouth that says *I Ruv You*. It sits on my bedside table next to the plastic pitcher of water, an evil grin on its little doggy face. Its beady eyes say, "No romance for you, Cancer Girl."

Does the white dog know it's also my two-year anniversary with Will? Exactly two years ago today, we went on our first date—burgers at Barney's, and *Casablanca* at the art house movie theater on Telegraph. He kissed me for the first time when Ilsa said to Humphrey Bogart, "Kiss me. Kiss me as if it were the last time." The theater shows it every Valentine's Day, and we went again last year, just before my first diagnosis. We were going to make it our tradition. We had it all planned out for tonight—the same burgers, the same movie—but that was before my leg fell apart and I ended up back in here. And now visiting hours are over.

I've been lying here since my parents and Jenica left. Kasey even made an appearance, but left quickly for a date with some new boy she just met. I could tell she didn't want to tell me about her plans, didn't want to talk about life going on outside these walls when mine's about to come to a close, but I pulled the information out of her. She couldn't look me in the eye as she told me.

My favorite night nurse, Suzanne, is on duty, and she keeps coming in to see if I need anything, if I want to speak to the counselor on call. Everyone is trying to get me to talk. It must be part of my care plan now. It must come up in big, blinking red letters whenever someone opens my charts on the computer: *Get her to talk about her feelings!!!* But I don't feel like talking. What's the point of having the same conversation over and over again? What's the point of talking if it doesn't change anything?

But I did tell Suzanne my leg hurts. I can at least talk about the kind of pain that medicine can fix. There's been talk about putting me on a PCA, "Patient-controlled anesthesia," which would give me control of my pain meds with the push of a button. But no one's willing to make that call just yet. Once that happens, it's over. There's no coming back from that.

I hear a knock on the door. "Dinner," Suzanne calls from the other side.

"I already ate," I say.

"It's a special treat," she says. "Close your eyes."

"I'm not hungry."

"Are your eyes closed?"

I close my eyes. "Yes." It'll probably be something heart-shaped. It'll probably be something pink. I wish I were sleeping. I wish I could just get rid of the rest of this sad, pointless day. I wish my leg wasn't throbbing. I wish these pain meds were stronger.

I hear Suzanne's shoes on the floor, the creak of the rolling tray. I swear I can smell the broken promise of my anniversary cheeseburger, and I feel the beginning of tears leaking through my closed eyelids. Crying over the hallucinated scent of a stupid cheeseburger? I must really be losing it.

Suzanne clears her throat. I pretend I'm sleeping. She clears her throat again. Her voice sounds low; I think she's coming down with a cold. "What?" I grumble, and open my eyes.

The lights are dim and in front of my bed is a tray covered with a lace tablecloth, candles, and a dozen red roses. On a real china plate sits a big, beautiful cheeseburger and curly fries.

I look around the room and find Will standing by the door. "Happy Valentine's Day," he says, and I immediately start crying. The floodgates are finally open. In a blink, he is by my side, his warm hands around mine.

"Are you okay?" he asks, his face squeezed into its too-familiar look of concern.

"Yes," I say. "Just surprised. Just . . . happy." I don't tell him that my leg is on fire. I don't tell him I've been trying not to cry for days. None of that matters in this moment. There is just happiness. There is just love. "How did you manage this?"

"I worked it out with Dan and Suzanne. They're awesome, by the way."

"I know."

"I brought *Casablanca*," he says, pulling his laptop out of his backpack. "And theater-size Junior Mints. But the deal is you have to eat all three and a half servings."

I lift my skeleton arm and pull him close. He is so sturdy, his back so muscled and solid, he feels like a different species than me. "I love you," I say with all the strength I have left.

His lips are soft on mine. I can barely remember what it felt like when my whole body would respond to his kiss, when it was strong enough to want something more than this weak grasp on survival.

"I wish I were stronger," I say, my tears in our mouths. "I wish I could—"

"Shh," he says. "You're perfect. This is perfect. Just like this." I nod, wanting so badly to believe him. "Except, the burger might have gotten a little cold in my backpack." It doesn't matter. We both know there's no way I'll be able to eat more than a couple of bites anyway.

I manage a laugh, and for a second, with his face so close to mine that he's all I can see, love breaks through the fog of the pain medication and everything does feel perfect. I can imagine, just for this moment, that things are back the way they used to be. Back before everything was almost over.

"Will," I say. "Thank you." I don't want to let go. Maybe if I keep him here, just like this, time can stop. Maybe we can stay here forever, a freeze-frame of perfection.

"No problem," he says, running his fingers down the back of my neck.

"Not just for this. For everything. For everything you've done for me this past year. For staying with me. You didn't have to. No one else would have."

He looks at me with his kind sky-blue eyes. "Evie, I love you. Leaving was never an option."

"But it's been so hard on you. You shouldn't have had to deal with all this. You should have had a normal life."

"I wouldn't have it any other way. I've gotten to be with you. That's all that matters."

I shake my head, but I know there's no use in arguing with Will's loyalty. It is pure and solid and so much better than I deserve.

"I am so lucky," I say, holding on to him as tight as I can. "I love you so much."

"I'm the lucky one," he says.

We stay like that for a while, me lying in bed with Will leaning over me, trapped in my arms. I wish he could climb into bed with me; I wish he could hold me with his whole body; I wish we could fall asleep together. But there's not enough room in my narrow hospital bed, and even if we tried to squish, there's the question of my leg and my catheter and my IV, all the things he could get tangled in.

He kisses me on the cheek. "Now how about this movie?"

"Okay," I say. It might be good to get a break from this intensity, let some fictional people take over the drama.

He sets his laptop on my bedside table and presses play. As he pulls the adjustable tray out across my lap, his elbow knocks over the pole that holds my IV bags. He reaches out to grab it but knocks the table instead, tipping the computer onto my broken leg.

They can hear my scream all the way in San Francisco.

I am on fire. I am blind with pain. Will is crying. His voice, distorted: *Help. Oh god. Evie.*

Nurse Suzanne to the rescue. Her hand on my shoulder. Walkie-talkie crackles.

Rubber shoes scuffle, so many pairs. The heavy silence of emergency. The whisper of nurses turning into angels.

I am falling, falling. Into the black hole with no ladder. Into the darkness with no way out. Into the pain that leads to more pain that leads to numbness that leads to—

four.

"I'M ON THE GOOD STUFF NOW," I ANNOUNCE WHEN WILL arrives with yet another bouquet of flowers. "Also, I think I hate flowers."

"Who hates flowers?" he says, kissing me on the forehead before setting his signature dozen red roses next to the million other wilting arrangements that have collected during the going-on three weeks I've been here.

"Cancer patients, that's who," I say. "Did you hear me? They have me on morphine now. They inject it right into my port, then *whoosh*!" He does not seem impressed.

"Are you okay?" he says as he caresses my face. His fingers feel like pillows.

"I wish people would stop asking me that." I try swatting his hand away but I miss. Nothing is where it's supposed to be.

"You scared me last night, honey." His eyes are wet. What is wrong with these people? I already had to endure my family's waterworks earlier today, but luckily I was nodding out through most of their visit. "You were in so much pain," he whimpers.

"But now I'm not," I say. I can't even remember what pain feels like. "So turn that frown upside down." I try to smile my biggest smile, but I'm not quite sure I get it right. I don't have the most precise control of my muscles right now. "My face feels like lasagna noodles." I open and close my mouth a few times to demonstrate.

"Be careful with that stuff, Evie."

"Or what?"

"You can get addicted."

Does he have any idea how ridiculous that sounds? "I'll go to rehab as soon as I get out of the hospital," I say. I think that's pretty hilarious, but Will looks like I just punched him in the nose. He doesn't know how funny I am. Stella thinks I'm funny. Outside, in his world, I am not funny. In here, I am a comedian. There is so much he doesn't know about me.

"This stuff is magic, Will. It's like I know there's pain, but I just don't care. It's so nice to not care for a change. I've wasted so much time caring."

Will ignores me and starts setting up a backgammon set.

"There is no way I'm going to be able to play that," I say.

What were we talking about? Lasagna? Why were we talking about lasagna?

He looks at me with his puppy-dog eyes and the room stops its throbbing for a second. "Evie," he says. "Do you remember what happened last night?"

"Of course I remember. You dropped a computer on my leg."

He flinches when I say that, and for a split second, I think I hear a distant echo of something that might sound like regret, but it passes and the room starts swirling its comforting swirl. I don't know why I never noticed how the lights pulse, how they flicker so minutely. I can see so many things now that I'm so slowed down. Like slow-motion photography. Like extreme close-ups on a nature show. Hummingbird wings. Snake tongues.

"Evie," someone says. Is it the narrator of the show? Or is it the snake? "Evie," he says again. "Where'd you go?"

Will. "In case you forgot, I can't exactly go anywhere right now."

"You can't even focus your eyes on me."

"I'm not mad at you," my mouth says, but I don't know why.

"Oh, Evie." Will is beside me, his face buried in his hands. I wish he would stop saying my name. Something must have happened. There are so many flowers.

"Well, if it isn't my two favorite Abercrombie models," says a different voice, and it brings a new soundtrack to this tragic scene. It brings dancing instead of this funeral dirge.

"Stella!" I say. And there she is, materialized out of the fuzz, sauntering into the room in her signature rock-chic ensemble. Her tight tank top shows off her boobs that have somehow remained perfect despite all the rounds of chemo she's gone through.

"Cheerleader," she says. "Hey, Loverboy."

"Will, look at her boobs!" I say.

"Evie!" he says with a voice that means I'm in trouble.

"Uh-oh," Stella says. "Looks like someone's been hitting the sauce."

Do I catch her and Will sharing a meaningful moment of eye contact? *She's on the IV drugs now, isn't she? Next stop, PCA city. This is the end, isn't it? Only a matter of days now. Hours, even.*

Well, whatever. Let them have their moment. Better than the usual of them not knowing what to say to each other, of Stella thinking Will's a boring tool and Will thinking Stella's a bad influence on me.

"They're not letting me out yet," I say. "They were supposed to let me out."

"They know what's they're doing, Evie," Will says. "They have to get your pain under control." God, why is he always so serious?

"Stella, you just missed a really good joke I said," I tell her.

"What was it?"

I try to think, but all I find in my head is cotton. "I don't remember."

"Sounds hilarious, babe."

Will is determined to set up the backgammon board. There are at least a million little black and white pieces for him to find the right places for. It's making me dizzy just looking at it. And not the good kind of dizzy. Not the warm whirlpool of forgetting I had before he got here.

"Will, stop it with the backgammon," I say. "I told you I'm not playing." I can't put my foot down, so I thump my fist instead. But it's harder than I meant it to be; I'm stronger than I'm supposed to be, and the game and all the pieces go flying. White and black buttons fall in slow motion to the ground, tinkling dully and rolling away to darkened corners where they will never be found.

"Oops," I say. I know I should look at Will. I should make this easier for him. I should soften the blow of all these things falling apart. But I cannot take his sad face anymore. I cannot risk his reflecting me in those glassy eyes and showing me a version of myself that is not as indestructible as I want to feel.

So I look at Stella. Strong, wild, beautiful Stella. She could probably be a supermodel if she wasn't such a feminist. "Stella, you're beautiful," I say.

"Don't tell me you're switching sides, Cheerleader. And with your boyfriend sitting right here. Scandalous!"

"Excuse her," Will says. Why is he crawling around on the floor? "She isn't herself right now."

"I'm myself," I say. "I'm totally myself."

"Maybe this *is* herself, Loverboy," Stella says as she picks up the huge photo of my cheer squad out of the jungle of flower arrangements. She looks at the photo and shakes her head, then puts it back down facing the wall. "I can't look at these fembots anymore," she says. "No offense."

Will looks up from where he's kneeling on the floor, his hands full of white and black game pieces, as if finding them all will make this day salvageable. He looks so tired. Is this new? Or am I only now noticing? Is it my special slow-motion super-vision?

But what if I don't want to see this? Why am I sad? I thought morphine was supposed to make all the pain go away.

"Get up," I say as kindly as I can. I try to focus on him, try to remember what it feels like to want to make him happy. "Come here." I reach out my hand for him. I see him take it but I barely feel a thing. I flex my skeleton arm and pull him to me—amazing how much power I have to move people. I smile, kiss his chin, and just like that, I make everything okay. I will hold his sadness if I have to. It is heavy, but at least I don't have to do it for much longer.

"You two are so cute," Stella sighs. "I wish Cole was here. We could, like, double-date or something. Do something superexciting like go to the cafeteria and share some fries. Cole's going through this weird phase right now where all he wants to watch is kung-fu movies, but I'm sure he'd join us in the playroom to watch *Toy Story 3* for the fiftieth time. He's a good sport like that. Though if I have to watch that movie one more time, I think I'll tear my eyeballs out."

"I like *Toy Story 3*," Will says.

"You haven't watched it forty-nine times."

"There you are, Stella," says a dreaded voice from the doorway.

"Crap!" says Stella. "Quick, hide me."

"Miss Hsu," Nurse Moskowitz bellows, "go back to your room right now. Doctor's orders are to rest. You know that."

"I'm not even tired. See, watch." Stella dances a little tap dance in her big black boots.

"Right now, young lady."

"But I put my boots on and everything. Do you know how long these things take to lace up?"

"Do you want me to call your parents?"

That makes Stella stop dancing. "Ooh, Nurse Ratched. You are diabolical." She makes a show of dragging herself out of the room. "Have to go back to my cell now, kiddos. Come over tomorrow, Cheerleader. We can drink Diet Cokes and braid each other's hair and talk about what we're going to wear to homecoming. So long, Loverboy. Stay gold, Pony Boy."

"Bye, Stella," I call behind her. The room is smaller and darker as soon as she leaves. The lights start pulsing again, but not in a friendly way.

"She's so weird," Will says. "I don't get how you two are such good friends."

I shrug. Something like pain twists in my chest. It has nothing to do with cancer or my broken leg. But one of the charming things about morphine is it comes in waves, so just when sadness comes sneaking around, a warm surge turns my blood cozy again.

A sound like *Uhhhghhh* comes out of my mouth. Like something deflating.

Will is a cartoon character, startled, a little furry animal with his eyes bulging out of his head. *Danger! Danger!*

"Everything's okay," I mumble. My eyelids are so heavy.

"What happened?" he says. "Are you okay?"

I don't want to talk to him right now. I don't want to darken this fluffy cloud with his worry.

"Morphine," I say. "Will you marry me?"

"Oh, Evie," Will says, barging in on the conversation.

"Stella, get me that flower over there."

"Stella's gone. This is Will. Are you okay?"

God, that question!

"Are you in pain?"

"The flower, please."

"Which one? There are a million flowers over there."

"Bouquet, second from the left. Little yellow flower on the bottom. You can barely see it." Even with my eyes closed, I know every millimeter of those flowers. I feel like I've been staring at them for years.

"This one?"

My eyes open. The room is just a cave. The machines are just shadows. Will hands me the flower and I hold the tiny, fragile thing pinched between my fingers. Amazing that my fingers know how to stay still while the room wobbles.

"Will, I'm dying." It comes out like water, liquid and cool.

"You know I hate it when you say that."

"No, really. I'm stopping treatment. There is zero chance that I'm going to live. Ask my parents." I am lucky because I don't have to feel his pain. I don't have to go with him inside where his heart is breaking. I can stay right here, floating, a safe distance from it all.

The sound I hear resembles "No," but it is more like a waterfall—crushing, deafening, love trapped and drowning beneath tons of violent water.

"Look, Will," I say. "This flower knows things. It's called a buttercup for a reason. Put it under your chin. Just like this."

I am blind. I see with my fingers. I can feel his afternoon stubble. I remember what it used to feel like on my cheek when we kissed. The best sandpaper.

"It paints you yellow if you like butter. Makes you glow. Right here. Right where I kissed you."

"Where?" The word sculpted out of tears.

"You can't see but I can. Your desire lit up like the sun."

"You're talking nonsense." I know from his voice that he's crying, but I will not look. I know I should feel sad with him, but the flower is the only thing I will let myself see.

"Other flowers tell other things. Do boys do 'She loves you, she loves you not?' with the petals? Guys play football, girls decapitate flowers. But we don't need to ask, do we? We already know the answer. Right, Will? Right?"

He is kissing my hand. His lips are wet with tears. Trembling. Wordless.

"It's so weird you give them to sick people, don't you think?" I feel my words and blood thicken. My tongue is a fat slug in my mouth. "As soon as you pick a flower, it starts dying."

"Stop it," Will whispers.

The world dims and spins its final spin. I am still and heavy, a windless fog.

"Will," I think I manage to say. "I give you all my flowers."

five.

THIS SLEEP ISN'T LIKE THE OTHER KIND OF SLEEP. IT'S BETter. It's magic.

In this sleep, I am not sick. I have never set foot inside Oakland Children's Hospital. I float around time and space, unburdened by gravity. The morphine makes me invincible—my bones are steel, my marrow is liquid silver. I am superhuman. Warmth spreads from the IV through the central line in my chest, into my head, down my spine, and deep into the rest of me, hugging me from the inside. I have never felt pain. I will never feel pain. I am cradled by peace. Liquid love pulses through my body. I am home.

This is the best kind of dream. It is the kind where I am in control, where I am both the director and the star. I can simply decide that the last year never happened—and voilà!—life is perfect once again. There was never Sick Girl, Cancer Girl. There was only ever Pretty Girl, Happy Girl. The cheerleader with the perfect boyfriend, the lifelong best friend, the parents who never fight. Here I am with my long hair and perfect skin. Here I am stretching before cheer practice, my hips solid and flexible. Here I am with the sun in my face, when everything is possible.

"You're so beautiful," my mother says. I feel her hand caressing the patchy peach fuzz of my head. The touch pulls me from the dream and I am in my hospital room, straddling both worlds. "So beautiful," she says again, and the words fly away like butterflies. I want to say "I love you," but it is too much effort to make my mouth move. My eyes open to slits and for a moment the peace drains from me; I know she is lying. In her eyes, I see myself reflected, I see the words that should have been said instead of "beautiful." All she knows how to say is "beautiful." She cannot say how pale my skin is now, how sunken in my cheeks, how sickly skinny I've become after so many rounds of chemo, after so many meals that refused to stay inside me.

No. She will not ruin my dream. She will not suck the peace out of my blood. Just focus on the hand softly dusting the pain away. Don't look inside her. Never look inside. Focus on something else, peer through the haze at something that takes you out of this time and place.

My pom-poms sit on a shelf in the corner, next to the giant photo of the cheer squad, signed by everyone. Even though Stella turned it backward, I can still see it; I have X-ray vision. There's me with my arm around my best friend, Kasey. Her little mouth sings, *Remember what it felt like to be part of something?* She squeezes me and I feel it, a warm hug around my waist. She says,

Remember what it felt like to be the top of the pyramid? Remember what it felt like to be certain no one would ever drop you?

Our happiness is bigger than everything. Our smiles are so strong they blow the stench of sadness out of this room. There goes my mom flying out the window. Bye, Mom! Go home and take a shower. Go out for a nice dinner with Dad. Get your nails done. Have a spa day. Get out of this place as fast as you can.

Evie! Kasey calls from the picture. *Evie!* the rest of the squad repeats. Their tiny, tanned arms are waving at me to join them. "I'm coming!" I tell them. I can smell the grass of the field already. I can feel the snug comfort of *North Berkeley Lions* written in blue across my breasts, the tightness of my long hair pulled into a ponytail.

It is the afternoon before the winning game that takes our football team to Regionals. We are getting in one last practice. I have the big finale flip of the halftime routine, but that is not what I am nervous about. There is a big party after the game, but that is not where I am going. Will's mom and dad will be out until late. We have been dating for eight months and I can't imagine it being possible to love anyone more than I love him. Our love is the stuff of fairy tales.

I wonder how long he has been planning this night—the fire in the fireplace, the candles, the red roses. I wonder how he managed to score this bottle of champagne. Our hands shake as we ting our glasses in cheers, as we say "I love you" for the millionth time. I wonder if he knows this will be the happiest day of my life, that in a year I will rely on a drug so I can come back here in dreams, that a chemical will help hold me in his arms in front of this fireplace.

That was when I was a different kind of invincible, a time before pain, a time before fear, sixteen years old and three months away from the doctor's visit that would be my death sentence. The biggest things on my mind that day were if I could pull off my flip in the cheer routine and whether it was true that the first time you have sex always hurts no matter how gentle, if there was still a chance of getting pregnant even with a condom, even after being on the Pill for two months in preparation.

I had been worried then about creating a life. It would be funny if it weren't so sad.

And now the pain comes back, like cracks in the sky. Shooting bursts like meteors. The sweet drifting turns into falling. I am crashing. I am no longer weightless. I am full of needles, full of knives. I don't know if this pain is physical, but it hurts so much I think it will kill me.

"Mom!" I cry, and I sound like I'm drowning.

Come back from the window. Put your hand on my face. Tell me I'm beautiful again.

six.

I AM TOO PRESENT. I AM TOO AWARE OF MY BOREDOM.

"What should we watch?" Caleb says. He's the only one of us who has his own laptop. We've been scrolling through the Netflix menu for fifteen minutes.

"Something scary," Stella says. "Or sexy. Something scary *and* sexy."

"I want to watch something funny," I say.

"Me too," Caleb says.

"You always want to do what Evie wants to do," Stella says. "Hey, can I borrow your laptop tonight?" She always wants to borrow Caleb's laptop.

"Why don't you use the computer in the teen lounge?" I say.

"Maybe I don't want Dan looking at what I'm doing."

"Is it illegal?" Caleb asks.

"No."

"Is it porn?" I ask.

"Jesus, what's wrong with you people? Who do you think I am? I'm just Skyping with Cole, okay? It's almost impossible to find a time we can both do it because he's so busy with school and work. My parents won't let him visit, so it's the best I got. I haven't seen his face in like three weeks."

"Okay," Caleb says. "You can borrow it."

"How is he?" I say. I've never met Cole, but I feel like I know him from hearing Stella talk about him for the several months they've been dating. I know he's in his second year of nursing school at Cal State East Bay, works at a coffee shop on Telegraph, and shares a two-bedroom apartment in downtown Oakland with a waitress/burlesque performer. I know he's vegan, loves to bake and watch movies, and dreams of backpacking across South America someday. I know he can calm Stella down when no one else can, not even me. I know he was born a girl, but has considered himself a boy for as long as he can remember. I know he gives himself a shot of testosterone every Wednesday night and has been for the past year.

"What about this one?" Caleb says, his attention back on the computer screen. "It has Will Smith in it. He's funny."

"Evie," Stella says, ignoring him. "It's nice to have you back in the land of the lucid. Though I have to say, Junkie Evie is pretty entertaining."

"I guess," I say. "I was just starting to get used to it, then Dr. Jacobs said I had to go back on the wimpy pills again."

"Dr. J is stingy with the narcotics. He's notorious for it. He's all about prescribing the bare minimum, then taking it away as soon as he thinks you don't need it anymore."

"But isn't it supposed to be, like, the one perk of being a terminal cancer patient, that you get free reign with the pain-killers?"

"You're preaching to the choir, girlfriend. He's a sadist." She laughs. "You never cease to surprise me, Cheerleader."

"Why? What'd I say?"

"Have you ever even been high before? Like smoked pot?"

"I got tipsy on hard lemonade once."

"Hard lemonade: the gateway drug to morphine. Oh, Evie, you're adorable."

"I think it's good," Caleb says.

"You think what's good? Hard lemonade?"

"No, Dr. Jacobs not giving out too much drugs. It's good for us to be here, like really *here*, as much as possible. Don't you think?"

"I'd rather not be too present for my dying, actually," Stella says.

"But you don't want to be a zombie for the time you have left, do you? If you're all high on painkillers, you miss the opportunity to say good-bye to the people you love. I want to make sure I can spend as much time as possible with my family. And you guys."

I don't like the direction this conversation is going. What happened to watching a movie? If I was still on the morphine, this wouldn't even bother me.

"I guess you're right," Stella says. "I'm sure Dr. Jacobs isn't going to let Evie be in pain or anything. I'm sure when it's really, *really* the end, they pump you full of everything."

"But Evie still has some time until then," Caleb says.

"Wow," Stella says. "We really know how to pick conversation topics."

It's quiet for a while after that.

"My parents want me to be at home," I finally say. "When it gets to that point. When it's really the end."

"What do you want to do?" Caleb says.

"I don't know. I want to be able to decide then."

"Did you tell them that?" says Stella.

"Yes, but Dr. Jacobs says that isn't realistic. Because at that point I might not be in any condition to make decisions." And then it hits me, a wave stronger and harder and heavier than the morphine ever could be, one that sucks the air out of me and replaces it with terror. I start crying. I feel everything slipping, falling, tearing away.

"What if it comes out of nowhere and I don't have a chance to tell anyone what I want?" I blubber. "What if they just take me out of here and I can't talk anymore and don't have control over anything and all I can do is lie there while they make decisions for me and I can't do anything about it? What if I can't say good-bye? What if—?"

I am crying so hard I can't see or hear or breathe. I feel Caleb's and Stella's arms around me. I feel us squeezed tight, fused into a ball of pain and sickness and love.

"You don't need to worry about us, if that's what you're

thinking," Stella says. "We know you love us. It's okay if you can't say good-bye."

"It's so funny," I say, wiping my snotty nose on the back of my hand. "I spend all my time in here wanting to go home, but now it's like I'm scared to. I don't want to go home just to die there."

"So stay here with us," Stella says matter-of-factly, as if it is a wonderfully simple decision. "Either way, we'll make sure Dr. J puts you back on the good stuff." I know her confidence is an act, but it still makes me feel better.

"Yeah," I say.

Caleb is crying quietly beside us. "Hey," I say. "It's not that time yet. I'm still here, right?"

He nods, his bottom lip trembling.

"I changed my mind," Stella says. "I think I want to watch a comedy too." She puts her feet up on my bed and leans back in her stiff hospital chair. "Jeez, Evie. Isn't there some way to clean under your cast? You're starting to smell."

Caleb picks the Will Smith movie, and we spend one more night together in my room, pretending to not all be thinking the same thing—that this could be the last time, that this won't be my room for much longer, that I will be replaced by another sick kid with more hope than me.

seven.

"STELLA, IT'S YOUR TURN," CALEB SAYS. WE'RE SUPPOSED TO be playing gin rummy, but Stella's been distracted for the past half hour, texting frantically on her phone.

"Hold on a sec," she says for the hundredth time, holding up one long, skinny finger with blood-red nail polish.

Caleb takes off his hat and rubs his head, like he's thinking hard about his hand of cards. He only takes his hat off when he's with us, in the privacy of one of our rooms. Cancer Kids can be particular about their hats. His is an Oakland A's baseball cap his dad bought him at a game last year, before his cancer came back. It's easy to forget he belongs here when it's on, but when he takes it off, you can see the trails of scars from old surgeries, the weird peeling and discoloration from recent radiation treatments, and you immediately remember he's not a normal boy.

Will just texted that he's eating pizza and playing video games with his football friends, Jenica is no doubt studying,

Kasey's going out on her second date with the new guy, and here we are, three seriously abnormal teenagers, sitting on my bed on a Friday night pretending to play gin rummy while every other person our age is out in the world doing things regular teenagers do, at movies or parties or having sex or eating dinner with their parents. Stella's texting again with an evil grin on her face, Caleb's organizing the piles of cards on the tray over my legs, and I'm looking out the window at the black sky, and this is as normal a life as I'm ever going to get.

"The vultures are out there again," I say. Caleb gets up and looks out the window at the news vans below. I can't actually get over to the window; I only know they're there because I saw it on TV.

"What is it this time?" he says.

"Three-year-old kid got shot in a drive-by."

Caleb crosses himself and mutters a prayer under his breath. We could talk about how sad it is, but what's the use? This whole building is full of sad.

Stella looks up from her phone. "Evie, you just got your painkillers, right?"

"You were right here when Moskowitz gave them to me, like, ten minutes ago."

"And your next dose is in, what, four hours? I mean, three hours and fifty minutes?"

"Yeah. So?"

"Caleb," she says. "It's time."

"Really?" He looks scared.

"Time for what?" I say.

"Are you sure?" Caleb says.

"Of course I'm sure, Caleb. What a stupid question. You know I'm always sure. Now come on. We only have three hours and forty-nine minutes."

He doesn't move. He looks paralyzed. I think for a moment he's under one of his brain tumor spells, but then he says, "I don't know, Stella. I don't think it's a good idea."

"Remember," Stella says gently, seriously. "It's for Evie. We're doing this for Evie."

He nods. He says, "Okay."

Stella slides off my bed, shuffles to the door, and looks both ways. "Clear," she says, and disappears out the door.

"What's going on?" I say. Caleb just shrugs and smiles his sweet smile.

Stella returns with a wheelchair. "Uh-oh," I say, knowing who it's intended for.

"Uh-oh is right," Stella says. "Now how do we get you in this thing?"

"First you have to tell me what's going on. Where are you taking me?"

"Nope, don't have to tell you. That's part of the deal."

"What deal?"

"The deal you made when you became my friend. Friendship with me comes with the agreement that I am allowed and expected to blow your mind on a regular basis, no questions asked. Don't you remember signing that contract?"

"Come on, you guys," Caleb whines. "Hurry up." Whatever rule breaking is about to ensue must be killing him.

"You heard the man," Stella says. "Hurry up."

I don't know what to say. This could end up being the very best or very worst thing that could happen to me. I look into her bright black eyes: "Seriously, Evie," and for a moment all her hard edges soften. "What have we got to lose?" She smiles, and for a second I see the young girl in her, and maybe even a little bit of fear.

"Okay," I say. What have I got to lose?

I instruct Caleb and Stella on how to handle my leg and various attachments. Stella is so gentle as she pulls the IV for the bag of fluids out of my port. "For the next couple hours, you can drink water like a normal person, can't you?" she says.

As Caleb hoists me into the chair, my pajama pants snag and pull all the way down, giving them a full view of *everything.* Stella breaks down laughing and Caleb nearly drops me. "I'm sorry that had to be your first experience with a vagina," I say, pulling up my pajamas, and that makes Stella laugh even harder.

"I'm going to pee my pants!" she cries.

"I'm going to pee my catheter," I say, and even Caleb has to laugh at that, even though he's finding it impossible to look me in the eyes. Only with them am I ever this funny.

"Oh no, I'm crying," Stella says. "Is my makeup smearing?"

"We have to hurry," Caleb says, as if being all business will cure his embarrassment.

"Yes," Stella agrees, collecting herself. "Phase two: Operation

Spring-a-Leak." That makes us crack up again, but Caleb's already on the move toward the door.

"I'm going to do this," he says, more to himself than to us.

"It's just like acting," Stella says. "You love acting. Think of this as your Broadway debut. Pretend you're Brad Pitt playing a ninja."

He takes a deep breath and walks out the door. "Jill," we hear him call in the direction of the nurses' station down the hall. "Can I talk to you?"

"Are you ready?" Stella asks me.

"I have no idea."

She smiles. "Good answer."

She pushes me to the door and we listen to Caleb explain to Nurse Jill that he is severely constipated and hasn't pooped in five days and can he please have a laxative? It takes all of our self-control to keep from bursting out laughing. We pop our heads out the door and Caleb gives a thumbs-up when Jill disappears into the nurses' office, then Stella pushes me down the hall in the other direction toward the elevators. She hits the down button and we wait there for what seems like forever, and I realize this is the most alive I've felt in a long time. That unfamiliar buzz in my blood is adrenaline. I didn't know my body could even make adrenaline anymore.

The elevator arrives right as Jill comes back out of the nurses' office with Caleb's laxative, and we get in just in time.

We're both breathing hard, me from excitement, but Stella seems genuinely out of breath.

"What's up?" I ask.

"Nothing," she says, but her face is pale and she's leaning on the side of the elevator. I've seen her sick before, but somehow she always managed to maintain an aura of fierceness, even when she was puking, even when she was stumbling around, tired and weak. But that reliable fierceness has suddenly faded, and now Stella just seems sick.

"No, really," I say. "You don't look good. We should go back."

"No!" she says with all her strength. "We're not going back. Not yet. You need this."

"Okay," I say. I know not to argue with Stella.

The elevator opens and she pushes me out. Luckily, the front desk doesn't face the elevators and everyone's preoccupied with the frenzy of reporters and news cameras, so we're free to sneak through the side door without anyone noticing. When we get outside, the night is crisp and clear. Stella seems energized by the fresh air, her weariness gone as quickly as it came. She pushes me around the side of the building, down Fifty-Second Street, and under the freeway and BART tracks. She waves in the direction of a big blue van idling across the street, and it makes a U-turn and pulls up right in front of us.

The guy who gets out of the driver's seat is thin and well-dressed in a sweater-vest and bow tie, with a wide smile that immediately puts me at ease. "This is Cole." Stella beams.

"I feel a little underdressed," I say. I am wearing a ratty old T-shirt and pajama pants with sledding penguins on them.

"You look great," Cole says with a surprisingly girlish voice.

He's so convincing as a boy, I almost forgot he's not quite one, at least not physically.

"Cancer chic," Stella says.

They roll me up a makeshift ramp into the back of the van. "This is Vincent," Cole says.

"The van?" I say.

"Yeah," Cole says. "As in Van Gogh."

"Get it?" Stella says. "Van. *Go.*" They laugh at the bad joke together and I ache for Will, for these silly things shared by people in love.

The inside of the van is cozy with a futon mattress, a beanbag chair and assorted cushions on an orange shag carpet. Stella pushes them aside to make room for my chair, then covers me with a blanket that smells faintly of mildew.

"Put your brakes on, Scooter," Stella says. "We're going for a ride."

"Is that a disco ball?" I say, noticing a sparkling orb hanging from the ceiling.

"It most definitely is a disco ball," Stella answers.

"You never know when you're going to need to dance," Cole says.

"How am I supposed to keep from falling over?"

"Watch this," Stella says. She pulls a giant clump of tangled bungee cords out of a plastic bag, hands half of them to Cole, and they start attaching my chair to door handles, metal hooks, anything they can find that's solid. Pretty soon I'm sitting in the middle of an intricate web that looks like it was spun by a deranged spider. Stella gives my chair a test push and it barely budges.

"Wow," I say.

"A feat of engineering," Stella agrees.

"You feel safe?" Cole says.

"As safe as I'm going to."

"Then let's get the hell out of here," Stella says. She slams the back doors closed and they get in their seats in the front.

"Wait a minute," I say. "Why am I facing the back? I can't see anything."

"Exactly," Stella says. I can hear the evil grin in her voice.

"Where are we going?"

"That's a surprise, obviously," she says. "Duh."

"Did you really just say 'duh'?" She doesn't answer. I feel the car pulling out of the parking lot into the street. "You're basically kidnapping me, you know."

"Technically, I think Cole's kidnapping both of us," Stella says.

"Sorry for kidnapping you," Cole says. "Are you okay back there?"

"Yeah. It's kind of bouncy."

"Are you going to puke?" Stella says.

"Probably not. Considering the fact that I'm supposed to die in a few weeks, I feel surprisingly good."

"La-la-la-la!" Cole sing-screams loudly.

"Cole doesn't like it when we talk about dying."

"Oh, sorry."

Sometimes I forget how uncomfortable normal people get when we joke about being sick. They don't understand that turning it into a joke is sometimes the only thing that makes it bearable.

"So," Stella says. "I have a very important question for you. What kind of music do you like?"

"Music? I don't know. I never really thought about it. I guess I just listen to whatever's on the radio."

"No," she says. "No no no no no no no. That is unacceptable."

"Definitely unacceptable," Cole agrees. "If Stella didn't love you so much, I might have to kick you out of this van."

"Yet it is exactly what I was afraid of," Stella continues. "That's why I prepared a very important lesson for you. And it is centered around this mix CD. You can't see it because you're tied up and looking at the windowless back door of a kidnapping van, but I am at this moment holding up a mix CD that I carefully constructed for you. Because I care about you, Evie. I care about your musical salvation."

"Okay," I say.

"That's it? Okay? Say it with a little more enthusiasm."

"Okay!" I shout.

"Louder!"

"Okay!!!"

"That's better. Now. I know you're familiar with angsty white boys singing about boy stuff and poppy girls with male producers showcasing their boobs instead of their brains. Right?"

"Sure."

"Forget them," she says with a snarl. "Listen to this. Girls in combat boots and fishnets picking up guitars and making their own music. Music for *us*. Do you understand?"

"I think so?"

"No, I don't think you understand. Hence the need for examples. Hence the need for this mix. Are you ready?"

"Yes?"

"Without further ado, song number one from Stella's Impossibly Awesome Kick-Ass Girl Mix." As she inserts the CD into the stereo, she adds, "You'll like this one. It's about cheerleaders and football and shit."

Simple drums and a driving baseline start the song. A girl's thin voice starts singing about a pep rally, about teenage dreams, something about white privilege. Then the guitars come in and the song really starts rocking. Stella starts singing along in her beautiful, fierce voice—about going crazy, about living big despite it all. The music is so loud I can feel it in my bones. I can feel it in my poisoned marrow.

"Do you hear that?" Stella screams. "Do you hear that rage? She's so fucking strong. She's so fucking *angry*." All I can see are the locked van doors in front of me, but I suddenly feel freer than I've felt in a really long time.

When the song's over, I realize I'm shaking. But not because I'm cold. Not because I'm sick.

"This song is, like, my anthem," Stella says. "It's all about questioning authority. Not believing blindly just because someone with power tells you something's true. That's all high school is. Doing things blindly. Following the rules. Wearing their stupid uniforms and cheering at their stupid games, as if that's the shit that's really important." Maybe I'm supposed to be offended. Maybe I'm supposed to be pissed at Stella for implying I'm one of the high school sheep for being a cheerleader. But I'm too grateful to be mad at her.

"I love it," I say.

"I knew you would. I knew it. That singer was in a band with Carrie Brownstein. You know Carrie Brownstein? From *Portlandia*? Oh my god, I am so in love with her. Sorry, Cole, but she's my free ticket. We each get a free ticket, right? Like, the one person we're allowed to sleep with and we'll be forgiven?"

"Mine's my eighth-grade history teacher," Cole says. "She had this really sexy lisp that I couldn't get enough of. I loved it when we covered the Civil Rights era because she had to say 'Mississippi' all the time."

"That's weird," Stella says. "But whatever." The next song she describes as a love song, but it's got none of the sentimental cheese you hear on the radio. It's about the hard parts of love, the ambiguities, the complicated stuff people don't usually sing about.

"These are real women playing real instruments making real music they wrote themselves," Stella says. "They don't all have perfect voices; you can hear them straining sometimes, but that's what makes them *real*. That's what makes it beautiful."

I can feel the car going up a hill. Stella gets quiet for the next few songs, speaking only to tell me who the artist is and a little history. As I listen to a gorgeous song that's nothing but an acoustic guitar, cello, and haunting voice, she says, "This one is from 1992. We weren't even *born* yet. Can you believe it? Everything cool has happened already."

"Maybe something even cooler is going to happen any minute now," Cole says.

"I doubt it," Stella says.

"What about your band?"

"That's very sweet of you, but it's kind of hard to rock when you haven't practiced in two months."

The van continues to go up, and I'm guessing we're somewhere in the Oakland or Berkeley hills. I feel my chair strain against the bungee cords, but I've never felt safer. It's disorienting not being able to see anything, but I kind of like it. It's like all that exists is the music and Stella's and Cole's voices and the feeling I'm being taken somewhere good.

Stella sings her heart out, but after a while she has to stop because she's out of breath. "The altitude's getting to me," she says. I remember that we are sick. We are not as invincible as these songs make us feel.

The van slows down. "We're here," Cole says, and does some kind of complicated parking maneuver.

Part of me wants to stay where I am, in the dark. The world in the back of the van is small and manageable; it's just me in this tiny space, with nothing and no one else to worry about. I don't even have to worry about me. I can let go because Stella's calling the shots. I can just let her lead. I don't have to care about how everyone's feeling. I can finally relax.

When the back doors open, I am on the edge of the world. All I can see are the lights of Oakland over a thousand feet below me, the Bay Bridge and the San Francisco skyline, even the Golden Gate Bridge in the distance. The moon is full and reflecting off the bay. Everything is clean and sparkling, the streets pulsing like arteries. From this height, everything down there seems to be working efficiently, as if the city is a healthy, flawless body. We can't see any of the dirt or crime or poverty. We can't see any of the disease. Up here, on the outside, everything is perfect.

With Cole's help, Stella hoists herself into the van and leans her back against my wheelchair. Cole follows and snuggles against her. We sit in silence for a while, looking out over the city, and I think I could sit here forever.

I hear some movement and look down. Stella is rolling a joint. I watch, mesmerized, as her thin, graceful fingers work. I've never seen anyone roll a joint. I've been around weed a few times, smelled it, seen it being smoked at parties, but it was never something I was all that interested in trying.

"I've never smoked before," I tell her.

"There's a first time for everything."

"What if we get caught?"

"This is Oakland. People smoke weed walking down the street."

"You don't have to if you don't want to," Cole says. "I'm not since I'm driving."

"No," I say. "I want to." For some reason, it suddenly seems like something I have to do. Like I have to prove to myself, to Stella, that I am someone who can be wild. I can break out of a hospital. I can get strapped into the back of a van and not care where I'm taken. I can smoke pot at the edge of the earth, inches away from death.

"I don't think I've ever broken a law before," I say.

"But you're not even breaking a law," Stella says. "That's the best part. It's not even illegal. You have cancer and this is a prescription."

"Dr. Jacobs gave you a medical marijuana prescription?" I can't believe it. Not Dr. Jacobs who took away my morphine. "Don't you have to be eighteen to get it yourself? Your parents actually go to the pot club to pick it up?"

"I didn't say it was *my* prescription."

"That doesn't sound very legal."

"Yeah, well, I have bigger things to worry about than a misdemeanor pot charge. It's all about perspective, you know?"

"Yeah," I say. "I guess, what's the point of following all the rules if you're just going to die in a few weeks?"

"Exactly!" Stella says. "Plus it really does help with the nausea. I couldn't keep anything down without it. It really is medicine. All those medical marijuana activists aren't just a bunch of potheads."

"Just most of them," Cole says.

"Are you nauseous right now?" I ask.

"No, this time it's purely recreational." Stella lights the joint and a sweet, herby smell fills the air. I watch her take a couple of small puffs and hold it in. She passes it to me and says, "Don't suck too hard."

"That's what he said," I say, and that makes them crack up. I take a little drag like she did, feel the smoke burn down my throat. I start coughing.

"You okay?" Cole says.

"I'm fine," I say, and hand the joint back to Stella. We pass it back and forth a few more times, and just as I think I've gotten the hang of it, Stella decides I've had enough. "I don't think I feel anything," I say.

"Just wait," she tells me.

I look out at the view and imagine I live up here permanently, that this is as close as I'll ever be to the city below. For the rest of my life, I will only see beautiful. I will never have to go down there again, never have to sit through another round of chemo or radiation, never have to get another surgery, never have to get another piece of metal drilled into my bone, never have to wake up in that hospital bed, never have to eat that hospital food, never have to see my mother cry, never have to hear another doctor try to explain how I am dying. I will keep floating up, farther away from the city, farther away from the pain. I will never go down.

"I think I'm high," I say. My voice sounds weird, lower than normal. Like a grown-up.

"Woo-hoo!" Stella cheers into the night. "Evie's high! Congratulations, Evie!"

"I don't want to talk about dying," I say.

"Who said anything about dying?"

"If we were in a movie about kids with cancer, this is the part where we'd talk about dying. We'd get all philosophical and some sad music would play and we'd have some sort of breakthrough and come to terms with something and it would be really cathartic. Then one of us would die."

"Fuck that shit," Stella says.

"Yeah," Cole says. "Fuckity-fuck that shit."

"FUCK! THAT! SHIT!" Stella screams. "Come on, Evie. Say it with us."

Together we scream, "FUCK THAT SHIT!"

"Come on, Cheerleader," Stella commands. "Put your back into it."

We scream it over and over, faster and faster, until it's a kind of chant, until we don't even know what we're saying anymore, just that we're saying it loud, together, and on top of the world.

"Fuck you!" someone yells outside, and we all laugh hysterically. Cole pokes his head out the back of the van.

"Some dude is parked down the road," he says. "Probably trying to put the moves on a girl and we're totally ruining the moment."

"Good thing for the girl we're here," Stella says, but we calm down.

"I wish the world looked like this all the time," I say.

"It can," Stella says. "It can be whatever you want it to. You get to decide how you live in the time you have left."

"Are you getting sentimental on me? Where's Stella? What'd you do with my friend Stella?"

"Sometimes she gets a little sappy when she's stoned," Cole says, and kisses her softly on the ear.

"I'm serious," Stella says.

It is too much for me to think about, so I watch the night sparkle.

"Are you going to live big?" Stella says with a softer voice than I've ever heard from her.

"What do you mean?"

"Promise me, Evie," she says. "Promise me you'll live big."

"I promise," I say, even though I have no idea what that means in the little time I have left. I reach out my hand and Stella takes it in hers. We sit like that for a long time, holding hands, looking out over the world made beautiful by our distance from it.

When we get back to the hospital, the news vans are gone, but a couple of police cars are still in front. "Do you think those are for us?" I say as Cole turns the corner to drop us off out of sight. "We're going to get in so much trouble."

"What can they do to us?" Stella says. "Withhold our pain meds? Refuse to empty your pee bag? It's not like they can ground us. We already can't do anything."

Cole helps me out of the van and gives me a long hug. "I'm so glad I met you," he says softly. "Stella loves you so much." His voice cracks and he turns away, but not before I notice the tears in his eyes. And then I remember, in the midst of feeling more alive than I've felt in months, that I am going to die. My life is almost over, even though I feel like something huge was just born.

"Oh, we can't forget Evie's mix," Stella says, and moves toward the van. She stumbles and Cole catches her just in time.

"I'm okay," she says with a laugh. "That weed was strong, huh?"

"Hold on to Evie's chair," Cole says. "I'll get the CD."

I look up at Stella and see something like fear in her eyes. I open my mouth to ask her what's wrong, but she puts a finger in front of her lips and says, "Shh."

"I'm going to walk with you," Cole says as he hands me the mix.

"No," says Stella. "I don't want you to get in trouble."

"It's not a choice."

"Fine," she says. "But only halfway. Just until we turn the corner."

Cole pushes my chair as Stella leans on him for support. Even though it's barely two blocks, we have to stop twice so Stella can catch her breath. The relaxed and friendly Cole I spent the evening with has transformed into someone serious and strong, someone Stella trusts to hold her up. Just like that, the magic of the evening disappears. Minutes ago we were weightless, but now we are so heavy we can barely move.

"Okay," Stella says when we reach the corner. "You have to go now." Cole holds her for a long time as they whisper their love, and I am suddenly so cold, I am freezing, and the only thing in the world that can warm me up is Will's arms around me.

"He can be such a drama queen sometimes," Stella says as

Cole walks away, but I can hear the sorrow behind her weak attempt at humor.

We turn the corner and are immediately assaulted by the blinking of police lights. Nurse Moskowitz is talking to a police officer. Her head snaps in our direction.

"Oh crap," Stella says. "Here comes Nurse Ratched."

"Where have you two been?" Moskowitz bellows as she comes storming toward us.

She grabs Stella's arm and I think she's going to start lecturing like she always does, the same tired old sermon she gives Stella every time she breaks the rules. But instead, she puts her fingers around Stella's wrist and takes her pulse. Her movements are almost gentle, which is not a word anyone would ever use to describe Nurse Moskowitz.

"Is all this fuss for us?" Stella says. "You shouldn't have."

"In my eighteen years here, I have never, *ever* had a cancer patient leave the hospital AMA. *Never.* Do you realize we had to put the whole hospital on lockdown? Do you have any idea how much trouble you caused?"

"A lot?" says Stella.

Moskowitz glares at us as she speaks into her walkie-talkie: "They're back. Send Burns down immediately with a wheelchair and some blankets. Call their parents and let them know we found them."

"I don't need a wheelchair," Stella says, and starts coughing so hard that Moskowitz has to hold her in a bear hug to keep her from falling down.

"Evie," Moskowitz snaps, and it makes me jump in my chair. She has never raised her voice at me. I am not the one who gets in trouble. "Didn't you stop to think how risky it is to Stella's health to leave the hospital like this? She needs round-the-clock care. What if something had happened? How would you feel then?"

I don't understand how this became my fault, but I say I'm sorry anyway. I look to Stella for some clue, but her eyes are glazed over and dim, like she used up every last ounce of strength she had in her for the trip, and now that it's over she's only a shell.

"We just went for a walk," I say as a policeman approaches.

"For two hours?" Moskowitz says. She puts her hand on Stella's forehead. "Jesus, you're burning up."

What's happening? What happened? Why is Stella so sick all of a sudden?

"We had cars patrolling the neighborhood," the police officer says, eyeing us skeptically. "It's surprising we didn't see you."

"It's not our fault you couldn't find us," Stella says from somewhere behind her fever.

I'm shocked she'd talk to a police officer like that, but he just ignores her. "I don't think we're needed here anymore, are we, Nurse? Unless you want to press charges."

"What?" says Nurse Moskowitz, preoccupied with checking Stella's vitals. "Jesus, no. Thank you, Officer. And sorry for wasting your time."

"Girls," he says. "Think a little before you do something next time, okay? I don't think you have the same freedom to be as stupid as other people."

I brace myself for Stella to say something horrible but it doesn't come. She's lost inside herself, somewhere infected and hot.

"Where is that goddamned wheelchair?" Moskowitz curses, and that's when I start crying. Even she is scared. Moskowitz is never scared.

"Stella?" I say.

The sliding doors open and Mr. Burns, the medical assistant, finally arrives with Stella's wheelchair. He and Nurse Moskowitz help her into it and cover us both with blankets. As they push us to the elevators, Moskowitz continues to berate us. "I can't believe you got Caleb mixed up in this with you. You know that poor boy would do anything you asked him."

We get into the elevator and she presses the button for the fifth floor. "And Evie, that you of all people would do this. I thought you were smarter than that."

"Don't blame Evie," Stella mumbles through her haze.

"Especially with Stella being neutropenic," Moskowitz continues. "She has virtually no immune system right now. Do you have any idea how dangerous it was for her to leave the hospital?"

My heart drops. "What? Stella, you didn't tell me that. Why didn't you tell me?"

"I have leukemia," she says flatly. "'No Immune System' is my middle name."

It's my fault. Stella did this for me. She caught something

while we were out and it's all because of me.

"Mr. Burns," Nurse Moskowitz says when we get to the fifth floor, "please help Evie back to her room and ask Nurse Jill to help get her back in bed. I'll take care of Stella."

"Yes, ma'am," he says, and starts pushing me away. I turn my head to watch Stella as Moskowitz wheels her in the other direction toward her room. She looks smaller than I've ever seen her, empty somehow. She raises her head and for a split second the light comes back in her eyes. She winks at me and I mouth *I'm sorry*, but she shakes her head. So I mouth *Thank you* instead, and she nods, satisfied.

I turn the corner into my room and Stella disappears from view. My hand tightens around the CD she made me, perfect and solid in my lap.

eight.

"I BROUGHT YOU A BAGEL," KASEY SAYS AS SHE LOWERS herself into the chair next to my bed. She places the paper-wrapped bagel on my bedside table, and the smell of garlic and herb cream cheese makes me nauseous. Not because I'm sick. Not because of my body. Because of the pale, tired light barely making it through the window. Because Kasey's skin is still somehow tan.

"Thanks," I say.

"God, I can't believe what you guys did last night," she says. "Your parents told me all about it on the way here. They were so worried about you."

"I feel really bad about that," I say, and I mean it. After everything they've gone through. After everything they've already suffered because of me.

"It was really stupid, Evie."

"I know." Like I need one more person to tell me that.

"Do you know what's going to happen to you yet?"

"My parents and Stella's are talking to Dr. Jacobs and the hospital director right now."

"They should kick that girl out of here."

Did she really just say that? "*That girl* has leukemia. I think it might go against the Hippocratic Oath or something if they kicked her out."

"Whatever," Kasey says, and I kind of want to throw the bagel at her head.

"I'm not really hungry right now," I say, pushing it away from me. She doesn't seem to hear me. She's looking at the bagel ravenously. "Do you want it?" I ask.

"Oh no," she says, breaking out of her trance. "I'm on a diet."

"You look hungry."

"I'm fine."

"You're too skinny."

"Really?" Her face brightens. "You think so?"

I forgot that in the outside world, that's supposed to be a compliment.

I decide to change the subject. "So what's happening? How are things going with that guy?"

"Pretty good. You know."

No, actually, I don't. I don't know anything except that he goes to Skyline High School and she met him at a party and it's awkward for her to talk to me about it because I'll be dead soon.

She's looking at her pink polished nails. "Did you get a manicure?" I say.

"Huh?" She looks up. "Oh yeah. Some of the girls from the squad got together last night at Taylor's and did our nails and facials and stuff. Lisa did mine. She did an okay job, but there's a spec of something on this one."

"That sounds fun," I say, but it doesn't. Compared to what I did last night, it doesn't sound fun at all. Normally, I would have loved a night like that. Before I got so sick, there's nothing I would have rather done than sit around with a bunch of girls, green goop on our faces, excited about my pores getting opened, excited to talk about boys, about school, about so many innocuous things, back when happiness was so easy, when it was just there all the time, hovering around us, waiting to be picked like fruit.

"Oh, Evie," Kasey says. "I wish you could have been there."

"Me too."

She shakes her head. "I shouldn't have told you."

"Why not?"

"It must be terrible for you to hear about the fun stuff I do without you."

I shrug. Maybe I should be upset. Maybe I should be jealous and heartbroken and yearning to be back in that world with her. But right now I'm too busy worrying about Stella. I'm worried about her getting weaker. I'm worried about what's going to happen to us for last night, what kind of punishment we have in store.

I want my morphine back.

"What's going on with you?" Kasey says.

"What do you mean?"

"It's like every time I see you, you're further away. And now you run off with that girl in the middle of the night, when you're so sick, when everything is so . . . fragile? It's not like you, Evie."

"It was eight o'clock, not the middle of the night," I say. "And all we did was walk around the neighborhood. I'm sick of being in here. I'm tired." My default line. No one can argue with a cancer kid who says she's tired.

So we say nothing. We sit there staring at the bagel neither of us is going to eat. There was a time not too long ago when we could talk on the phone for hours and never run out of things to say. Now we struggle to have a conversation longer than five minutes. And soon we won't be able to have a conversation at all.

"Hey, bitches!" Stella's voice breaks the silence, and I take a big breath of relief. Even Kasey looks grateful for the diversion, and I know she can't stand Stella.

Stella's in the doorway with Caleb behind her. But she's in a wheelchair. Stella's never in a wheelchair. At least she's still wearing real clothes and her signature red lipstick. But even all that color isn't enough to hide how frail she is, how unlike herself.

"Like my new ride?" she says.

I open my mouth but nothing comes out.

"Hi, Kasey," Caleb says.

"Hi, Caleb." Then, after a pause, like she has to talk herself into saying it: "Hi, Stella."

"Pep Squad," Stella says. "So good to see you."

Kasey doesn't try to hide her suspicion.

"Let's get Evie into her chariot."

Caleb gets one of the medical assistants to help me into a wheelchair. It's not nearly as difficult as it has been. I woke up this morning and it felt like my arms suddenly decided they have muscles; I'm actually able to help hoist myself up out of bed. But that's not all of it. It's like last night changed something even deeper, like everything inside me has been turned upside down, or like the balance of the universe is off somehow. Whatever it is, I am not the same person.

"Girl, you're a machine," Stella says.

"Yeah," agrees Caleb. "You look really strong today."

Kasey looks at them, and then at me, trying to see what they saw so easily.

As Kasey and Caleb roll us into the hallway, I whisper to Stella, "Have you heard anything?"

"Nope."

"They're still in there?"

"Yep."

"God, what could they be talking about?"

"Probably how they're going to give us extra cancer as punishment."

"At least Dan's with them, though. Right? He'll be on our side."

"I hope so."

"Did you hear from Cole? Did he get away all right?"

"He's fine."

"What are you guys whispering about?" Kasey says.

"Nothing," we say in unison.

We pass by five-year-old Shanti's room. She's been in and out of here her whole life with sickle-cell anemia. Her door is open and we can see her tiny figure wrapped up in blankets, attached to a bag of blood.

"Hey, Evie," Kasey says in a thin, desperate voice. "Remember that time we toilet-papered David Halloway's house in fifth grade? And your mom made us go over there and apologize and clean it up?"

"Yeah?" I say.

"That was hilarious," she says, but her voice trails off almost before she finishes.

"That sounds really funny," Caleb says, and I wish I had some of his sweetness right now. I wish I could at least try.

We pass eleven-year-old Leo's room. He just got out of the surgery that removed his right arm below the elbow. On the other side of the curtain is his roommate Jonathan, four years old and here for his first round of chemo.

And now we've reached the end of the hall. We're face-to-face with a too-cheerful painting of monkeys hanging from a tree under a smiling sun. There's nothing to do but turn around.

"We could go down to the teen lounge," Caleb says. "They're doing crafts in there right now."

Stella sighs as Caleb and Kasey face our chairs the other way. "Remember my hair, Evie?" Stella says.

"Yeah. You could have sold it for someone's cancer wig," I say, and we all laugh at the irony. Everyone except Kasey.

"I stored all my power in my hair," Stella says dreamily. I only now notice something off about her, something slow and hazy. She has the pain-meds look. She has the look of being half-gone. "Now I keep all my power in my hat."

"It's a good place for it," I say.

"But you can take a hat off," she says, and I know there's some hidden meaning there, but I don't want to think about what it is.

"So where do we want to go?" Caleb says. "Cafeteria? Teen lounge?"

"Or how about the teen lounge?" Stella says. "Or maybe the cafeteria?"

This is a joke we say multiple times a day. It has never been funny.

"Let's race," I say. "Whoever makes it to the nurses' station first wins."

"Now you're talking," Stella says.

"I don't know," says Caleb.

"Are you crazy?" Kasey says behind me. I almost forgot she was there.

"Come on," Stella says. "Live a little." Another cancer ward joke that is not funny.

"No," says Kasey.

"Okay," Caleb says. "But we can't go too fast."

"Three out of four is a good start," Stella says. "Pep Squad, what do we have to do to convince you?"

"No," Kasey says again. She steps out from behind my

wheelchair and faces me, furious. "I'm not doing it. You could get hurt."

"It doesn't matter," I say, with a laugh in my voice that is much crueler than it should be. "We're already in a hospital."

She practically stamps her foot. "I'm not going to help you be so reckless. You have to be careful. Your leg. It's fragile." Her voice is shaking; her hands are fists by her side; her eyes are full of fear. I forgot she's not like us; she can't laugh this world away. She's still holding on. She still thinks there's some way for us to control it.

"I'm sorry," I say, taking Kasey's hand and squeezing it. She relaxes a little. "No racing. You're right."

"Thank you," she says. We hold each other's eyes for a moment and our shared past comes rushing back to me. It fills me up with a warm, thick sadness, and I realize I miss Kasey. I miss us. Even though she'll never be able to fully understand the Cancer Kid world, she was my world for far longer than I'll spend in here.

Stella starts coughing. Deep, cavernous coughs that shake her whole body.

"Stella?" Caleb says.

Stella shudders so hard that her hat falls off, revealing her pale, bald scalp. She stretches her neck, mouth opening and closing, gasping for air, tendons straining. She is a baby bird, shivering, featherless.

"Nurse!" Caleb calls. He shuffles as fast as he can to the nurses' station.

Kasey picks Stella's hat off the floor and places it gently on her head. She puts her hands on Stella's thin shoulders, says, "Shh." She wraps her arms around her and holds her as her body quakes. The kindness of this kills me and I start to cry. My beautiful girls. I reach for them but they are so far away.

Caleb comes back with the nurse on duty. She's new and we don't know her. She is all business. It shouldn't be her. It should be someone who loves us. Dan should be here. Even Moskowitz would be better.

"Excuse me," the nurse says, using her hip to push Kasey out from behind Stella's wheelchair. "Dr. Bernstein is on her way. I've got to get Miss Hsu back to her room." She wheels Stella away from us, her shoes squeaking in double-time. I want to run after them. I want to do something. But all I can do is sit in my chair, watching as Stella's bony back disappears down the hall, listening to her cough rattle the walls.

"Oh my god," Kasey says. I am crushing her hand in mine.

"It's going to be okay," Caleb says. "It's going to be okay." But none of us believe him.

nine.

"IT'S A GOOD SIGN THAT SHE'S STILL IN HER ROOM," CALEB says. "They haven't had to take her to . . ." His voice trails off midsentence and his eyes are confused, searching.

I put my hand on his arm. "Caleb?"

After a few moments, he's able to make eye contact and come back to me. "Sorry," he says. "I got stuck."

"Don't be sorry. You have nothing to be sorry about."

"How long was I gone?"

"Just a few seconds."

"I must look like such a freak."

"Not at all. And you're right, by the way. When you said it's a good sign that Stella's still in her room." I can always count on Caleb to see the positive in everything, even if his brain isn't fully working.

We've been sitting in my room watching TV for the last hour. The meeting with our parents was cut short by Stella's emergency, then everyone was distracted, so I guess we've avoided punishment for now. I saw the relief in Kasey's eyes when my parents came in and she knew her shift with me had ended. She does not have endurance for things like this. She has not been woken in the middle of the night by the loudspeakers calling "Code Blue"; she has not had to witness parents finding out their kid didn't make it through surgery; she has never seen a stretcher wheeled down the hall carrying the too-tiny sheeted figure.

But that doesn't make it easier for us. It doesn't make it less painful. Just less shocking. There is a place inside us already ready for this kind of pain. But it is still pain.

Will called from baseball practice, but even he couldn't quite figure out what to say. What is a guy—even one as sweet as Will—supposed to say to his girlfriend when her secret best friend forgets how to breathe? My parents were kind enough to hold off on the lecture when they found out about Stella, and went home early to have dinner with Jenica. Now Caleb and I are just waiting for someone to tell us something, even though we know they're not allowed to because of some stupid patient privacy law that does not recognize the need-to-know of best friends.

Around seven, Nurse Suzanne comes in. Caleb jumps up and gives her a hug. "Hey, buddy," she says. "Rough day, huh?"

"Have you heard anything?" I say.

"She's doing okay," she says. "You know I can't tell you any more than that."

"Can—," Caleb says, then pauses for a long time with his

mouth open as his brain tries to find where it hid the next word. "See?" he finally says.

Suzanne puts her hand on Caleb's shoulder. "Maybe tomorrow," she says. "I told her only one visitor tonight and she's asking for Evie. Sorry, kid."

He nods, smiling so sweetly I can almost believe his feelings aren't hurt.

The first thing Stella says when Suzanne wheels me into her room is, "I look like Gollum."

"Space Gollum," I say. Tubes stick out of her nose and the portacath in her chest, connecting to various machines and bags of fluids. Her bald head is bare. "You look like a cyborg." She is half machine. The monitor shows her heartbeat. The beep of her pulse harmonizes with the wet sucking of her oxygen machine.

"Space Gollum," she chuckles. As well as someone with tubes in her nose can chuckle. "You're funny, Cheerleader."

"Why aren't you wearing your hat?"

"Don't feel like it."

Stella's propped up in bed, her hospital gown hanging off her thin frame. Her shoulder sticks out, barely as thick as a golf ball. In all these months we've been in and out of the hospital together, I've never seen her in a hospital gown. She has never let herself look this sick.

"Nice dress," I say. First rule of being a Cancer Kid: we have to say the obvious things everyone else is too afraid to say.

"They cut off my favorite jeans," she says. "Can you believe that? They didn't even have to do anything to me below the waist, but they cut them anyway. These assholes in here are always trying to get me naked."

"'Cause you're hot."

"Are you flirting with me? Better not. Cole will kick your ass. Ha-ha." Her voice breaks and her eyes get shiny. "Fuck!" she says, rubbing her eyes. Even though she is weak, her voice manages enough anger to push the sadness away. "My fucking parents. He's never seen me in here. He can't come now. I won't see him before—" She covers her face with her beautiful hands, but her long fingers are too thin to hide behind. "Fuck!"

"We'll sneak him in," I say. "Give me his number."

"No." She shakes her head. She looks up at me and smiles. "It's okay. Don't worry about me. You worry about enough people already."

Just when I think the silence will consume us, Stella says, "They got me on some good drugs."

"Yeah?"

"I basically feel like a giant marshmallow."

"That's good." I look around Stella's room and see so much familiar—the counter and sink, the tiny closet, the computer and monitors, the blood pressure machine, the TV on the wall, the bed with all its rails and buttons, the other half of the room where it's all repeated.

"Where's your roommate?" I ask.

"They moved her in with Gwyn down the hall. Good riddance is what I say. When that girl wasn't crying, she was snoring. And her mom smelled like hot dogs."

Neither of us acknowledges what we know the move really means. They only make someone change rooms if they think their roommate is dying.

Stella hasn't decorated her side of the room like most of us long-term patients. There are no pictures of Cole or her friends and bandmates, none of whom her parents approve of. Stella wouldn't let them baby her with stuffed animals or, god forbid, religious paraphernalia. The only sign of her is her hat, alone, on the bedside table.

"You know what's weird?" Stella says. "You never come to my room. I always come to yours. You've always been the sickest one. We've always had to come to you." I don't know what to say to that. "Now look at you," she says, smiling. "You're going to be running in a few days. Or what is it you do? Cheerleading? Can that be a verb? You're going to be cheerleading in no time."

"I'm not sure that's the first thing I'd do if I could walk."

"Oh yeah, you'd have to screw that cutie boyfriend of yours."

"Stella!"

"That's what I'd do. Except not your boyfriend. Mine."

"It's weird you call him your boyfriend."

"Why? That's what he is."

"Sorry, it's kind of confusing to me."

"Maybe it's good to be confused sometimes."

"You never seem confused."

She considers this for a moment. "I get confused sometimes. About all sorts of things. But I just don't let it win. I figure it's better to make a decision and do something rather than just sitting around thinking about it forever. Even if it turns out to be the wrong decision. Then at least I'll be moving. At least I'll learn something, right? You don't learn much sitting on your ass waiting for a sure thing."

"You are very wise, Space Gollum," I say as I take her hand in mine, even though I know she hates mushy stuff.

"Shut up," she says, swatting my hand away. "I don't need you pining away at my sickbed. Suzanne!" she shouts into her intercom, shockingly loud for someone who needs tubes in her nose to breathe. "Come take this wench away. I need my beauty sleep."

Suzanne appears seconds later. "Bye, wench," Stella says as she pushes the button to lower the head of her bed. "Smell you later. Seriously, you should get that cast checked out. I think there's a dead rat in there."

"I love you, Stella," I say as Suzanne wheels me out of the room.

I expect a witty comeback, but what I think I hear are sobs.

ten.

I'M WAITING FOR MY PARENTS TO GO HOME SO CALEB and I can go through with our surprise for Stella, but they won't leave. They're too worked up about today's visit with Dr. Jacobs.

"She's gaining strength," Dr. Jacobs told them in his professional passionless monotone. "I know the plan was to send Evie home as soon as her pain stabilized, but if it's all right with you, I'd like to keep her in here a few more days so we can run some tests just to see what's going on. *If* anything's going on."

"I thought you said I was done with tests," I said. "I thought you said the goal was to minimize my suffering now."

"Well, that's the thing," Dr. Jacobs said, addressing my parents even though it was me who asked the question. "Evie is doing a lot better than anyone thought possible. She seems to have turned a corner. Very suddenly, I might add. She seems to be getting stronger even though her condition should be quickly deteriorating."

I heard Mom gasp.

"But I don't want anyone to get too excited just yet," Dr. Jacobs continued. "She's probably just feeling better because we stopped the chemo. I'm afraid if we let her go home right now, she might push herself too hard because of a false sense of wellness and end up accelerating her decline."

Despite Dr. Jacobs's attempt to rein in their hope, of course my parents jumped at the opportunity. No one even asked me what I wanted. So they sucked my blood and sent me off to radiology for a bone scan. Mom and Dad are working themselves into a tizzy, even though they should know by now it's going to hurt more later when the tests show I still have the same broken body as before.

For so long, my life was on hold. Now my death is on hold, and it's just as irritating. What a bizarre thing for life to feel so inconvenient. How unnatural to want to get it over with.

"How's Stella doing?" Mom says now, trying to make conversation. "I wanted to say hi earlier but she was sleeping."

"I don't know," I say. "She's okay, I guess."

"Her parents were livid in the meeting yesterday," Dad says. "It's like she can't do anything right in their eyes."

"Poor girl," Mom says, shaking her head. I don't know if she's referring to the cancer or her parents, but either way, she's right. "You know I love Stella, but sometimes I'm afraid she just doesn't think."

"You're wrong," I say, my voice trembling with an unfamiliar feeling. "It was a gift." I feel like I've been possessed by something foreign, something outside myself. I am shocked to realize it is anger pulsing through my body, sharp and vivid, like a drug. I can see how people could crave it. It's like what Stella said about the music, about the women singing. My anger makes me strong.

"What was a gift, honey?"

"What Stella did. Taking me outside. She thought it through. She did it for me." My voice shakes with a desperate need to be understood. "You don't know what it's like being stuck in here. Trapped, like a prisoner. She wanted me to get off of hospital grounds once before I died, so I could feel freedom again, just for a second."

"Oh, honey," Mom says. "It was very sweet, in her way. But I wish she would stop to think about how her actions affect others, that's all. What you two did was kind of selfish, Evie. We were really scared."

Again, that taste of anger. Ever since I got sick, all I've done is think about how everyone else is feeling. All I've done is try to protect them from their fear, protect them from mine.

But my rage dissipates as quickly as it came, leaving only sadness in its wake. "Are you mad at me?" I say. As intoxicating as it is, I don't want anger, theirs or mine. All it does is create conflict. All it does is tear people apart.

"Oh, Evie," Mom says, grabbing my hand.

Dad puts his arms around me and squeezes tight. "Sweetheart," he says. "We could never be mad at you."

My parents finally leave and I immediately call Caleb's room and tell him to come over.

"Did you bring everything?" I ask when he gets here.

"Laptop, check," he says. "Giant piece of red velvet cake from the cafeteria, check."

"I made a bouquet out of my best flowers," I say. "I think that's everything. Is she awake?"

"Yeah, I walked by her room and the door's open and the lights are on."

"Did she see you?"

"I don't think so."

My surprise for Stella isn't nearly as epic as hers was for me, but it's the best I can do with limited time and resources. Caleb carries the supplies as I wheel myself down the hall. Nurse Suzanne gives us the thumbs-up from where she's sitting at the nurses' station. It's sweet how seriously Caleb is taking this, tiptoeing down the hall in a semi-crouched position. He flattens himself against the wall outside Stella's door, then looks at me and nods. I nod back in the silent language of covert operations. He reaches his arm in and turns the dimmer down on the lights. I open the laptop and punch some keys to get it ready.

"Hey!" I hear Stella's voice from inside. "What's going on?"

As we enter the darkened room, I see her writing something on a piece of paper, but she quickly hides whatever it is under her hat on the bedside table.

"What're you writing?" Caleb says.

"None of your beeswax. What's with the mood lighting? What the hell are you two up to?" But her attempt at feistiness makes her cough so hard it shakes the bed and rattles the table next to it. "I'm okay," she gasps, waving off Caleb's doting. "I'm okay." She takes a deep breath to collect herself.

Caleb sets the cake and flowers on the table. "For you, madam," he says.

"Are you trying to woo me?" she says, wiping her mouth with the back of her hand. Her wrist is so skinny it barely seems strong enough to hold on to her hand.

Caleb takes the computer from me and sets it in front of her. The screen glows with Cole's smiling face.

"Hello, beautiful," Cole says out of the computer's tiny speakers.

"Oh!" Stella gasps, raising her skeletal hands to her mouth. Her eyes well up with tears.

"We wanted to have candles," Caleb says. "But Nurse Suzanne said no open flames around oxygen tanks."

Tears are streaming down her face and she's gasping for air.

"Stella?" Cole says from inside the computer. "Are you okay?"

"Can you breathe?" I say. "Do you need us to get Suzanne?"

"I'm not suffocating, I'm crying," she says. "Jesus, can't you people tell the difference?"

Stella is not supposed to cry.

She wipes her eyes and sits up a little straighter. She looks into the computer screen and her face relaxes into a smile. If it were anyone else, I would say she was almost blushing. But this is Stella, and she doesn't do things like that. But there is a sudden peace in her eyes that takes her out of this room, takes her away from all these machines and sterile whiteness, takes her out of her weak, emaciated body. For a moment, she is somewhere else, somewhere with Cole, and she is not sick.

I know what that feels like. Sometimes with Will, even when I've been so sick I could barely sit up, I would see him walk through the door and I'd be suddenly be strong and flawless, as if the sight of him healed me. I wish he were here. I wish he would wrap me in his arms and make all of this less scary.

"Let's give them some privacy," I say, wheeling myself backward out the door. Caleb follows and shuts the door behind him.

He takes a seat in a spare wheelchair and parks it next to mine. We are sitting in the hallway outside of Stella's room, staring at the white flatness of her closed door.

"I wonder what they're talking about," Caleb says.

"What would you say to your girlfriend?"

"I don't know. I've never had a girlfriend."

"Oh."

The brightly lit hall reverberates with the sounds of TVs. The nurses and medical assistants are huddled around the nurses' station, laughing at something on a computer screen. It might almost seem cheerful to someone who wasn't stuck here, who didn't know what kind of suffering is going on behind these walls.

"Evie?" Caleb says after a couple of minutes.

"Yeah?"

"I'm scared."

I look over at him and his baseball hat is on his lap, the scars and bumps and discolorations of his scalp exposed, vulnerable.

"Me too," I say.

"Can I hold your hand?" Caleb says.

"Okay."

He reaches over and threads his warm, thick fingers through mine.

Given the circumstances, I don't think Will would mind.

NOW.

if.

Dear Stella,

I know you're putting your makeup on, getting ready to visit me. Soon, I will hear your big boots clomping down the hall. I will hear you whistling at Dan and it will make me smile even before you can see me.

The good news is I think we're off the hook for our escape the other night.

If I write you this letter, it means you can't be gone. A letter has a destination. It makes you exist. You will read it and laugh, and then I will watch your beautiful hands fold it into a heart.

In the world of this letter, there is no such thing as a coma. Your voice has not been reduced to the sucking of the CPAP echoing in your empty room. Your eyes are not closed, your eyeliner and mascara not smeared away. There is not your limp hand resting on the blanket over your stomach, the tubes connected to the port in your chest, your fingers naked, all your rings removed.

But in the other world, the world outside of us, it is another story. A sad story. In this world, Dan wheels me over to the window, as though a change in scenery could somehow make you less gone. He tries to get me to talk, but I am somewhere far away, somewhere I do not have a voice. Here, the world looks different, wrong. It is dirty and hostile and falling apart, not beautiful like the view from the hill. It is not beautiful like when you are in it.

In this world, your parents walk stiffly to the front door of the hospital. Their faces are stone, showing nothing of what's inside, showing nothing of what it feels like to have a vegetable for a daughter. But then a flash of light—Cole rushing behind them, your knight in shining armor. And then a standoff, three figures at the sliding doors, fighting over who's allowed to love you. Your parents block the way. Cole is the hero, trying to save you. You are his Sleeping Beauty, waiting for the kiss that will bring you back to life. I call to him, but I, too, am a princess. I am Rapunzel locked in a tower. No one can hear me this far up, behind these thick windows that cannot open. We are beyond saving.

He was gallant, Stella. You need to know that. He tried to get around them. He did everything he could. But your father is bigger than Cole. And when the father of the girl you love shoves you to the ground, it is impossible to get back up. When security guards automatically side with the grown-ups, you are already defeated.

But don't worry. That is somewhere else. That is the world we don't belong in. In this world, our world, Cole is with you right now, and you are playing guitar softly while he runs his fingers through your long hair that has never fallen out. It is summer and you are singing. We are at the top of the hill looking at the world in all its glowing perfection, and your voice is making me brave.

Stella, it is so hard to stay with you. I keep shuttling back to the place where you are not. I am sick here so close to the ground. I am nauseous and trembling. But this sick is not from the cancer, not from chemo or dehydration or various medications. This is a new kind of sick, something sweet and feverish, something that comes with a sudden urge to tear this cast off, run down the hall, and jump out the window. Something in my bones, my muscles. I'd give anything to move. I know what wild animals must feel when they are caged. This room—this life—it is so small, so safe, so sterile. I want to scratch the paint off the walls. I want to run. This is something primal.

Stella, we are deer running through someplace wild. No. We are wolves.

I look at the framed picture of the cheer squad you

turned backward. All those girls with their faces to the wall, surrounded by wilting flowers. All those girls who have never known real pain. All those empty smiles. All those perfect lives. Their flawless world is miles away now, across vast deserts, mountains, oceans—unreachable. I will never find my way there again. That is not my world. Not that little universe captured so cleanly in that cheap frame. There's no way in, no portal between this world and theirs.

I bend and twist and stretch my body until my reaching fingers touch the frame. Muscles throughout my body, weak from disuse, strain back to life. I grab the picture, hold the hard, flat thing in my hand, then throw it across the room. Satisfaction pours through me as the glass shatters against the wall. My blood cools. The room expands just a little. Just enough to breathe. Just enough to stay alive.

I don't know which world is broken. Which world is yours? Which world is ours? Which world is the one I'm in right now?

Glass is on the floor. If I could walk, it would cut my feet.

Stella, which world is the one where you're not dead?

Love always,
Evie

eleven.

"COME ON, EVIE. JUST TRY IT," CALEB SAYS. WE ARE IN HIS room because there are too many kids in the teen lounge, but even in here with the door and curtains wide open, I feel claustrophobic.

"No, Caleb. I am not going to pray with you."

"But it works, it really does," Caleb says. "There are studies."

"It works doing what? Does it bring people back from the dead?"

He flinches.

"I'm sorry," I say, and I am. Why am I being mean to the one person left in the world who can come close to understanding what I'm going through? "I just don't understand what I'm even supposed to pray for."

"You can pray for comfort," he says. "You can pray for peace in your heart."

A surge of anger burns through me. "Really?" I can't help

the acid in my voice. "What about cancer? Can it make cancer go away?"

He lowers his eyes. I've hurt him, but he's still trying. "Actually," he says softly, "there have been cases of people being cured of all kinds of things, including cancer."

I roll my eyes. They are so swollen from crying, they are just slits. Stella died yesterday, and Caleb has made it his mission to comfort me. But all I seem able to do is treat him like crap.

"No offense, Caleb, but that's bullshit."

He takes a deep breath and looks at me with more kindness than I deserve. "I'm sorry you feel that way."

"Me too." I wish I believed as he did. I wish I had faith that God was taking care of me, that God gave a shit about any of us. I wish I believed there was a good reason for His taking Stella.

Caleb takes my hand in his. "I pray for you, Evie," he says. "I pray for you every day."

"Well, stop," I say. I pull my hand away. "I don't want your fucking prayers."

He looks like I slapped him. I hate myself.

"I'm sorry," I say. "I don't know what's wrong with me."

"It's okay," he says with a timid smile. "We're all grieving. We just do it in different ways, I guess."

"Hey, kiddos!" Dan says too cheerfully from the doorway. He's been popping in on us practically every half hour, along with the chaplain (aka the Grim Reaper), a social worker, a therapist, and all sorts of people who want to know if we want to talk about our loss. I assume this is just one of these visits until I notice a new glimmer in his eye. He's staring right at me with a maniacal look on his face.

"Evie, my dear, I'm going to steal you from Caleb," he says, and practically sprints over to grab the wheelchair. He wheels me out of the room before I even have a chance to say good-bye.

"What's up?" I say.

"Your folks are here."

"That's what you're excited about? They come here every day."

"Dr. Jacobs is here," he says.

"Ugh."

He just laughs as he delivers me to my room, where Mom, Dad, and Dr. Jacobs are waiting for me.

"Oh, Evie," Mom says, hugging me. "Dr. Jacobs told us about Stella. I am so, so sorry."

"Thanks."

"I should send Mrs. Hsu some flowers." Even after all this time, they never got to be on a first-name basis.

"Sure. That'd be nice." As if flowers could change something. As if anything Mom does could really help. Mrs. Hsu's daughter is gone forever, and I'm next.

Dad takes his turn hugging me. "How are you holding up, honey?"

"Okay, I guess." How do I even start to answer that question?

"That's actually not why I asked you to come this morning," Dr. Jacobs interrupts. Could he be any more of a dick?

"Oh," Mom says, startled. She narrows her eyes in suspicion.

"What is it?" It's never good news when Dr. Jacobs calls them to the hospital.

My stomach drops. I can't handle any more bad news. Not now. Not yet. I am too raw.

We all look at Dr. Jacobs. We are all holding our breath, waiting to hear what new trick the cancer has played on me.

There is a crack in the usual stone of his face, a fissure in the professional emotionless doctor demeanor. Is that his lips turning up? Is that a *smile*?

"The test results came back," he says.

"And?" Dad says.

"I can't quite get my head around it yet, but Evie's blood counts and proteins look normal. And the bone scan didn't show anything except healthy bone and the implants exactly where they're supposed to be. I think she'll be ready to get her cast off any day now."

Mom and Dad look at each other. Their faces are blank, shocked. They are trying to process this impossible news.

"Her blood counts, Doctor," Mom says. "What does that mean?"

"Well," says Dr. Jacobs, looking at me sympathetically. "It means I want to do a bone-marrow aspiration."

"No!" I say.

Imagine the most painful thing in the world. Then multiply it by a thousand. That's what a bone marrow aspiration feels like.

"Evie," Dad scolds.

"Wait," Mom says, her lips finally breaking into the smile

she's been fighting. "You want to check her bone marrow? You think something may have changed?"

"The cancer in her bone marrow should have affected her blood work. But as I said, her results matched those of a perfectly healthy kid."

"Oh my god," Mom gasps, and starts blubbering. Dad blinks back tears and squeezes my good knee a little too hard.

I feel nothing. I feel numb. Stella is dead and they're talking about me being a "perfectly healthy kid."

"Now, I don't want everyone getting too excited just yet. We won't know anything for sure until after we get the results. But there's a chance Evie has more time than we originally thought. I've never seen anything like it, but it's possible the chemo finally kicked in, to use precise medical terminology."

Did Dr. Jacobs just make a joke?

"Oh, thank you, Dr. Jacobs!" Mom cries. I know she wants to hug him, but luckily she's controlling herself.

I zone out as they talk about the test. I try not to imagine the big fat needle slicing through my skin and fat and muscle and bone. I stare at the wilting flowers I spend so much time staring at. Why hasn't anyone removed them? Can't they see that they're dying?

"We need to throw away those flowers," I blurt out.

"Oh, okay, honey," Mom says, confused. "We'll deal with that in a minute."

When Dr. Jacobs finally leaves us, Mom and Dad hover around me, beaming at each other like they just accomplished a great feat as a team—an Olympic relay race, the Super Bowl. And I'm the baton or the football, an inanimate object that gets passed back and forth, a prop without which the game wouldn't exist.

In a few minutes I will become a pincushion for their needles yet again. I will be strapped down and drilled into and sampled so they can look for good news.

Stella just died and I might live and I don't know how I feel about any of this.

twelve.

I COULD BE ANYONE, JUST A REGULAR KID WHO BROKE HER leg doing something normal like riding a bike or climbing a tree. Dr. Jacobs says it's healing perfectly. Miraculously, no major nerves or blood vessels were damaged; the tissue remained healthy and supple while I was bedridden. The only thing that shows up on X-rays now is the small metal plate in my pelvis and the titanium rod and six screws holding my thigh together.

My white blood cells are at normal levels after being virtually nonexistent. According to the tests and multiple retests, there is cancer exactly nowhere in my body. Nowhere. Nothing. Zero. Zip.

There has been a mistake. Or a miracle. Or some twisted combination of both. Another one of God's jokes—but I don't know if I should laugh or cry.

I am the only kid on the cancer ward without cancer. My room is empty. All the decorations have been taken down, all the flowers finally thrown away. I am sitting on my hospital bed, waiting to be discharged.

I've already endured Caleb's tearful good-bye. I promised him I would visit and text, that we'd meet for coffee as soon as he gets out, but all I wanted was to get away as quickly as possible. I don't belong here now.

Mom is in the hall somewhere, looking for someone to officially sign me out. Jenica and Dad are bringing the car to the front, my suitcase packed and in the trunk. Will and Kasey both wanted to come, but I told them not to. My leaving is already getting too much attention as it is. Plus, we have all the time in the world now. This may be the last hospital room I see for a very long time.

I should feel something. Happy. Grateful. But I keep thinking about how the last thing Stella probably saw was a ceiling identical to this one, an empty expanse of flat, lifeless white. I keep thinking about how she was alone in that room, being kept alive by machines. Until she wasn't.

After I leave, the hospital sounds will continue without me—the constant beeps, the doors opening and closing, the rattles of equipment being rolled up and down the hallway, in and out of rooms. The low, serious drone of doctors and parents; the high, cheerful voices of children; the hospital's peculiar duet of laughter and crying.

I hear squeaking wheels and the shuffling of little feet. A girl I recognize from movie nights appears in my doorway, wearing pink footy pajamas that probably used to fit her but now droop off her emaciated frame. She has the look of a lifer, one of the kids who have basically been raised here. I think she's somewhere around six or seven, but it's so hard to tell the age of the gravely ill. Teenagers can stay prepubescent for years; little boys can look like haggard old men.

Only a few stringy wisps of white-blond hair are left on her head. Stella would always have a fit whenever people failed to shave their heads when they got to this point. "No self-respect," she'd complain. "It hurts my eyes." But maybe this girl's parents have more important things to think about than their daughter's hair.

She is dwarfed by the oxygen machine she drags behind her. A floppy stuffed rabbit rides on top.

Before I have a chance to say anything, she walks over and climbs onto my bed.

"Hi," she says.

"Hi."

"I'm Carla."

"Hi Carla, I'm Evie."

"I know." She retrieves the stuffed rabbit from its perch on the machine and holds it out to me. "This is Piggy."

"Hello, Piggy." I shake his little soft hand.

"Can I sign your cast?"

"Okay." I don't tell her that I'm getting it removed tomorrow.

She pulls a pen out of a hidden zippered compartment in Piggy's back. She has come prepared.

She bites her lip in concentration as she writes the wiggly

words in a clean space between the faded names of kids who have come and gone in the three weeks I've been in here: "To: Evie. Love: Carla," then circles it with a heart.

"That looks nice," she says, nodding her head.

"It does."

She scoots closer to me. "I have what you had. Ewing's sarcoma." The heavy words sound so strange in her tiny voice. "It was in my arm but now it's in my lungs, too." She holds out the rabbit and points to its chest. "Here," she says.

"I'm sorry," I say.

She looks around my empty room. "All your stuff is gone."

"I'm leaving today."

"I know."

"Oh?"

"Everybody knows."

"Oh."

"Evie?"

"Yes?"

Her big eyes blink twice. If they made a sound, it would be *plink, plink*. "Can I touch you?"

"Why do you want to touch me?"

"Piggy and I were thinking that maybe some of your miracle will rub off. So maybe I can be cured too."

Before I can even think about what I'm doing, I throw my arms around Carla and press her hard against me. I can feel her brittle bird bones through her skin. If I let go, she'll disappear. She'll shatter and turn into dust.

"Ouch," she says.

I release her quickly. "Are you okay? I'm so sorry." I look her over for signs of harm.

"This just got knocked a little," she says as she adjusts the tube in her nose.

"I'm sorry. I don't know why I did that."

She just shrugs her shoulders. "You probably needed a hug."

"I guess."

She slides off the bed and puts Piggy back in his spot on top of the oxygen machine. "Okay, bye," she says unceremoniously. I fight the urge to grab her again.

"See you later," I say, trying to act casual, struggling to not lose it in front of this kid.

She tilts her head to the side and studies me. *Plink, plink.*

"Probably not," she says flatly. "I don't think the hug worked. I don't think miracles are contagious."

My mouth opens but no words come out. I watch her shuffle out into the hall, the oxygen tank following her like a loyal pet.

thirteen.

MY BEDROOM IS LIKE A MUSEUM. EVERYTHING IS EXACTLY where it was when I left for my walk with Will at Lake Merritt what seems like forever ago. I can tell Mom washed my sheets because my bed is made, but other than that, it's like time stopped that sunny afternoon. The book I was in the middle of reading is still lying open on my bedside table. My school sweatshirt is still hanging on the back of my desk chair. A dirty sock lies lonely in the corner.

I know it hasn't really been that long, but I imagine a layer of dust coating everything. It's my room, but I feel a strange reluctance to touch anything, as if I'll get in trouble for disturbing the exhibit. None of these things feel like they're mine. All these patterns and textures, all these colors besides white, all these smells besides hospital disinfectant—it's too much. I feel dizzy. So I reach over from my wheelchair and turn off the lights. The darkness makes it a little more manageable.

Dad left my suitcase in the middle of the room, where it now sits awkward, almost menacing. It strikes me that I don't even want to open it, don't even want to let the contents touch this air. I will never wear those clothes again, never use that toothbrush, never brush my hair with that comb. That is all Cancer Girl's stuff. Not mine.

I wheel myself over to the suitcase, wanting to move it somewhere out of sight. Maybe I can push it deep inside my closet, where it will be lost, unopened, and I'll never have to think about it again. But that's when I notice something on my desk that wasn't there before, a square package slightly bigger than a shoebox, wrapped in brown paper and a postage label with my address on it. The return address is the hospital.

Before I even open it, I know it's from Stella. It's just like her to send me a package from the dead. As I unwrap the paper, a familiar smell hits me so hard I choke on my own breath—Stella's smell. The musky men's cologne she somehow managed to make smell so feminine.

I open the box to find Stella's hat—the smooth black felt fedora, with the oval brim and center crease, like something Al Capone or Indiana Jones would wear, except this one has a special Stella flair with the shiny black ribbon around the crown, holding the iridescent green and blue peacock feather. It is mine now, the place where Stella kept her power. My hands shake as I lift it up, as I discover a second present hidden under it, a small wooden box, a little girl's treasure chest. When I open it, another familiar smell escapes—the box is stuffed full of more marijuana than I could imagine anyone ever being able to smoke.

A folded note sits among the densely packed buds. I open it to find the smooth, graceful handwriting of a ghost:

Dear Evie,

Don't forget to live big. Make me proud, Cheerleader.

Love,
Stella

"Honey!" Mom's voice calls from the living room. "Will's here!"

I don't have time to hurt. I don't have time to miss her.

I put the hat on my head and it fits perfectly. I imagine I absorb some of Stella's power as it hugs my thin, patchy hair. I hide the box of weed in the back of my underwear drawer and wheel myself into the hallway, my arms stronger than they've been in months.

Maybe Will can make me feel better. Maybe he'll take me into his arms and squeeze some joy into me. But what I really want to do is get into bed and sleep for as long as it takes for me to feel like doing all the things I used to love doing. I want to sleep until I can forget that Stella's gone.

Will's face lights up when I enter the living room. He hands me yet another bouquet of red roses. The too-sweet smell overwhelms me as he leans over to kiss my cheek. I feel so small, like I'm his child.

"How are you feeling?" he says.

"Fine," I say. "Tired. Ready to get out of this chair. Ready to get my cast off tomorrow."

We come dangerously close to awkward-silence territory, but a knock on the door saves us just in time. Kasey walks in without waiting for anyone to answer, a right she earned a long time ago from being my best friend.

"Evie!" she cries, and runs over to hug me. For a moment, it feels right, and I wish we could just go to my room and lie on the floor in our pajamas and pretend it's two years ago. But instead, it's now, and no one knows what to say.

"Well," Mom says. "Your dad should be here any minute with the food."

"Isn't that Stella's hat?" Kasey says with a hint of a frown.

"Do you like it?"

I can tell the answer is no, but she manages a smile and nods. I haven't had a chance to see what I look like, but I know this isn't exactly the style of a varsity cheerleader.

"What does everyone want to drink?" Mom chirps.

"Water's fine for me," Kasey says.

"I have iced tea," Mom says. "Milk. Orange juice. We might have a couple of cans of Coke in the back of the fridge."

"I'll have iced tea," Will says. "I bet Evie wants iced tea too. Right, Evie?" He grins at me, like he expects an award for remembering that I like iced tea, and I'm pretty sure old Evie would have been touched, but I'm not.

"Yeah," I say. "Sure." Mom disappears into the kitchen.

"How's baseball going?" Kasey says to Will.

"It's all right. Keeping me busy, I guess. But I have to admit, I miss football season."

"Yeah, me too," Kasey says. "Cheering for the basketball team just isn't the same."

They laugh. I don't. I can't even try to pretend I care about sports.

"Do you guys want to sit down or something?" I say. "We're just sort of standing around. I mean, you. You're standing. I'm already sitting. You know what I mean."

"Oh, Evie," Kasey says, flicking my hat. "You're so cute."

The front door swings open and Dad yells, "Dinner's here!" He's carrying bags full of takeout boxes, and the sweet, spicy smell of my favorite restaurant, Burma Superstar, fills the house. I'm so excited that I forget to be annoyed with Kasey for being so patronizing.

"Awesome," Will says.

"Have a seat, everyone," Dad says. "Plates are already on the table. I'll grab some serving spoons." Mom emerges from the kitchen with our drinks just as he's going in, and she giggles her surprise at their perfect timing, and he kisses her.

"I hope I have a relationship like your parents when I grow up," Kasey says to me. "They're, like, perfect."

"Yeah," Will says. "They're pretty perfect." He looks at me in a way that says he thinks we could be that perfect too. And now, for the first time in forever, we can actually allow ourselves to think in those terms, to think about us having a future.

Jenica skulks out of her room and joins us. We all sit down

as Dad unpacks the bags of deliciousness. The smell of coconut and curry waft around the dining room, and my mouth actually waters. This is definitely not hospital food. I am hungrier than I can remember being all year.

"Did you get the walnut shrimp?" Jenica says, systematically inspecting each of the takeout boxes.

"Oh, oops, sweetie," Dad says. "I forgot."

"But that's my favorite," she whines. "You know that."

"There are a lot of other great dishes. What about the shrimp and eggplant?"

She frowns as she serves herself. I can almost hear her adding this to her long list of resentments of me, as if I am responsible for Dad's mistake. Now that I'm back, there's suddenly room for more than love and sadness, and we can fall back into our good old sibling rivalry.

Luckily, I am able to lose track of the dinner conversation as I stuff my face. "Oh my god, this is so good," I say. "I forgot what real food tasted like."

This seems to make Mom and Dad happy. They share one of their looks.

"Evie, how are you feeling?" Kasey says, moving the food around on her plate. She only has some greens, a couple of pieces of broccoli, one shrimp, and about a tablespoon of brown rice.

"Good," I say. "Hungry." My parents do their look again, like they need to congratulate each other on everything I do that resembles healthy teenage behavior.

Kasey doesn't seem satisfied by that answer. She wants

something bigger, deeper, more cancer-y.

"It's so great to have you back," Will says, placing his hand on mine. He leaves it there, on my hand holding the chopsticks. He is keeping me from my food. "How does it feel?" he says.

"Good," I say, pulling my hand away to continue eating.

Jenica and I are the only ones eating. Everyone else is just sitting around looking at me.

"So, Kasey," Mom says, always the first to rescue us from uncomfortable silences. "How is the cheer squad this year?"

"Oh, great," she says. "There's a freshman who made varsity who's been training as a gymnast for the *Olympics*." She looks at me guiltily. "But of course, it's not the same without Evie. We all miss her so much."

I give her a broccoli-toothed smile.

"Dr. Jacobs says that if physical therapy goes well, Evie could be down to a cane in just a few weeks!" Mom says. "She's healing so fast."

"Wow," says Kasey.

"She's so strong," says Will.

I have gotten so used to people talking about me in the third person.

"Our little survivor," Dad says.

"Our miracle," Mom says, her voice cracking at the end as her eyes well up with tears.

It goes on like that for another hour. I focus on my food and try not to feel guilty for not feeling the gratitude I know I should. A week ago, I thought I wouldn't live more than a month, yet now

I find myself annoyed that I'm going to be limping around with a cane like an old lady. As we sit around the table sampling the ice-cream flavors Dad picked up from Tara's—avocado, lavender, white pepper chocolate chip, and Mexican chocolate—my leg starts hurting. It's probably nothing a couple of Advil can't fix, but I'm grateful for the Norco prescription they gave Mom when I left the hospital. It's up to me when I need it. All I have to do is ask.

I want to hug Mom when she shoos Will and Kasey away after dinner. "I know you two want to stay and hang out with Evie, but she needs to rest." They take turns hugging me and telling me how great it is to have me back. I want to agree with them, but something inside me says not so fast. I'm not the girl they remember. I'm not anyone they know.

After they leave, the house is quiet. Mom helps me with the humiliating task of going to the bathroom. "Just a few more days and you'll be on crutches and you can do this on your own," she reminds me from outside the door after she gets me situated. Even with the door closed, I am never alone.

I wish Dr. Jacobs hadn't told her to hold my prescription. I wish I could be in control of how much and when I take it. If it were up to me, I'd take three pills right now, but that is not an option. I'm only allowed a maximum of two every four hours. So I ask Mom for two. I don't tell her I already took a few Advil. I don't tell her about the theory I'm testing: maybe the Advil will take care of the dull ache in my leg; maybe the Norco will then be free to work its other magic and make the rest of my life a little softer.

fourteen.

I MISS YOU, SAYS CALEB'S TEXT. I START TO WRITE *I miss you too*, but then I delete it and change the channel on the TV.

I just got home from getting my cast off and now we're waiting for the physical therapist to show up. Luckily, Orthopedics is on the first floor right by the entrance to the outpatient hospital, so I didn't have to go up to the second floor; I didn't have to go near Oncology or the injection clinic where Stella and I spent so much time together. It was weird to be across the street from the inpatient hospital where I spent the past few weeks, the place where Stella died, where Caleb still is, where Dan, Nurse Moskowitz, Dr. Jacobs, and everyone else are still showing up every day to hang out with sick kids. I used to be one of those kids, one of the sickest, but today I was just someone getting a cast taken off. In and out in less than an hour when only a few days ago I was dying.

Two days into life outside the hospital and, so far, I'm not impressed. I watch the same mind-numbing daytime TV I watched in the hospital. I take naps. Mom asks me five million times per hour, "How are you feeling?" and five million times I answer, "Fine." I answer, "No, thank you," to her "Do you need anything?" Helicopters could take lessons from her in hovering.

I'm avoiding texts. All those *I love you, babe*s from Will. All those *So happy you're back!*s and *Can't wait to see you!*s and *When are you coming to school?*s from everyone else. All those exclamation points.

This is really exciting stuff. This is what it feels like to be a miracle.

I change the channel on the TV again. I look for something new. Something louder.

After a few episodes of yet another reality show about rednecks, the physical therapist—a large, butch woman named Sandy—arrives with pages and pages of physical therapy instructions. Mom's beside herself, offering the poor woman beverages, snacks, my unborn child, anything, like Sandy is doing us a huge favor by coming over, like she's the most generous person in the world, like it means something more than just her doing her job.

She and Mom help me upright so I can practice using the crutches. It's weird being suddenly vertical after a month of sitting and lying down. The muscles in my legs wake up from their deep sleep. They are groggy. They want to go back to bed. My leg doesn't feel like it's mine. It's someone else's, someone weaker, someone who stole my strong leg and replaced it with this pathetic, shriveled, unused thing.

Mom watches as I take a couple of practice laps around the living room. I don't think her butt is even touching the chair, she's so tense and springy. Her hands are in front of her mouth, palms together like she's praying. I don't think she's breathing. As if holding her breath could keep me upright. As if exhaling could blow me over.

My leg cramps. I lose my balance and Sandy catches me under my armpits. Mom springs up and hovers closer. I can feel her propellers buzzing.

"Honey, are you okay?"

"I'm fine." Sandy helps me to the couch. Why am I out of breath? I hobbled maybe twenty feet total.

"You have to take it easy," Sandy says. "Start out small and gradually work up to longer distances. It's all in the instructions here." She taps the pile of printouts. "Now why don't we try out some of these exercises?"

She shows me how to point my toes and flex my feet. She shows me how to stretch my quads and hamstrings. This is remedial stuff. This is stuff for old people. The infirm.

I can't even touch my toes. A year ago, I could do splits. On both sides and the middle. In the air.

"Good job!" Mom cheers at nothing.

Sandy leaves us with my rehab instructions and my therapy schedule. Mom's eyes glisten with possibility while mine cloud over with exhaustion. My phone dings with another text, but I ignore it. Time for another nap.

if.

Dear Stella,

I have to go into the hospital in a few days to see Dr. Jacobs. I'm only getting blood tests, but for some reason he feels it necessary to talk to me. If he wants to see me so bad, I don't understand why he can't just take the elevator down a few floors and walk across the street to the outpatient building where they do blood tests just fine. It's like he wants to torture me, making me go back to the inpatient building, back to the cancer floor, back to that place with all the memories. It's just a thirty-minute appointment, but still. I'm trying not to think about it.

I'm doing laps around the house like a caged beast. I hobble in circles until I'm so exhausted I can barely make it back to the couch. Sandy said to take it easy, and I'm sure she means well, but she doesn't know what the hell she's talking about. I doubt she's ever been trapped in her house like a prisoner. She certainly hasn't ever had my mother as a prison guard, constantly offering beverages.

My armpits are chafed and red from the crutches. Physical therapy and all my circles around the house have made me sweaty. Even with the removable soft brace that replaced my cast, I still haven't managed to take a proper shower in weeks. I'm sure you'd have something crude to say about the way I smell. I know I'm disgusting, and I know I should do something about it, but somehow it seems easier to stay in pajamas all day since all I do is sleep and watch TV anyway.

Sometimes I want to shake everyone until the smiles fall off their faces, those smiles that try to say everything's okay now, the hard part's over, Evie's alive and everything is back to normal. No one wants to talk about how incredibly un-normal it actually is, how no one knows how to talk to me now that I'm home, now that I'm not Cancer Girl anymore.

If I'm not Cancer Girl, who am I exactly? Crutches Girl? Gimpy-Leg Girl? Should-Have-Died-but-for-Some-Reason-Didn't Girl? Going-to-Get-Better-Soon-but-Right-Now-Is-Still-Pretty-Useless Girl? Caged-Lion-in-a-Too-Small-Cage-at-a-Second-Rate-Zoo Girl? Everyone is so damn polite all the time. My family, my best friend, my boyfriend, these people who are supposed to know me better than everyone—they can't do much better than small talk and pats on the back. They stare at me with their weepy eyes and sigh. Even Will seems scared to touch me; the only affection I get is quick, dry pecks on the cheek. It's like he's afraid of breaking me. I miss the way he used to touch me. I miss feeling wanted, really wanted, *not just cared for, not just doted on. Everyone thinks I'm still so fragile. Don't they realize I survived? Don't they realize how tough that makes me?*

No one knows what to do with me now that I'm alive. There's no protocol for how to treat someone who comes back from the dead. There are so many books about grief and loss, about saying good-bye to the people you love. But there is no book about taking back that good-bye.

Maybe things will get better when I go back to school in few days. Maybe something will happen besides this monotony of waiting. Maybe people will remember who I really am. Maybe I will too.

Love,
Evie

fifteen.

MOM HAD TO RUN TO THE STORE, SO I'M HOME ALONE. IT hits me that I haven't really been alone in a month. I've either been in the hospital with a nurse checking on me every hour, or here with Mom's constant attention.

Now this is it, my chance to escape. Just for a few minutes, then I'll get back in my cage like a good pet.

I turn off the TV. The house is quiet. Mom will be back from the store soon. Will is coming over after baseball practice. I have half an hour of freedom.

I pull on a sweatshirt and tie an old running shoe on my good foot. I pull a clean pair of sweatpants over my leg brace. I look at Stella's hat sitting on my desk and think about putting it on, but I ultimately decide it would be cruel to subject it to being seen with this outfit.

The doorknob is solid and cold in my hand. It feels illicit. I have been reduced to this: the most exciting thing that's happened to me in days is opening the door to leave my house.

I hobble out onto the sidewalk. The air is cool and breezy with early spring. This quiet residential street I used to so easily walk down is suddenly an obstacle course of cracked sidewalk, tree roots, and cars parked in driveways. A sensible voice inside my head tells me this isn't a good idea. I've only been upright for a few days. I've only practiced with these crutches in my very flat house with walls and furniture all around to grab on to whenever I get tired. I've always had someone to catch me.

But there's another voice, the wild beast voice. The one that's so sick of being caged. It says, *What the hell?* It says, *Maybe a little danger is exactly what you need.*

It says, *What would Stella do?*

Stella would strut down this sidewalk like she owned it.

I try on her confidence. I imagine what it feels like to be a rock star, to be strong and fierce and fearless. I look at all the hazards in front of me and tell myself I'm not afraid of falling.

So I walk. It feels good to be moving. It feels good to be going somewhere besides in a circle. My leg is already stronger. My muscles are already coming back. I barely even slow where a tree root breaks through the concrete. I slide past a traffic cone with perfect grace.

I turn the corner onto a major street and the wall of sound and exhaust from a passing bus throws me a little off-balance. But my arms have gotten strong and I manage to right myself with my crutches. A cyclist narrowly avoids me on the sidewalk and I yell, "Ride in the street, you fucking asshole!" Stella would be proud.

I walk and I walk. Most people ignore me, but a few people look with confusion and concern. It's not very often you see a girl in sweatpants with patchy cancer hair hobbling down a busy street on crutches. But whatever. Let them look. This is the best I've felt in weeks. I feel like I could walk forever. I could keep going and going and never come back.

I manage to go five full blocks before I start feeling weak. I turn around and see the expanse of sidewalk I'll have to travel before turning onto my street. It's farther than I remember. Isn't it supposed to be the other way around? Isn't the way back always supposed to feel shorter?

I make it one block before I realize I should have turned around a lot sooner. I lean against a tree for support. I white-knuckle the crutches. Sweat is pouring down my face and my leg is wobbly. I didn't bring my phone with me. Something could happen. Something could happen and no one would know.

I'm standing in the middle of the sidewalk four blocks from my house and I feel farther away from home than I've ever felt. I can't go back and I can't get away. I'm stuck here, in this limbo place where you're only supposed to pass through. And I can't move. I'm exhausted. My leg folds and I manage to slide down the tree onto the ground. My braced leg slides out from under me. I'm sitting in a puddle of who knows how many dogs' pee. My hand is in something wet and squishy.

I cry because I can't move. I cry because I'm trapped. I cry because my body is a cage, with a door that opens and closes whether I want it to or not. I'm alone inside, while everyone I love is on the outside, pointing, watching, feeding me things through the bars, waiting for me to do tricks. And even though the door opens, I know I can never get out. There's a moat around me I cannot cross.

I wanted to be fearless like Stella, but I'm terrified. And she's still gone.

"Hey, girl," says a tall man with long dreadlocks and a Caribbean accent. "Whatchu doin down dere?"

"Nothing," I say.

A woman stops. Her dog sniffs at me. "Are you okay, honey?"

"Why she cryin'?" the man says to the woman.

"I don't know. Honey, why are you crying?"

I shake my head. I don't look up. I don't want to see them staring at me down here in my cage.

A guy on a skateboard stops. A girl on a bike stops.

"Do you need us to call someone for you?"

"Do you need help up?"

"Do you want to use my phone?"

They're all looking, waiting for me to tell them how to help me. But I don't know. I have no idea what I need from anyone.

"Evie!" calls a familiar voice down the street. My heart jumps. "Evie!"

"Is that you?" the woman says. "Are you Evie?"

"Evie!" Will's voice calls from blocks away. My savior. My knight.

"Over here!" the man yells in his direction.

"Evie?" says the woman, crouching down in front of me. She

holds her hand out, like I'm some dog she's testing to see if it's friendly. "Do you know that boy? Are you safe?" I look up and the concern in her eyes is real. Everyone's concern is real. Their concern is always so real.

I nod. I wipe my face with the back of my hand. Whatever wet, squishy thing it was in smears on my face, and it makes me start crying all over again.

Will runs up, his skin still shiny with sweat from practice. "Evie, what happened?" But I can't speak through my tears.

"I think she fell down or something," says the kid on the skateboard.

"Are you hurt?" He crouches down and I reach my arms up, like a toddler who wants to be held. "Oh, Evie," he says, letting me throw my arms around his neck. He somehow picks me up, cradled in his arms, as if I am the three-year-old version of myself, and I am both grateful for his strength and disgusted with myself for feeling so helpless, for needing him to rescue me.

"Did you fall?" he says.

I shake my head no. "I just got tired," I say into his chest. "I just had to sit down."

"I got to your house and your mom was freaking out. She was getting ready to call the cops. Why did you leave the house? Why did you go so far? Why didn't you tell anyone?"

"I wanted to go for a walk."

"You can't do that, Evie. You can't just go. Not now. Not anymore." There is an edge to his voice, but it is not anger. It is fear. That is my prison. It is everybody else's fear.

"I'm sorry," I say, and then I'm crying so hard I can't say anything else.

Will carries me the entire way back home. I couldn't get out of his arms if I wanted to. I hide my face in his neck and breathe in the musky warmth of his post-practice sweat. I remember when this smell used to turn me on, when one whiff of it would make me dizzy with desire. It is the smell of his strength. But now that means something entirely different than it used to. Now I don't know how it makes me feel.

I want him to stay, I want him to never let me go, but eventually Will has to leave to have dinner with his own family. Even though I can do it myself, I let Mom help give me a sponge bath. She cries as she wipes the dirt and whatever else is on my face. She says, "I was so scared when I got home and you weren't here. I don't know what I'd do if something happened to you."

But you do know, Mom. You've known for a long time. It's my living *you don't know what to do with.*

I tell her I'm tired and don't want dinner. She helps me into my pajamas and tucks me into bed before Dad even gets home.

"Does it hurt?" she says, stroking my hand. I tell her yes and she gives me two Norcos. But it is not my leg that needs them.

As soon as she leaves, I take Stella's magic box out of my sock drawer where I've been hiding it. I pull out the two pills I've been saving for an emergency, the ones I hid in my cheek after Mom gave them to me yesterday.

This is it. This is the emergency. This is the pain I need to not feel.

sixteen.

HALFWAY THROUGH LISTENING TO STELLA'S CD, I REALIZED I was no longer solid. My body had turned into steam. It turned into the opposite of pain.

And then sleep.

Then my mom shouting, "Evie, wake up!" in the middle of my head. "Evie, we're going to be late for your appointment with Dr. Jacobs." Her shrill voice, scraping my skull.

And now back to zero pills. Now an anxious emptiness I don't know how to fill. I remember the school assembly about prescription drug abuse. I am fully aware that's what I'm doing. But after everything I've been through, I'm really not that worried about taking a few extra Norcos once in a while. It's amazing the kinds of things people worry about, all their stupid ways to be careful and avoid getting hurt. Wear your seat belt! Look both ways when crossing the street! Don't abuse prescription painkillers! But I had cancer. *Cancer.* Survival is hard work, and sometimes survivors need a little help dealing with all the surviving they're doing. Some have support groups and counseling; Caleb has church and faith and Jesus; and I have my pills.

I also have a box full of weed sitting in my sock drawer, waiting for me to figure out what to do with it.

On my way to the hospital, my anxiety grows with every block we drive closer. The air is getting denser, like we're entering some other dimension with different gravity that wants to crush the breath out of my lungs. Mom is listening to NPR, and they're talking about a civil war somewhere in Africa, about starving orphans, refugees, mass graves. How can she listen to this all day long? How can it be background noise on her way to the grocery store or post office? How can she hum to the tune of murdered babies and genocide and the international community not wanting to get involved?

Things have been happening all over the world and I know nothing about them, and I don't want to. Turn the radio off. Put cotton in my ears. I don't want to hear it. All these things so much worse than what has happened to me. I know I should be grateful I am alive. I should be grateful for my mom and her car and the stupid hospital and doctors and their great medical training. I should care about the orphans. I should care about something, anything. But I don't. I can't. It's caring that's the problem in the first place. It's caring that gets hearts broken.

As soon as we enter the hospital lobby, I can't breathe. All those parents' faces. All those kids. All those supposed-to-be-cheerful decorations.

Mom is ridiculous, strutting in and greeting the security guard like they're old pals. "Hi, Al! It's been a while." She's desperate to find someone she recognizes. She wants to gloat. She wants everyone to know her kid isn't dying anymore. She's showing me off.

"After we see Dr. Jacobs, we can go see Caleb and some of your friends," she says. "Would you like that?" She is talking too loud. Her voice bangs around in my head and makes my brain hurt.

I shake my head because it's impossible to speak when you're not breathing.

She doesn't understand. She thinks the hospital is just a building, just a place. She doesn't understand how dangerous it is. It takes people and doesn't give them back.

I fight the pounding in my chest on our way up the elevator. How can she not feel it? How can she act like this place didn't almost take me, too?

Breathe.

I close my eyes and conjure Stella. I hear her voice. I feel her hand, cool on the back of my neck. We're in the chemo dungeon, sitting side by side on those horrible beds with tubes pumping poison into our chests. And when I have to lean over the side to puke in the bucket, she is somehow next to me, even though she is as strapped in as I am. I always got sicker than her. She was always the one helping me.

"Pretend we're getting pedicures," she said once. "These chairs are like those ones, don't you think? The big, cushy ones. Except without the massagers." She always talked nonsense while

I was puking, and I was always grateful. "I wonder if anyone's ever gotten off on one of those chairs. Like what if you're sitting there getting your nails done, and some housewife came in her panties in that exact same spot just a few minutes ago."

"Gross," I managed to say through my heaving.

"You know what's gross? The contents of your stomach. What have you been eating?"

I try to imagine she's with me in the elevator. She's with me in the exam room while Nurse Moskowitz draws my blood. She pretends to knock her hand while she's inserting the needle into my portacath. "Oops," she says. "Did that hurt? Hope we didn't puncture a lung."

She stands behind Dr. Jacobs doing obscene things as he asks me his questions. "How are you feeling?" he says.

"Okay," I say. A lie. There's no way I can even begin to truthfully answer that question in a way he can understand.

"How is the pain?" he says.

"Still pretty bad," I say. Also a lie. But I know how these things work. As soon as I say the pain's gone, he takes away my pills.

He doesn't like that answer. "It should be getting much better," he says. "You shouldn't need the Norco for much longer. Ibuprofen should really be enough." But he's only a doctor; he doesn't know anything about pain. "You only have two more refills, right?" he says.

"I don't know. Mom is the one keeping the bottle."

"Yes," Mom chimes in. "The bottle says two more refills."

She seems confused. This is nothing like the conversations she's used to having about me.

"Evie," Dr. Jacobs says. "How many have you been taking per day?"

"I don't know. Probably around six or eight." I don't tell him sometimes I save pills up so I can take three or four at once.

"That seems like kind of a lot."

"The prescription says up to twelve a day."

"That's for severe pain. You shouldn't be having severe pain anymore." He's looking at me the way he looked at Stella all the time, with his eyebrows raised and his chin folded against his neck, looking over his glasses like he knows I'm hiding something from him. "Can you rate your pain for me on a scale of one to ten?" he says.

"When? Right now? I'm not in any pain because I just took a pill before we left." I can hear him thinking, *Smart-ass.*

"What about when you ask your mom for a pill? What is it then?"

"I don't know. Maybe a three or four? I thought I was supposed to stay ahead of the pain. That's what you always said before. So I take a pill before it hurts too bad."

"That was before. You shouldn't be having anywhere near as much pain as you were having before."

I shrug my shoulders in my best angsty-teen impression. I imagine Stella behind him, giving me the thumbs-up.

"I want you to taper off the pills so you're off of them by the time we check in next month, okay?" he says. "Do you think you can do that?"

"Sure. Okay."

"Nurse Moskowitz will get you a handout about how best to do that. Mrs. Whinsett, can you help Evie keep track of how much she's taking?"

"Of course," she says, because she knows that's the right answer, but I can tell she doesn't understand what Dr. Jacobs is so worried about. This doesn't have anything to do with cancer.

"Now I bet you want to say hi to Caleb," he says. "I think he's down in the teen lounge with Dan."

My throat closes up and I can't breathe again. My heart pounds fast in my chest. It pounds so hard I can hear it. It pounds so fast it will jump out of me. I shake my head. That's all I can do.

"I'm sure he'd love the surprise," Dr. Jacobs says. "He's been pretty down lately."

Something inside me cracks a little. A fissure threatens to spread and break me into pieces. But somehow I manage to say no. I manage to say I'm not feeling well and want to go home.

The thought of seeing Caleb, even just texting him, makes my throat close up. As Dr. Jacobs and Moskowitz leave the exam room, a train car full of history comes barreling toward me, heavy and reckless with things I want to forget.

"All right," Mom sighs, turning away from me to grab her purse. "Are you ready to go, then?" But when she turns back, I'm leaning forward with my head between my knees. I'm sucking in air but none of it is getting to my lungs. I can't see. I can't feel anything except the absence of breath. I have to get out of here. I'll die if I don't.

"Evie!" Mom says, her hands instantly on my back. She instinctively starts rubbing the way she's always done when I'm sick, ever since I was a little girl with the flu. The tightness in my chest releases, just a little. I try to stand up, but I'm too dizzy. "I'll go get Dr. Jacobs," she says, turning toward the door.

I grab her arm. "No," I say. "Please, Mom. He'll make it worse."

She sits down next to me on the exam table and continues to rub my back. "Oh, honey," she says. "You're having a panic attack. Just breathe."

"I'm trying!" I am sobbing now. I am sucking in huge gulps of air that are going nowhere.

"Come on, count with me. In—one, two, three, four. Out—one, two, three, four."

I do what she says. Over and over until the world becomes solid again. Her hand smooths a circle on my back. I let her comfort me. I let her remind me how to breathe. When my panic finally subsides, she collects me in her arms. We sit like that for a while, rocking. Maybe I can let myself be held. Just this once. Maybe it's okay to be weak, but only sometimes.

I keep my head down as we walk out of the hospital and back to the car. Luckily, we don't run into anyone I know. The farther away we get, the better I can breathe. Mom tries to talk to me on the car ride home, but she gives up when it's clear that I am only capable of silence.

All I want when we get home is to be alone, but I'm not even allowed to lock the bathroom door when I take a shower. "In case something happens," Mom says. In case I fall. Her fear, ruling me.

When I remove my brace, my leg is shriveled and gross, white and dry and scaly, like some kind of albino reptile. I have special, gentle, fragrance-free soap. I have instructions to be careful. I have a big jagged hole in my leg, the flesh at the incision still purple and raw and weeping, laced together with black stitches. Inches away on my hip is the faded smaller scar from my first surgery to remove the sarcoma when it was still a little dainty thing, before it spread. I am spotted with other scars from laparoscopic procedures and biopsies. I have been cut apart and stitched back up. I am Frankenstein's monster.

I wash gently like I've been instructed. My skin is tender everywhere, not just at the incision. There is an army of microscopic cells working overtime to repair this damage, to give me back my leg, to make all of this pain and history go away. Then I'm supposed to walk again like nothing happened, like every other normal girl. And I'm supposed to do things normal girls do, like go to school, drive a car, eat dinner with my parents, fight with my sister, maybe even have sex with my boyfriend one of these days. But all of it seems so stupid. The cells are wasting their time. What's the point to all their hard work if all I'm going to do is take a math quiz in a few days, or go to the movies, or take the garbage out, or ride a bike, or babysit, or maybe get a job someday making a big corporation richer? What's the point of any of it?

Stella would know. She would know exactly what to say to make me not feel so lost and crazy.

I have to find out where Mom is hiding my pills.

seventeen.

"ARE YOU NERVOUS?" KASEY SAYS.

"A little." I'm in the passenger's seat of her car, my crutches in the backseat, my gimpy leg stretched out in its brace, on my way to my first day of school in almost six months.

"Everyone is going to be so excited to see you," she says.

"I'm just excited to get away from my mom."

"Oh, come on, she's just happy to have you home. She likes taking care of you."

"She needs a better hobby."

Kasey's laugh is too loud for such a lame joke.

A minefield of hugs is waiting for me at school. Hugs everywhere. Open arms and tearful eyes around every corner. I smell so much body odor, so much laundry detergent and deodorant and cheap perfume. By the time I get in the door, I am already sneezing from the artificial fragrances.

"How are you?" they say. *(Depressed.)*

"How are you feeling?" *(Shitty.)*

"You look great." *(Liar.)*

"We missed you so much." *(Oh, really? Then why didn't you visit me in the hospital?)*

But of course I don't say any of these things. I smile and let them hug me.

Am I really back? My body's here, but I don't feel connected to it. My mind is somewhere else, a place where time stopped. What was the last class I went to? What was the last homework I turned in? What is my locker combination? Everything feels surreal, like the world is going on without me, and I'm a ghost, invisible. Everyone's smiling, but they look right through me.

Will is waiting at my locker with a single red rose, and despite my growing disdain of his flower choice, I warm a little at the sight of his big, handsome grin. He kisses me on the cheek, takes my bag from Kasey, and hoists it over his shoulder with a pleased look on his face. Part of me is grateful, proud to still be the one on his arm. But part of me wishes I didn't need his help. Part of me wants to say I can carry my bag by myself.

First period is European History. We're somewhere in the Reformation now, but the last thing I remember is the beginning of the Dark Ages. My teacher is weepy and interrupts herself in the middle of her lecture to tell me to take all the time I need to get back in the swing of things, to come see her for help anytime. She says this in front of everyone while they all stare at me. Maybe she knew someone who had cancer. Maybe someone she loved died from the same thing I had. That is the only excuse for her behavior.

The whole cafeteria claps when I enter at lunchtime, and I want to die.

I probably shouldn't say that.

I sit between Kasey and Will. The same old people are at the lunch table as were here six months ago, plus a freshman girl who managed to work her way up, and minus Alex Monroe who moved to the East Coast last month. "What else is new?" I say, and everyone kind of looks at each other and shrugs.

"Alison and Justin broke up," someone offers.

"Oliver Kent got expelled for selling weed."

"Missy Chang almost got on *Teen Jeopardy!*"

"Keyshawn Duncan came out."

"The theme for this year's prom is 'A Night in Paris.'"

I can't believe I came back from the dead for this.

Will has baseball practice after school and Kasey has cheer. She invites me to come along and watch, but that's just too depressing.

My exciting after-school activity is riding a stationary bike or hanging out in a lukewarm swimming pool with Sandy the physical therapist. She says she's amazed at how fast I'm progressing. She calls it a miracle. My parents call it a miracle. Everyone throws the word around like it explains everything: a miracle's doing all the work, not me. They don't say anything about how I stay long after my physical therapy appointments are over to keep working, how I go to the pool even when I don't have appointments, how I come home exhausted and sore and strong, how

I'm down to one crutch weeks before expected. They think I'm tired in the evening because of weakness. Mom puts her hand on my forehead to check my temperature. Dad says maybe I should rest after school instead. But I spent the whole past year resting. I am done with rest.

In the water, I am weightless. Nothing hurts. I am not clumsy. I don't need crutches. I can do flips like I used to, but now they're in slow motion—dreamy, graceful. In the water, I am not broken and I do not need anyone's help.

But then I return to reality. I eat dinner with my family and listen to Jenica complain. "Evie tries to get herself killed hobbling around the neighborhood and you practically throw her a party," she whines. "I get an almost perfect score on the SATs and no one says anything." Even two weeks later, she's still harping on my not getting punished for that. At least she doesn't paint a smile on her face and pretend everything's perfect like Will and Kasey and everyone else I know.

This is my life now: Conversations stop when I enter rooms. Words are replaced by empty smiles, as if I am too fragile to be included, as if I need to be protected. People talk to me like I'm a child. I'm getting stronger, but no one sees it. When I make jokes, people look at me like I'm speaking a different language. Apparently, dying girls aren't supposed to be funny. And apparently nobody got the memo that I'm not dying anymore.

I'm supposed to fit back into their world *and* I'm supposed to live up to my role as Cancer Girl. No one seems to realize I can't do both of those things at the same time. Those people all went on living while Cancer Girl was dying. Their lives went forward while hers stayed still. She spent the whole last year just surviving while they all went on having lives, and now she's so far behind she'll never catch up. And I don't even know if I want to.

Everyone seems closer now because they bonded over my impending death, but the irony is that I got left out of that bonding. Kasey and Will are practically best friends after spending all that time worrying about me together, and even though they're supposed to be the two closest people to me, I feel I can barely have a conversation with either of them. Now that I'm back, no one knows what to do with me, and I don't really know what to do with them.

The pain pills aren't coming fast enough. I need more than I used to. I've started feeling sick in the morning before I take my first pill. I looked up how to roll a joint on YouTube, but I'm too chicken to try to buy rolling papers.

Caleb keeps texting, and I keep starting to write back and erasing it. I'm not a part of his world anymore, either. I'm a traitor to Cancer Kids by getting well. I'm an alien among everyone else. I'm not dead, but I'm not really alive. I fit nowhere. And I'm so sick of feeling sorry for myself.

if.

Dear Stella,

When I can't sleep, I listen to your CD and look out the window and imagine I'm somewhere else, like I've been plucked out of this life and put somewhere brand-new, where I don't have a history, I don't even have scars, I'm reborn, like I just came out of the factory, still warm from where my parts got glued together. And the future is infinite because the past hasn't come with me, because it's not dragging me down like an anchor, not pulling me back into itself. Until that day comes, until the magic happens that wipes my memory and my body clean, I will never be able to truly be free. I will always be marked, always defined by what I survived.

Remember how I told you my parents don't fight? Well, things have changed. They try to keep their voices low, but it's pretty impossible to not hear the constant bickering about money, about the hospital bills they'll never be able to pay off, about not knowing how they're going to pay for Jenica's college, about having to get a second mortgage on the house. And then we all sit down for dinner and pretend everything's okay, even though Mom's face is still striped with tears, and Dad's grinding his teeth, and Jenica's looking at me with daggers in her eyes. And I want to tell her, Well, you should have thought of that a year ago, so you could have killed me before I got sick and saved us all a lot of trouble. You'd have plenty of money to pay for college and nobody's life would have had to stop so mine could keep on going.

God, I am so sick of my own thoughts. I limp through my days listening to this whiny voice in my head complain about how nobody understands me. Whenever Will or someone at school offers to carry my books, I want to punch them in the face. I know they're just trying to be nice, but I am so sick of being pitied. I'm so sick of being defined by having been sick.

If you were here, you'd want to slap me. I want to slap me. I'm doing nothing with this life I should be grateful for. I'm doing nothing to deserve it. I don't know who I am and I don't know where I belong. I want to find myself, but I don't know where to look. I feel like I'm disappearing.

I want to make you proud, Stella. Is that weird? I want to be someone cool enough to deserve our friendship. I want to live large enough for both of us.

I want I want I want I want.

I'm taking good care of your hat, by the way. Maybe someday I'll actually be brave enough to wear it outside of the house.

Love,

Evie

eighteen.

I PAINTED MY CANE BLACK WITH PURPLE STRIPES IN ART class today. The teacher patted me on the shoulder and said, "That's nice, Evie." The first thing Kasey said when she found me in the hall was, "Isn't that kind of goth?"

I got my math quiz back, which I'm pretty sure I answered maybe two questions right on, and instead of a grade, the teacher drew a smiley face and wrote, "Good try!" like I'm in kindergarten.

But at least I can drive now. And at least my parents are still in this weird phase where they're afraid to say no to me, as if they're afraid that upsetting me will bring the cancer back. Mom hands me her keys and I close the front door behind me before she's finished saying, "Be careful." I have Stella's magic box with me, even though I still don't have a pipe or rolling papers or even a lighter. I heard someone talking once about smoking out of an apple, but I have no idea how that works.

I have nowhere to go, so I wander. I drive up to Telegraph by the university, past the jaywalking college students and fake homeless kids. I drive down College Avenue, with all the moms in yoga pants pushing strollers. I drive down Fortieth past the hipster coffee shop and the restaurant where mac and cheese costs fifteen dollars, past the BART station, past the Emeryville strip malls, onto Mandela Parkway and into the West Oakland ghetto.

I think, *What would Stella do?*

I stop at a corner store. I park Mom's Prius behind a shiny purple low-rider with giant tires. I walk straight to the counter and ask for rolling papers and a lighter. The man behind the bulletproof glass barely even looks at me. His eyes are glued to the fuzzy TV in the corner. He hands me my purchases through the hole in the glass. I hand him money. That is all. Easy-peasy.

I am giddy as I get back into the car with the contraband in my pocket. But as I put my seat belt on, I realize how ridiculous this is. I bought a lighter and rolling papers. Big deal. I don't even know if that's illegal. And I don't think I even know how to work a lighter.

I keep driving, under the BART tracks and freeway, to where civilization stops and is replaced by silent warehouses and giant parking lots full of semitrucks and shipping containers. The giant Port of Oakland cranes tower in the distance and there is no one, not a single soul, anywhere.

I realize this is exactly where I want to be—away from people. Away from anyone who thinks they know me. I park in an almost empty lot next to the entrance to the Bay Bridge trail. I take out my phone and review a YouTube video about how to roll a joint.

If Stella were here, she would laugh her ass off.

After many tries and several soggy, ripped rolling papers, I manage to create something that looks reasonably enough like a joint. I can't figure out how to get a flame out of the lighter until my thumb is sore and scraped raw from trying. I light the joint and inhale like I remember, but I only get a sour taste of soggy smoke before the thing goes out. It is too drenched with my spit to stay lit. I try a few more times until I've accomplished a couple of good, crackling pulls, but I still don't know if I've done it right. More smoke fills the car than seems to have made it into my lungs.

I feel embarrassed even though no one can see me. I don't feel stoned, I feel stupid.

I can't stand to sit in the car with myself any longer. I'm annoyed by my own company. So I pull the hood of my raincoat tight around my head and get out of the car. It's windy, wet, and cold out here by the water, and there are no bikers or walkers anywhere on the trail. But it's better than being inside with myself. Better than being with other people who want me to be something I'm not.

I inch along the paved trail. The world sounds different out here, empty. There are no voices, just cars traveling fast on the freeway above my head. Just my cane clunking along the pavement. I walk past chain-link fences guarding vacant lots. I walk past old sun-bleached warehouses with peeling paint and broken windows.

I don't know how far I go before I realize I'm really, really high. Ten minutes, maybe. All of a sudden my feet feel heavy and I need to sit down, but everything around me is wet and dirty and exposed. The freeway is too close and the cars sound too fast. I am too alone. This is the kind of place girls like me get lost and are never found again.

I turn around to return to the car, when I notice a set of stairs that go underground. It's the only place I can see that might be dry, and I can't imagine walking any more right now. I feel dizzy. I smoked too much. All I want is a cave. A dark, dry place to catch my breath. A place to hide.

I make my way down the stairs slowly, my bad leg threatening to pull me down. I pass an orange cone and a sign that says TUNNEL CLOSED. I'm out of breath when I reach the bottom; the muscles in my arm burn from holding so much of my weight with the cane. Black stenciled letters on the white painted wall read ADMIN BLDG, TOLL PLAZA, BUS STOP with an arrow pointing the only direction there is to go. I hear my breaths echo as I stare into the concrete tunnel, just wide enough for three people to pass through side by side. Pale light shines in from outside and illuminates enough to tell me I'd need a flashlight to go any farther. Any other time, I'd be terrified. I'm aware of this, aware that the logic of this moment is completely backward, that I am crazy for favoring this place over a short walk to return to the safety of my car.

The sounds of my cane clacking and the padding of my feet bounce off the walls. As I make my way deeper into the tunnel, I can hear the muted traffic of the freeway above me, so many tons of steel overhead. It is strangely comforting, like some urban version of being inside the womb—hard, cold, dirty, and possibly dangerous, but tight and close and full of white noise just the same.

I find the place where the light almost ends, where there is barely enough to see my hand in front of my face, barely enough to see proof that I still exist. I am almost in the darkness. I am almost completely underground. I am somewhere no one can find me.

The tunnel's so loud with the pulsing of the freeway that I don't hear the footsteps. I don't see the flashlight. I don't see the man coming out of the shadows.

And then it is too late. He is too close. His face is clouded by cigarette smoke. He is getting closer.

Fear sobers me, makes my senses sharp. But I forget I am lame. I forget about my leg and my cane, and I try to run. My good leg moves as it should, but the other is too slow, the stride too short, and I trip. I fall. My palms scrape as I collapse onto the concrete. The cars thunder overhead, the tunnel is so narrow, and the man is running, he's coming fast. He is here, in the dark, and I am gone.

"Hey!" the man says. His voice is young. I try to crawl. Dirt grinds into the wounds in my hands. I am getting nowhere.

"Hey, wait," he says. I should scream, but nothing comes out. This is the part of the nightmare where I'm supposed to wake up. Before the real pain comes. But I am still here. I will not wake up from this.

I close my eyes. I pull my legs to my chest. The darkness of the world swirls around me and I wait for it to suck me in.

"Oh my god, I am so sorry," the voice says. It does not sound like the voice of a killer. But I still can't open my eyes.

"Shit, you're really freaking out." The voice gets closer. He is kneeling down next to me. I flinch and pull away.

"I am such an asshole. I should have said something when I saw you so you'd know I was there. Usually this place is super well-lit, but the lights are all out for some reason."

Silence. I'm supposed to say something. But I'm still a ball. Still blind. Still shaking.

"Oh, man," he sighs. "I'm going to hang out here until I know you're all right. Is that okay? I mean, I can't really just leave you here like this, right?"

I have no choice but to look up.

I blink and the smoke clears and I see quite possibly the hottest guy I have ever seen in my life.

He smiles. "Hi," he says.

"Hi?" I croak. My throat is sandpaper.

"Are you okay?"

I can't say anything. I don't know the answer.

"This is me," he says, shining the flashlight to illuminate his face. "See? I'm a nice guy." It's hard to tell in the weird lighting, but I don't think he's lying. He looks like he's around my age, with light brown skin and short dreadlocks. His eyes are greenish-gray with eyelashes that go on forever. They are deep eyes, kind eyes. They are eyes you want to have see inside you.

I sit up and take a deep breath. I feel the cold ground solid beneath me. The knife blades of fear in my chest are replaced by something slightly less sharp. His shoulder is inches away from mine. I feel a warmness radiate from where we almost touch. I think I just went from fearing for my life to crushing on a stranger in ten seconds.

He jumps up, stubs out his cigarette, and offers me his hand. "I think you're going to be okay."

I take his hand and let him help pull me up. I'm still a little dizzy and have to hold on to the wall for support. "Oh, here," he says, bending over to retrieve my cane from the ground. He hands it to me like it's something as normal as a purse or a grocery bag, with none of the pity I see in everybody else's eyes.

"Thanks," I say.

"I'm sorry I scared you."

"I wasn't scared. You just surprised me, that's all."

He laughs. "Okay, tough guy."

His laugh immediately puts me at ease. The tunnel lightens. The heaviness of the weed I smoked turns to air, and now I know why it's called getting high. I am floating. I can't even remember being scared.

"What are you doing down here?" I say. "Do you carry a flashlight with you all the time?" My voice is strong. Am I flirting?

"As a matter of fact, I do keep a flashlight in my car in case of emergency, along with a first-aid kit and blankets. You never know when you're going to need a Band-Aid or an emergency nap." I notice his jacket is some kind of neon green vintage Windbreaker, with a logo for El Dorado Bowling Club on one side and ALFONSE etched in pink cursive on the other. I can't believe I was ever scared of this guy.

"And I could ask you the same thing," he continues. "An unlit tunnel under the freeway is not exactly the safest place. What are *you* doing down here?"

What should I say? What's the right answer? What's the witty thing to say? What's the thing that will make him like me?

No. Stop it. I'm sick of caring what everyone thinks. I'm sick of trying to make everyone happy. What if I just told the truth? What if I just showed him exactly who I am?

What would Stella do?

"I just wanted to get away from people," I say.

"Yeah, me too. People can really suck sometimes."

"Yes, they can."

"Guess we didn't find what we were looking for." He grins. I could melt in that grin. We hold eye contact for what seems like forever.

The combination of pot, adrenaline from almost getting murdered, and hanging out in the shadows with a cute boy makes me giddy. I am suddenly fearless. "Can I have a cigarette?" I say. I have never smoked a cigarette in my life.

He raises his eyebrows as he pulls a pack from his back pocket and offers it to me. I pull out a cigarette and place it between my lips. "Who *are* you?" he says as he lights it for me.

I inhale and cough like the amateur I am. I inhale again and force myself to keep the smoke in. I feel the poison enter my lungs. I welcome the sting. I fight my body's instinct to cough, to push the poison out. I smile at the ridiculousness of a cancer survivor smoking cigarettes. I am happy to be ridiculous.

I reach out my hand. "Evie Whinsett. Nice to meet you. Is your name really Alfonse?"

"I wish. That's just my alter-ego. My real name is Marcus Lyon." We shake for much longer than necessary.

"Well, Miss Evie Whinsett, I was about to head back to the parking lot. Do you want to walk with me, or are you staying here to see if any other creepy guys come out of the shadows?"

"One is probably enough for today."

We start walking. I am strangely not embarrassed by my cane. He doesn't even seem to notice it. He doesn't look at me with the patronizing stare of everyone who thinks I'm fragile. He offers me his arm when we get to the stairs and, without thinking, I take it. I let him help me. But with him, it doesn't feel like I'm surrendering. His help doesn't come with any baggage or expectations.

It has stopped raining. The world outside the tunnel is still empty and gray, except now Marcus is in it.

We walk without talking. I like the silence between us. I like not feeling pressured to fill it. I like that he keeps a flashlight in his car for emergencies. I like that he called me tough.

There are only two cars in the parking lot—my mom's Prius and an old, banged-up gold Mercedes station wagon.

"That's Bubbles," Marcus says.

"You named your car Bubbles?"

"My brother named her, actually. I inherited her from him.

But she's the color of champagne and has an excellent disposition, so yeah, Bubbles. Isn't she beautiful?"

"She's . . . unique."

"Which is the best kind of beauty, don't you think?"

"It's the only kind, really."

Silence consumes us. This is the time we part. This is the time we say good-bye and then never see each other again.

"Well, bye," he says. "Stay out of tunnels with broken lights."

What would Stella do?

I am bold. I am a girl who is fearless.

"Wait!" I say as he turns to walk away. He turns back around and I say, "Would it be weird if I asked you for your number?"

His lips break into a grin. "Not weird at all."

I pull out my phone. He tells me his number and I type it in. I text: *This is the girl you found in the dark.* "Now you have mine, too," I say.

"All right, then," he says. Somehow I stay standing as I melt into his eyes. "Until later, Evie Whinsett."

"So long, Marcus Lyon."

He walks to his car on the other side of the parking lot as I get into mine. We meet head-on as I turn to exit. Before he passes me, Marcus flashes his high beams, catching me in the light, and rolls down his window. I can hear him yell, "You're a star!" I'm suspended in his high beams, glowing, all lit up. Then he drives away, taking the light with him.

For a moment, I am blind as my eyes adjust.

"Nice job, Stella," I whisper to the darkness.

nineteen.

IT'S FRIDAY NIGHT AND I'M SITTING AT A TABLE WITH WILL AT "our" restaurant. For the last two years, whenever I've been out of the hospital and well enough to eat, we've come here at least once a month. I used to think it was romantic, going to the same place all the time, ordering the lamb kabobs for him and the veggie combo plate for me and switching halfway through. But now it seems boring, like we're an old married couple who's been together for fifty years. And if we're going to have an "our" place, shouldn't it be somewhere special and intimate, a place no one knows about, somewhere we discovered together? The food here is good and all, but it's big, loud, crowded, and kind of a Bay Area mini-chain. I'm pretty sure they premake everything at a central location and assemble it at each restaurant when it gets ordered.

The waitress comes to take our order and Will orders the same thing he always gets. I order something new.

"You've never gotten that before," he says when the waitress leaves. He looks concerned, like I've just told him I feel sick.

"I feel like trying something different," I say, but I can tell he's still worried. It's such a small thing, but it seems like part of something bigger, proof that Will refuses to accept that I've changed, that I'm not the same Evie he fell in love with.

He reaches across the table and takes my hand in his. The firm grip I used to love now seems crushing. "You seem distant tonight," he says. Maybe it's the three pills I took before he picked me up. Maybe it's because I don't really want to be here. Maybe it's because I can't stop thinking about Marcus.

"I'm sorry," I say, and I truly am. I should be better to him. I should love him more. I should love him as much as I used to.

"It's okay," he says, and beams, always so forgiving. "You're going through a lot. It must be so hard adjusting back to normal life."

"It is."

"I want to help you. I want to make it easier for you."

"I don't know if it's something you can fix, Will."

He shakes his head like he thinks I'm silly. Of course he can fix it. He's Will Johnson, boyfriend extraordinaire. "I have a surprise for you," he says. I half expect him to pull out more red roses. "I quit baseball. I can be with you more now. I can take care of you."

Oh my god.

"No, Will. You can't do that."

Our food arrives. The skin on my pomegranate chicken is brown and gelatinous with sauce. I am so not hungry.

"It's okay, Evie. Baseball was never really my sport, anyway. It was just something to do in the spring when football's over. I'd rather be with you."

"But I have physical therapy after school all the time."

"I thought it was over now."

"My appointments with the therapist are over, but I still have to do it on my own." This is only partially a lie.

"I can come to the pool with you. I can help."

"Will, I don't think—"

"Let's stop talking about it, okay?" he says with that same confident grin, the one I used to find so comforting, but now it strikes me as condescending. "Let's just enjoy our dinner. We can talk about it later."

I don't say much through the rest of dinner. Will doesn't even seem to notice. He fills the silence with updates on movies he's seen, gossip about people at school, other things I'm having a hard time caring about. When he puts his arm around me as we walk to his car, I am startled by a surge of anger. It starts in the pit of my stomach and burns all the way up into my eyes. I have to remind myself that this is Will. This is my boyfriend. This is the guy I'm supposed to be in love with.

"Want some ice cream?" he says as we approach the block-long line of young couples waiting for the overrated Berkeley artisan ice-cream shop that's not nearly as good as my favorite, Tara's, just down the street in Oakland. I am usually proud to be part of one of these pretty, wholesome couples. But not tonight. Tonight I feel like an imposter.

"Let's just go to your place," I say. "Your folks still do that thing Friday nights?"

"Sure." He smiles sweetly. "Okay, honey."

Before I got sick, and during my periodic windows of recovery, Friday night was our special night. Will's parents have some weekly Christian mingle thing they do at church, so Will and I would have the house to ourselves for three hours while they drank decaf coffee and ate stale cookies. I couldn't wait to run up to his room and spend the night in his arms.

But when we get there, he leads me to the living room and asks what kind of movie I want to watch.

"Who said I wanted to watch a movie?"

"We don't have to watch a movie," he says. "Why don't we continue that conversation we were having earlier? About me quitting baseball so we can be together."

I sigh. "I don't want you to do that, Will."

"Don't you want to be with me?"

"Of course I want to be with you," I say, but at soon as it comes out of my mouth I realize I don't mean it. "I don't want you giving up stuff for me. I want you to have your own life."

"Evie," he says, holding my hands in his, "you are my life."

I want to run. I want to get out of here, away from him, away from the gaze of his eyes that see someone else when they look at me, someone who no longer exists. But instead, I kiss him. I kiss and kiss and kiss him. Maybe if I taste him, maybe if I feel his skin against mine, I can remember what I felt like before all of this. Maybe if we are just our bodies, I won't have to feel whatever this is I'm feeling.

But he stops me. He pulls away and removes my hands from where they were attempting to unbutton his pants.

"What?" I say.

"I don't think you're ready."

Again, the anger. Rage like a fireball burning through my body. "Don't you think I should be the judge of that?" I pull my hands out of his and push him. I want to push harder. I want to shove him so far away that I can't see him anymore, so he can't look at me with those big blue eyes so full of pity, eyes that used to make me feel so beautiful but now just make me feel small. Invisible. Powerless.

"Evie," he says. "I don't want to hurt you. I want to take care of you."

"I can take care of myself," I say as I stand up.

"Honey, sit down. Let's talk about this."

I grab my cane and purse from the floor. "I'm done talking."

"Okay," he says. "You need space. I understand. I'll call you tomorrow morning."

"No. Don't call me."

"Or better yet, why don't I come over? I'll bring lattes and those cinnamon rolls you like."

"Did you not hear me?" I shout. "I don't want you to call me. I don't want to eat cinnamon rolls with you. I'm done. It's over. We're over."

"I know you don't mean that. You're just tired. You'll feel different tomorrow after you get some rest."

"Don't tell me how I feel, Will." I start hobbling to the door. "You have no idea how I feel." I wish I could stomp away. I wish I could storm out, make a more dramatic exit than this lopsided shuffle. I wish my every move weren't punctuated by the pathetic *clackity-clack* of my cane.

"I'll call you tomorrow," he says, getting up and rushing to open the door for me. He's a gentleman even as I'm breaking up with him.

"Will," I say, looking him straight in the eye so he can't misunderstand. "Listen to me. I can't be with you anymore. Too much has changed. We're too different."

He puts his arms around me and holds me close. "I'm not going anywhere," he whispers into my neck, the garlic and vinegar of dinner on his breath mixing with the musk of his cologne and threatening to suffocate me. "I love you and I know you love me. I'll be here when you're ready. We've been through so much. We'll get through this, too."

I pull away and just stare at him in disbelief, at that stupid grin that hasn't faded. He's so confident, so sure I could never stop loving him.

"Bye, Will," I say, and walk out the door.

"Let me give you a ride," he says.

"I live three blocks away. I can walk."

"Let me walk you."

"No." I may not be able to stomp away, but I can slam the door behind me.

if.

Dear Stella,

At this very moment, your favorite fallen cheerleader is smoking a joint out her bedroom window like a real teenage rebel. Ha! Aren't you proud of me? Scented candles are my new best friend, especially the ones that smell like gingerbread cookies. The only problem is they make me really, really hungry.

I had a lovely visit with my school principal today. I think my cancer-survivor sympathy may be starting to wear thin with the administration. Principal Landry thought of all the different ways to ask me how I'm doing, and I thought of all the different ways I could say "fine." I could tell she was trying to seem caring, but really the point of the meeting was to tell me I'm in trouble because I'm failing my classes. Except the way she said it was a lot nicer: I'm not failing, I'm "falling behind." I've been "lethargic in class" (i.e., stoned). And instead of saying I'm an ungrateful asshole, she said she's disappointed that I haven't accepted my teachers' offers of help or been working with a tutor. "We're a team, Evie! We all want you to succeed!"

But she's missing one very important thing—I'm not on their team. No amount of their wanting me to succeed is going to make a difference if I don't give a shit. They live in a fantasy world where the most important things in a teenager's life are getting good grades and going to college, but no one realizes I stopped living in that world a long time ago. It isn't real. None of it is real.

It's over with Will, by the way. Another casualty of my survival, I suppose. I think it was over a long time ago, but I was a little too busy dying to notice. Like everyone else, he loved that dying girl more than he loves me. The girl who loved him back died in that stupid hospital and this new me rose out of her ashes, and I am so sick of his doting and chivalry, all his "honey"s and "sweetie"s. It's pathetic. He's pathetic. I feel pathetic when I'm with him. And I am sick and tired of feeling pathetic. I wish I could say I don't even miss him, but that would be a lie. I miss us fitting together. I miss being part of an "us."

But in happier news, I finally found where Mom's been hiding my painkillers. What is it about drugs and sock drawers? She's so blind, she doesn't even notice the missing pills. I have a feeling I could get away with murder these days and she'd just pat me on the back and say I'm having a hard time adjusting to my new life and maybe I need a nap. Poor, sweet, loyal Mom.

The bad news is the bottle says only one refill left. I don't know what happens after that. I don't want to think about it. I'm trying to be careful with your weed, but it's going a lot faster than I'd like it to. I'm going to have to figure something out soon. I sure as hell can't go buying stuff from anyone at school. Not Evie Whinsett, Cancer Girl, squeaky-clean Will Johnson's girlfriend (no, ex-*girlfriend!), buying drugs from the bad kids! It would be a scandal! But maybe a little scandal is exactly what my life is missing.*

Speaking of which, I called Marcus. I waited a couple of days to see if he'd call me, but then I figured, fuck it—I'm the one who asked him for his number, right? So I'm the one calling the shots, and if I feel like calling him I'm going to call him. I don't care about being proper or playing hard-to-get, or any of those other stupid games. And FYI, he's as hot on the phone as he is in person. He's got this low, satiny voice and really smart, sarcastic sense of humor that makes Will seem so dull and childish. And guess what? We're going out tomorrow. WE'RE GOING OUT TOMORROW!

I'm failing all my classes except art, but I'm not

really worried about it. It's pretty great how good I feel right now despite the fact that my life is kind of falling apart.

Love,
Evie

twenty.

I TOLD EVERYONE I'M VISITING CALEB AT THE HOSPITAL after school. Even Will, despite my repeatedly reminding him we're broken up, feels entitled to this information, not to mention the fact that he still sits next to me at lunch and insists on carrying my bag. Everyone—Mom, Dad, Will, Kasey, Jenica—agrees visiting Caleb is an excellent idea, as if their opinion matters. I'm sure Caleb would also think it's an excellent idea, but he knows nothing about it and I haven't talked to him since the day I was discharged.

I keep thinking about this time in the hospital a couple of days after I broke my leg. Some player from the Oakland A's was coming in for a charity-visit-slash-publicity-photo op, and Caleb was freaking out like a little boy. He ran off to get his hat signed while Stella and I stayed in my room. I remember saying, "Could he be any more adorkable?" and Stella said, "You know he's in love with you, right?" I told her to shut up, but she said, "He worships the ground you wheel on."

Every time I ignore one of Caleb's texts, I think of this, and it makes me sick. He keeps texting even though I never text him back. I have turned into such an asshole, and he is still so loyal, so forgiving.

"Tell Caleb I say hi," Mom says as she drops me off in front of the hospital. "Give him a big hug for me."

"I will," I say. I walk slowly to the too-familiar sliding doors, waiting for Mom to pull away before I turn around and walk toward Telegraph.

I am meeting Marcus at a coffee shop. In preparation, I spent an hour last night rolling and rerolling a joint until it was perfect, which I will hopefully smoke with him. I practiced with the lighter to make sure I still know how to use it. Maybe this is not what normal people do before dates. But I have come to the conclusion that I am no longer normal, and I have a feeling Marcus isn't either.

I am wearing Stella's hat for extra strength. It helps me to not hyperventilate as I wait outside the café for Marcus to show up. It hugs my head and tells me to calm down. It says "Shut up" to the voice that keeps telling me he's not coming. I lean against the side of the building as cool as I can. I poke at my phone to look busy. I pretend I'm texting something important.

"Hey," says a familiar voice. I look up and Marcus is even better-looking than I remember. The sky is clear today, and it brings out the green in his eyes and the smoothness of his skin. He's wearing a faded T-shirt for a boy band from the eighties.

I realize it's been several moments since his greeting and I haven't responded because I've been too mesmerized by his beauty. "Hey," I finally manage to say.

"Cool hat," he says.

"Cool shirt," I say.

"Have you ever heard these guys' music?"

"No."

"It's horrible. It's like poison. It'll make your ears bleed."

"You're a big fan, then?"

"The biggest."

"Want to go inside?"

"Sure."

So far, so good. One minute into our date and I don't think I've humiliated myself too much yet.

I look around the café as we wait our turn to be at the counter. The place is full of hip, beautiful people staring at silver Apple laptops.

"I wonder what all these people are working on," I say. "Novels? Dissertations?"

"Probably just fooling around on the internet," Marcus says. He points to someone whose screen is facing us. "See, that guy is scrolling through someone's vacation photos. And that girl is looking at pictures of cats."

"They're really good at pretending they're working."

"Yeah, they even bring books and stuff as props."

"Evie?" someone who is not Marcus says. "Oh my god, you're alive!"

I look up and my breath catches in my throat. It is Cole,

Stella's boyfriend, standing behind the counter waiting to take our order.

"Cole," I choke out. "Hi."

I want to run, but I don't get the chance. Cole hurries around the counter and throws his arms around me and squeezes so tight I can barely breathe. Everything was going so well, but now worlds that were never supposed to meet are colliding.

"Marina," he says to a woman behind the counter when he finally lets go. "Okay if I take five?"

"Sure, honey," the woman says. "Take your time."

"Want to go outside and talk?" Cole says eagerly, his eyes bright with emotion. "It's so great to see you. You look so healthy."

I look at Marcus, who is smiling but confused. "I'll just be a couple of minutes," I say. "Go ahead and order."

"Let me get yours, too. What do you want?"

"A latte. Thanks. I'll be right back."

I hold my breath as I follow Cole outside.

"That's not Will, is it?" Cole says. "He doesn't look anything like what I pictured."

"No, that's not Will."

"Did you guys break up?"

"Yeah."

"I'm so sorry. Stella said you were so in love."

He said her name. "Things change, I guess."

"Evie, it's so good to see you." He hugs me again. I just want to get this over with. The longer it lasts, the closer we are to talking about *it*. About her.

"I tried to get into the hospital when I found out Stella died," he says. I can't do this. I can't listen. I need him to shut up. I need him to stop saying her name. "Dan called to tell me, even though I know he wasn't supposed to, but somehow Stella convinced him. Her parents didn't invite any of her friends to the funeral. Can you believe that?"

I can't breathe. Fear turns into claws that strangle me from the inside.

"Evie?" he says. "Are you okay?"

"No," I say. And before I have a chance to figure out why I said that, I start crying.

This is not supposed to happen. I am not supposed to be this weak.

Cole throws his arms around me and I hug him back. It feels so good to be in someone's arms who knew her. It almost feels good to be crying, to share this pain with someone who understands. I could have been doing this all along with Caleb. We could have been helping each other get through this together. I need to call him. I need to make things right between us. I need him.

"I miss her so much," I say, and it feels like the only honest thing I've said since I've gotten out of the hospital.

"Me too." Cole sniffles. "In some ways, her being in the hospital got me ready. I already had some practice getting used to her being gone. But no one can ever really be ready for something like that." He takes my hand. "I never had a chance to thank you. For that night when you set up the Skype date for

Stella and me. I can't tell you how much that meant to us. It was the last time we got to talk."

That seems so long ago, back when I was someone else. Back when I was someone kind and generous. Back when the world still had Stella in it and I was supposed to be dead.

This is not safe. Talking to Cole is not safe. Letting him in will only hurt both of us. I feel myself harden. Whatever opened up inside me when I saw him closes. My tears dry.

"I have to go," I blurt out. I need to flee. I need to escape before more memories come.

"Oh," he says, flinching. "Okay?"

"I'm sorry," I say, but it's too late. I can't take it back. I want to scratch my eyes out. "It was good to see you, Cole. Really good to see you." I start backing away. I wish he would stop looking at me like that, with such kindness and warmth, as if I deserve it.

"Her hat looks good on you," he says.

"Thanks."

"Maybe we can get together sometime," he says. How could he want to hang out with me, when it's my fault she's dead? She never would have snuck out that night if it weren't for me. I was the reason she put herself at risk.

"I have to get back to my friend," I manage to say without breaking into tears.

A sudden fury burns through me. Wait a minute—it's Cole's fault too. He shouldn't have agreed to pick us up. He knew it was dangerous. He knew Stella could get sick, but he did it anyway. How could he be so selfish?

"Yeah, okay," he says. "I guess I have to go back to work."

I can't even meet his eyes when I say good-bye. My feet feel like lead as I walk back into the café, and I can feel Cole's eyes burning their sadness into the back of my neck. I am a horrible person. He didn't deserve that. He loved her as much as I did, maybe even more. He deserved kindness. He deserved someone who would at least hug him back. Why did I have to be so mean?

I find Marcus sitting at a table with our drinks. "Can we go outside?" I say, trying to look as cheerful as possible. "It's such a beautiful day, we should go somewhere, don't you think?" Somewhere far from here. Somewhere without walls. Somewhere I can smoke this joint burning a hole in my purse. I must get out of here. Now.

"Sure," he says. "Let me just get these to go."

I walk out the door without telling Cole good-bye. I take deep breaths. I count in—one, two, three, four. Out—one, two, three, four. I struggle to keep myself from bolting down the street.

"Who was that?" Marcus says as he meets me outside. "You looked like you saw a ghost."

"Nobody," I say, but that is so, so far from the truth.

Marcus doesn't push it. He says he has the perfect place to take us.

"The graveyard?" I say as Marcus turns left off of Pleasant Valley into Mountain View Cemetery.

"Have you ever hung out here?" he says. "It's the most peaceful place in all of Oakland. Trust me. It was designed by the same guy who did Central Park in New York City."

We climb the hill on a narrow, winding road, passing ancient gravestones and giant, ornate tombs like little stone palaces, with famous Bay Area names—Ghirardelli, Merritt, Crocker, Chabot, Tilden.

"Some of these are a hundred and fifty years old," Marcus says.

"I never knew this place was so big."

"Yeah, it's the whole side of the hill. I love going for walks around here. Especially at night."

"They let you in at night?"

"Well, no. Not really. I sort of let myself in."

We finally crest the hill and Marcus parks on the side of the road next to a grassy area under a huge, old oak tree. "Wow," I say as I take in the view. "You can see the whole Bay from up here." It is so similar to another perfect view, one that burned itself in my memory the night that changed everything. I see the same outlines and shapes, the same landmarks, but this one is full of colors and textures and details, while the other was made of just darkness and light.

Marcus pulls a blanket out of his trunk and lays it out on the grass. "See?" he says. "Emergency nap blanket." We sit there in silence, drinking our lukewarm coffees. The only sound is the fluttering of leaves on the trees and the occasional bird chirp. This is way better than any park.

"It's so much easier to think when you're surrounded by dead people, don't you think? Live ones are just so loud." He has no idea how true this really is. "Evie," he says. "I have a serious question for you."

Uh-oh. "I have a serious answer."

"Okay," he says. He is silent for several moments, then says, "That was the dramatic pause. Did you like it?"

"Very nice."

"Ready?"

"Yes."

"What three things would you take with you in the apocalypse?"

"Hmm," I say. For some reason, it seems like a perfectly reasonable question at this moment. "It depends on what kind of apocalypse."

"Zombie."

"Sturdy boots. A good backpack. A machete, definitely. To cut off their heads."

"Biblical."

"Boots. Backpack. And a Bible? No, probably still a machete."

"You're very practical."

I am starting to like this feeling of being nervous and excited all at once. It's like the tingle in my chest when my pain pills kick in. It's the thrill of feeling something different.

"I have a question for you, too," I say, making my voice sound way braver than I actually feel.

"Hit me."

I try to act as cool as possible. I don't even look at him. "Do you smoke weed?" I say.

He laughs so hard he nearly spits his coffee out. The tingle in my chest shuts off, squeezes tight. Did I read him wrong? Funky car, ironic T-shirts, misfit attitude—does that not fit the profile of a pot smoker?

"What's so funny?"

"I don't think anyone's ever asked me that before. I guess I'm not used to hanging out with somebody who doesn't already know my reputation."

"Which is what, exactly?"

"I'm basically considered the school stoner."

Relief spreads through me. "Is that an accurate assessment?"

"I guess. Though when I think of 'stoner,' I think of someone who's stoned all the time. I'm only stoned *most* of the time."

"Are you stoned right now?"

"Nope. Thought it might not be the best way to impress a pretty girl."

The compliment makes me brave. "Do you want to be?"

"Are you offering?"

I open my purse, find the joint I tucked inside an old breath-mint tin, and present it to him in the palm of my hand. It is such a silly little thing, like a white twig, but I am ridiculously proud of it.

"Well, aren't you full of surprises?" Marcus says with a smile. "Ladies first."

"No, you. I insist. You're my guest." I hand him my lighter.

"All righty then."

I watch him as he lights the joint and inhales. He's obviously done this more than a few times. I try to match his confidence and ease when it's my turn. I imagine the ghosts of all these dead people around us, watching us, laughing at me.

"So what's *your* label?" he says, holding in his smoke. He exhales and I'm lost for a moment in a cloud of his breath. "If I'm the school stoner, what are you?"

I cannot tell him I'm a former cheerleader. I cannot tell him that, until a few days ago, I was the girlfriend of the varsity wide receiver. I cannot tell him I sit at the popular table. And I definitely can't tell him about Cancer Girl.

"I'm not really anybody," I say. "I'm kind of a loner." I know no one would ever describe me this way, but it's what feels the most true.

"Ah, yes," he says. "Mysterious, beautiful loner. I bet all the jocks are secretly in love with you."

You have no idea.

"So where do you go? Berkeley High? North Berkeley?"

"North Berkeley. What about you?"

"You'll never guess."

"Oakland Tech?"

"Think richer."

"Skyline?"

"I, my dear, am a Templeton man."

"What? Are you serious? Don't you wear, like, suits to school? Aren't you supposed to be planning for world domination? Why are you hanging out with a mere mortal like me? I had no idea you were so fancy."

"You want any more of this?" He holds up the half-finished joint.

"No, I'm done."

"I'm not fancy," he says, stubbing it out on a gravestone. "My dad's the fancy one."

"What's so fancy about your dad?"

"He's the chief judge of the United States District Court for the Northern District of California," Marcus says in a hoity-toity voice.

"Wow, that is fancy."

Marcus shrugs.

"That must make it extra hard for you to break the law."

"Not really." He hands me the joint. "I'm pretty good at it, actually."

"You know what I mean. It must be extra bad if you get in trouble, right?"

"Let's just say that as long as I don't get caught, what I do in my spare time is not my father's top concern."

"My parents either."

"Yeah? Why's that?"

I have to think about this for a moment. I have to decide just how much I want to let him in. I decide I can tell him the truth while leaving out some of the details. "It's like they have this idea about who I am and they really want to believe it. So they're very selective about the stuff they notice."

"I wonder if all parents are like that."

"Some more than others, probably."

"They can't ever really *see* you," Marcus says, looking into the distance, his eyes glassy and heavy. "No matter what you do to get their attention. They'll only ever see what they want to see."

"What doesn't your dad see about you?"

He smiles but it doesn't mask the sadness in his eyes. "This is really good weed."

"It's medicinal."

"Where'd you get it?"

"From a friend."

"Can she get more?"

"She moved away, unfortunately." For a second, I wonder if I could believe this. If I say it enough times, maybe I can convince myself it's true.

"Too bad. The weed I get is pretty good, but not as good as this."

"You're not going to answer my question, are you?"

"Tell me about your leg."

Of course. It had to happen sometime. "It's not that interesting."

"So tell me."

Part of me wants to tell him. The weed and the view and his arm touching mine makes me want to tell him a lot of things. But not this. If he can keep his secrets, I can keep mine.

"Car accident," I say. "Pretty boring."

"Was it gory?"

"Not really. My mom's car got sideswiped on the freeway, we ran into a barrier, and my leg got knocked around. There wasn't even any blood." It is way too easy to lie. I could get used to this.

"You act like it's no big deal."

"It's not, really. It's not like it makes me special or anything. No one will even know in a couple of months when I'm off the cane and have healed completely."

The sky is turning the orange-pink of almost sunset. There's nowhere I'd rather be than right here, right now, and I can't remember the last time I felt that. I think Marcus is happy too, but there's an edge to his happiness, like he can't quite accept it, like there's some deep residue of an old sadness that won't let him go. I want to touch his sadness. I want to reach inside him and pull it out and tangle it with mine.

"Most people spend all their time trying to convince people they're special," he says. "But you're trying to convince me you're not."

I lean against him, his whole side warm touching me. The back of his hand brushes mine. I tilt my head without thinking, resting my cheek on his shoulder. We fit together perfectly.

"You know what, Evie Whinsett?"

"What, Marcus Lyon?"

"I don't like many people, but I like you."

The sky explodes in color and light.

"I like you, too."

"Okay, good."

"Good."

I don't want to leave. I could stay in the cemetery forever. Marcus and I could live in one of the stone crypts, plant a little vegetable garden out front, steal from people's picnics when they're not looking. We already have a blanket. What more could we need? We could stay here until we get old and die, then we'd already be in the perfect place to get buried. But I promised Mom I'd be home for dinner.

I get Marcus to drop me off in front of a restaurant a couple of blocks away from Children's Hospital, where I say I'm meeting a friend. He offers to park and stay with me until she arrives, but I manage to convince him I'm fine on my own.

"You're so tough," he says before I step out of the car. If only he knew.

I turn to leave, but he reaches out and catches my hand in his as I move to open the door.

"Wait," he says.

"For what?" I say.

"I don't know. I'm just not ready to let you go."

We lean in to each other. Our foreheads touch. His musky smell makes me dizzy. "Evie," he says, and it sounds like the first time my name has ever truly been spoken. His breath gives me life. He names me.

I am wearing Stella's hat. I am fearless. I know how to get what I want.

I tilt the hat up and lean forward. I place my lips on his.

His mouth feels perfect on mine. Warm. Soft. Delicious. I could inhale him. I could eat him up.

I leave his car in a daze and float back to Children's. I can't get the grin off of my face and I don't try. I don't care that Mom's car is already there when I round the corner, that she sees me come from somewhere besides inside the hospital.

"Where were you?" she says as I get in the car.

"I left early. I went for a walk while I was waiting for you."

"In this neighborhood? At this time of night? Are you sure that's safe, honey?"

"It's not even totally dark yet. Plus, I'm tough," I say, leaning my seat back and putting my good foot up on the dashboard. "God, Mom. Haven't you figured that out by now?"

twenty-one.

KASEY'S COMING TO DINNER TONIGHT. MOM INVITED HER without even telling me. These days, Will can just decide we're not broken up and act like nothing happened, and Mom can decide to invite my friends over for dinner, and I don't get a say in any of it.

I'm in my room, still giddy from a phone conversation I had with Marcus right after school. Unlike everyone else in my life, he talks about real things. He has opinions on issues besides prom dresses and sports teams and school gossip. It's like everyone else I know is in black and white and he's the only person in full color. Everyone else is a robot and we're the only real people with real thoughts and real feelings.

When I get excited, I have to listen to this song from Stella about all the things the establishment wants to do to control us. I turn it up really loud and jump around my room on my good leg hitting things with my pillow.

This is what I'm doing when Mom knocks on the door and says, "Dinner's ready, honey. Kasey's here." It feels like they're forming an army and Kasey's been recruited for their side. It's four against one in the Whinsett family now.

I need reinforcements. I need strength. So I take Stella's hat from my desk and place it on my head.

"That's interesting music," Mom says when I open the door. "What do you call that?"

"It's called music, Mom."

"It's kind of . . . aggressive, don't you think?"

"Assertive is not the same thing as aggressive." I wish Marcus had heard me say that.

Kasey hugs me when I come to the table. "How long have you been here?" I say, and I realize too late that it probably sounds rude.

"I just got here," she says. "Like a minute ago." She smiles a less than sincere smile. "What's with the hat?"

"It was Stella's."

"I know. But why are you wearing it?"

"She gave it to me."

I sit down and start serving myself without waiting for the others.

"Evie," Dad says. "Aren't you going to take your hat off for dinner? I think that's the polite thing to do."

"Sure." I hang it off the back of my chair and stuff my mouth with rice pilaf.

I eat as Kasey and Jenica talk about prom, which is rapidly

approaching. I don't know when they got so friendly. I guess they're best friends now too.

"I just think it's so neat that your school includes juniors," Mom says. "At my high school we only had a senior prom."

"Tell me about it," Kasey says. "I've been looking forward to this since I was, like, nine. And I can't believe I get to do it again next year, too! I get to go dress shopping twice."

She is totally serious. Prom will be the highlight of her life.

"Honey, did you call Will back yet?" Mom says to me. "It must be important if he called on the house phone."

"It means she's not returning his calls to her cell," Jenica says. "Right, Evie?"

"Why aren't you returning his calls, sweetie?" Mom says.

"I've been busy."

Kasey looks at me with surprise. "You didn't tell them?"

"Tell us what?" Dad says.

"Oh god," says Jenica, rolling her eyes.

"Tell us what?" Dad repeats.

I stare at my plate, at the grilled chicken breast turning hard and cold. "Will and I sort of broke up."

"What? When did this happen?" Mom says. "Why didn't you tell us? Honey, are you okay?"

"I was wondering why we haven't seen him lately," Dad says. "Oh, Evie. I'm so sorry. You must be devastated."

"Why do you automatically assume he dumped me?" I say. "I broke up with him."

"But why?" Mom says.

"I don't want to talk about it. It's not that big of a deal."

"Not a big deal?" Jenica says. "You've been together for two years. He's practically a part of our family." So now Will's a part of their army too. Whinsett family: 5. Evie: 1.

"It *is* kind of a big deal," Kasey agrees, looking at her plate.

"Kasey, can you explain this?" Mom says, because apparently I can't speak for myself. "Do you know why this happened?"

"I don't," she says sadly. "I really don't. Will is such a perfect boyfriend. He loves Evie so much."

"I just need some space right now," I say. "To figure some things out. It's not a good time for me to be in a relationship. I need a break. Is that a crime?"

"What have you been busy figuring out?" Jenica says. "All you do is sit in your room and listen to that girl's horrible music over and over and talk on the phone."

"Physical therapy takes up a lot of my time," I say. "And how is my relationship any of your business, anyway?"

"Who are you talking to on the phone?" Kasey asks.

"And now you're wearing her hat," Jenica adds.

"Why are you guys ganging up on me?"

"What, are you, like, a lesbian now?" Jenica snarls.

"Are you fucking serious?" I scream.

"Evie!" says Dad. "Lower your voice. There will be no cursing at the dinner table."

"Dad, did you hear what she just said? What about Jenica being homophobic at the dinner table? What happened to this house being a hate-free zone? Just because I wear a hat and listen to certain music doesn't mean I'm a lesbian, or that there'd be anything wrong if I were. That is so closed-minded of you. God, Jenica, you're so stuck in the gender binary."

She smirks at me. It's the smirk she gets when she thinks she's smarter than everyone else. "Do you even know what that means? Define 'gender binary' for me."

"Evie," Kasey says, at least with some kindness in her voice. "I think we're all a little worried, you know? Will is such a great guy, and you were so happy for so long. It doesn't make sense for you to break up with him, especially after everything he's done for you."

"What has he done for me?"

"You can't be serious," Jenica hisses. "You ungrateful bitch."

"Jenica!" Mom says. "Language!" She is crying now. Dad jumps up and puts his arms around her, but she pushes him away.

I look at Kasey for some support, but her eyes are narrowed in anger now too. My heart drops. It's really true—no one here is on my team.

"He stayed by your side this whole time," Kasey says softly, as if she can't believe the horror of her own words. "The whole year you were sick. He could have any girl he wanted. Anyone. And he stayed with you."

I have never felt like such an asshole in my life. I look around the table but no one will meet my eye. "I never asked him to do that," I say, my best attempt at an excuse, but that just makes it worse.

"Yeah," Jenica says, standing up from the table. "You never asked any of us to love you, did you? It's all our fault. We're idiots." She storms away from the table and down the hall. The sound of her bedroom door slamming rattles the silverware on the table.

"I think I should go now," Kasey says, standing up from the table. "Dinner was delicious, Pam." She starts crying as she says this. Mom reaches out and pulls her close and I watch from the other side of the table as my dad wraps them in his arms for a group hug. I caused this. I'm the one who drove them away from me and into each other's arms.

"Evie," Dad says. "I think you should go to your room."

I get up and limp away, back to my dungeon. I will leave their sadness in this room. I will not take it with me.

I ditch my cane at the table. I don't need it anymore. I am tough, like Marcus said. I can do without it. I can do without any of them.

twenty-two.

MY LEG DOESN'T REALLY HURT ANYMORE, BUT I'M STILL TAKing the painkillers. Every day, multiple times per day. I don't have a choice. If I don't take them, I start feeling sick, like I'm getting the flu; my legs ache and my stomach churns and I feel like I want to crawl out of my skin. The pills don't really get me high anymore; they just make everything a little more bearable, a little smoother around the edges. They make the way my parents look at me not hurt so much. They make school not as excruciatingly boring. They make my "friends" not as mind-numbingly dull. They help me to not care that I'm so behind in all my classes that no amount of tutoring is going to keep me from failing.

Mom just got my last refill, then Dr. Jacobs said no more, I'm cut off. Then I don't know what happens. She keeps bugging me about the outpatient support group meeting I'm supposed to go to, where a bunch of Sick Kids and survivors sit around in a circle and talk about cancer. Why would I want to talk about cancer? I've spent enough of my life talking about cancer.

It feels like my world is on hold until I see Marcus tomorrow. First, I have to spend this afternoon with Kasey, doing the kinds of thing the old me used to love. I want to have fun, I want things to be good between us, but I'm not feeling very optimistic. Things have been tense since the blowup at dinner last week, but we've managed to patch things up enough to pretend we're going to repair our bond with some good old-fashioned girl time. I wish it was as important to me as it is to her, but the truth is, all I can think about is Marcus. All I want to do is see him.

So I take four pills before Kasey gets here, a preemptive strike against whatever I may feel in her company. I know I should be rationing, but desperate times call for desperate measures. My leg doesn't hurt, but there's a new kind of pain, one that only comes when the pills fade away, like a fist tearing my heart through my stomach, and the noise it makes is *IwantIwantIwantIwant.*

I hear the doorbell, and Mom's and Kasey's high-pitched greetings. I take a deep breath and remind myself to be kind. It's not Kasey's fault I'm someone else now.

She opens my door without knocking. "You're not even dressed" is the first thing she says.

"I didn't realize we're in a hurry."

"We have an appointment," she says. "And they're busy on weekends." Kasey's treating me to a pedicure. Whoopee.

"I can't figure out what to wear. All my clothes are, like, pre-cancer old." I couldn't care less about clothes, but I know Kasey will buy this excuse.

"Let's go shopping!" she says. "You totally need a new wardrobe now that you're getting your body back. We can go to the Bay Street Mall after we get our pedicures."

"But I'm broke," I say, pulling a pair of jeans and a black T-shirt out of a pile of what I hope is clean clothes. "And I don't think my parents have any extra money lying around."

"I'm sure they could spring for a new pair of jeans at least. Those ones are so ripped."

"I don't think so," I say, pulling the clothes on. "They're really stressed about money right now."

"A sweater, then. Something cheerful for spring. On the sale rack." Her smile clouds as she notices the look on my face. "Or we can just walk around and try stuff on."

I put Stella's hat on and look at myself in the full-length mirror. I look cool. I look tough. I see the reflection of Kasey behind me, in her short white skirt and tight pink sweater, her blond hair cascading across her shoulders.

"You're not going to wear that hat, are you?" she says.

The pills have started their softening. I can name the look on her face "bitchy," but it does not hurt me.

I turn around and strike a pose. "It's my signature look."

She tries to smile, but I can tell it hurts her face. "So what do you think? Pedicures, then mall? We don't have to spend any money. We can walk around. Or I could even buy you something."

"God, Kasey. I don't want to go to the fucking mall." The cruelty in my voice surprises me.

I watch her face as the seasons change from forced

cheerfulness, to surprise, to shock, to hurt, to anger. White, cold, freezing anger.

"Fine," she says, grabbing her purse from my bed. "Then I guess you don't want to get pedicures, either. That's stupid too, isn't it? That's just something your old bimbo cheerleader friends do."

"Stop. I'm sorry. I didn't mean it like that." I say the words, but my heart's not in them. I know I'm supposed to feel something, but I don't. The pills took care of that.

"No, whatever, it's okay. I know I'm not as cool as Stella. I know my life is totally boring, that all my problems are pointless compared to yours. I get it." She stops and faces me, her face red and blotchy and stained with tear-smeared makeup. All I can think is she'd be horrified if people at school saw her this ugly. "I miss you," she says, and for a second my armor cracks. For a second my heart breaks and I see my old friend, the girl who knew me better than anyone, the girl I couldn't live without.

"I miss you too," I say, my head suddenly clear. I want to hug her. I want to wrap her in my arms and make everything the way it used to be.

"You don't realize how hard this has been for me, too," she says. And my armor is solid once again. How dare she? How dare she compare her pain to mine?

I'm a tornado. I'm a hurricane. I'm a whirlpool of rage. "Oh, I'm sorry. I'm so sorry my cancer has been an inconvenience to you. What, has my dying gotten in the way of cheer practice and finding a new boyfriend?"

Her sadness, suddenly gone. Her anger is big enough to match mine. "Evie," she says. "You're not dying anymore. Get over it."

The sharpest silence I have ever heard as we stare each other down.

"Shit," she finally says, looking away. "That sounded really bad."

"I can't believe you said that."

"You know what I meant. I want you to be happy. But frankly, your attitude lately sucks." She takes a step toward me and I take a step back. "Like, shouldn't you be a little bit grateful that you're cured and you're going to live? Isn't that supposed to make you happy?"

"I am happy."

"No you're not. You're the least happy I've ever seen you. You were happier when you had two weeks to live."

"Well, maybe you'd prefer it if I could go back to that. Maybe everyone would like it better if I was sick again. Then you'd know what to do with me."

"Stop."

"I think maybe you should leave now."

"You can't be serious. You can't really think that. You can't really think anyone wishes you were still sick."

"I don't know what I think."

"We love you. We all just want you to be happy."

"I want you to go."

She reaches her hand out to touch me, but I slap it away.

"Go!" I scream. I don't want her to see me cry. I don't want her to be here when the pain breaks through. I can feel it bubbling up, somewhere in my stomach. When it makes it past my throat, I know I'll be a goner.

"Fine," she says, and turns away. When she gets to the door, she faces me. "You can keep pushing everyone away if you want. But we may not still be here when you decide you need us again." She walks away, slamming the door behind her.

If I move fast, the feelings can't catch me. I grab Stella's box out of my sock drawer and stuff it in my bag. I wait an unbearable five minutes to make sure Kasey's gone. I grab Mom's keys from the bowl by the door and walk out without telling anyone I'm leaving.

twenty-three.

I'M WITH MARCUS AND MY WORLD IS BACK IN COLOR.

Flowers burst out of the ground in every shade imaginable. The sky is a shocking, electric blue. We are zooming through the winding roads of the Oakland hills, going up, up, up, to the part of the city where everything glows with possibility.

"I think my parents used to take me here when I was little," I say as Marcus pulls into a spot at the Lake Chabot parking lot. "We'd bring a picnic and rent a canoe."

"That sounds so nice and wholesome."

"Yeah, that's my family. Nice and wholesome. Yours isn't?"

"Let's start walking," he says, perfectly aware that he's avoiding my question.

It is a warm, perfect day. It is so beautiful I can almost forget about my fight with Kasey yesterday. I can forget about getting stoned in Mom's car while my phone buzzed with her unanswered calls. When I got home, the house fell into what has become a usual routine. My mom, beside herself with worry, wanting me to sit with her on the couch and talk. Wanting to try to understand why I felt the need to take her car without asking. Dad furious, pacing and throwing his hands in the air. "What gives you the right? Do you have any idea how much we worry? Do you think your actions have no consequences?"

Well, yes. So far, my actions have had no consequences. Even this. Anyone else would be grounded for sure, but Mom happily gave me a ride to the hospital to "visit Caleb" again, as if yesterday never happened.

"Are you sure you're up for this?" Marcus asks as we start down a dirt path toward the lake.

"It was my idea."

"Your leg can take it?"

"It's not like we're climbing a mountain. We'll just walk until we find a nice secluded spot."

He doesn't question this. He doesn't say anything about how I'm still limping. Unlike everyone else, he trusts my judgment about my own body.

Maybe my hip is a little sore. Maybe I sort of regret giving up my cane so soon. Maybe it's tricky maneuvering around these rocks and roots, and maybe this is a lot harder than I thought it would be, but there's no way I'm going back. The air smells like warm soil and eucalyptus, the sun is glistening off the water, Marcus is holding my hand, I have a joint in my pocket, and I'm not worried about anything.

"Where's your cane, by the way?" Marcus says. "That cane was cool."

"I decided I don't need it anymore."

"Okay, tough guy," he says, squeezing my hand. A duck quacks good-naturedly somewhere out of sight.

"I like it when you call me 'tough guy.'" I stop walking and pull him close. I place my lips on his. His kiss erases my pain.

"Hey, I think I see the perfect place," he says. He holds my hand as he leads me off the trail.

After fighting our way through bushes and spiderwebs and nearly sliding down a steep ravine, we make it to a hidden beach just big enough for us. The view of the main beach is blocked by a fallen tree. Marcus adjusts some branches to hide us from the trail. No one in the world knows we are here. We are a secret.

Marcus lays out his blanket and pulls a picnic of wine, bread, cheese, and fruit out of his backpack. "FYI, this is a hundred-dollar bottle of wine," Marcus says as the cork pops. He pours me a plastic cup full.

"Just when I thought you couldn't get any fancier." I take a sip, but to me it tastes the same as something that came out of a box.

"Fresh from Judge Lyon's custom-made temperature-controlled wine cellar."

"Very impressive," I say, lighting the joint I brought.

"Yeah," Marcus says. "Too bad I'm not. Impressive, that is."

"I find you very impressive," I say, passing him the joint.

"I think you and my dad have slightly different standards,

unfortunately. You probably don't have as much interest in my being 'a respectable example of an educated black man in America.'" He says the last part in a very low and very serious voice.

"I guess not," I say.

"I doubt everyone is really paying all that much attention to me, so I'm not that worried about it." He takes a long pull from the joint. "Plus he makes me go to the whitest school in the entire Bay Area, so I'm pretty sure that makes him a hypocrite. The only other black kids in my class are these adopted twins who have two white Jewish moms, and another kid who's, like, royalty from Kenya or something. We're not exactly the epitome of African-American culture." He hands me the joint. "But Judge Lyon has pretty much given up by now and leaves me mostly alone."

"I wonder how he'd feel about your incredibly white girlfriend."

"Well, he married my mom and she was white. Or haven't you noticed my smooth, milky complexion?" He bats his eyes.

"*Was* white?"

"Was. Is. She's not in my life anymore, so past tense seems appropriate."

"I'm sorry."

He shrugs and picks up a eucalyptus seedpod and throws it in the lake. It lands with a less than satisfying plunk. He looks at me and smiles. "So that other thing you said. About you being my girlfriend."

"Oh." Shit. "I said that?" *Shit shit shit.* "I, um—it just came out. I guess I'm stoned. Wow, I'm embarrassed."

"Don't be," he says, putting his arm around me and pulling me close. He says nothing more, doesn't confirm or deny the label.

We finish the joint, the view turns into a postcard, and I gradually forget my embarrassment. We could build a little fort out of sticks and branches and steal some fishing poles from the bait shop. We could stay forever on our hidden beach and no one would ever find us.

I lay my head on Marcus's lap and he runs his fingers through my short, patchy hair.

"Your hair is so soft and fluffy," he says. "It's like a baby duck. I've never felt anything like it."

He doesn't know this is a result of the chemo. Maybe I want him to know. Maybe I'm ready. But first, more pressing issues. "Do you think you could find me some Norco? Maybe some Oxycontin?"

His hand freezes on my scalp. I can feel his body tensing under me.

"No way," he says. "I don't fuck with that stuff. Do you?" I can hear the worry in his voice.

I turn my head to look up at him. The sun frames his face like a halo. "What? No," I say, trying to smile as reassuringly as possible. "I heard it was fun so I thought maybe you wanted to try it with me or something. But if you don't want to, that's cool."

"Don't touch that shit, Evie." Despite the warm sleepiness that wants me to stay lying down, I can tell this is serious enough for sitting up. "Promise me. Heroin, Norco, Oxy, they're all the same. Meth and cocaine, too—these are all off-limits. Okay?"

"Why?" I say.

"Because they fuck you up big-time. You can't do that shit recreationally. It owns you."

"I think you're being a little dramatic."

"I'm being serious. Promise me. Please."

The concern in his face is real; his worry is sweet, not oppressive like everyone else's. I say, "Okay, I promise," because it seems like he needs it so much.

"Thank you," he says. "I feel like I can trust you. You're the first person I've been able to say that about in a long time."

A knife turns in my chest. I don't want to lie to him. I can't abuse his trust.

I know I should get off the pills. Maybe soon. Maybe I'll start cutting down. Maybe next week. My promise to Marcus has to mean something. But I'm not ready. I can't quit yet. I'm too scared.

He looks out over the lake. A family in a paddleboat floats by. The parents don't see us, but the little boy waves. Marcus waves back.

"Someone hurt you," I say. I am sick to my stomach thinking I could be that person, if he ever knew.

"You could say that."

"Tell me."

He's quiet for a while, lost in his own private world. I want in. I want him to let me in.

"Do you want to go swimming?" he finally says.

"Isn't it illegal? Isn't this a reservoir or something?"

"Yep," he says, unbuttoning his pants.

"Whoa there, stud," I say as he pulls them off. I notice a tattoo on his shin. The letters DL in messy black-blue, as if they were stabbed there with a pen. And a date, just a month from now, of last year.

"What's DL?" I say. "Who's that?" I know it's stupid to be jealous of someone he knew before me, but I can't help it. I hate her, whoever she was. I hate that he loved her enough to make her permanent on his body.

"Someone who hurt me," he says, and pulls his shirt over his head. His smooth, muscled chest is all I see for a moment, and I am breathless. But that warm electricity is quickly extinguished when I notice the scars on his arms. The area between his elbow and shoulder, the part covered by a T-shirt, is scored with uncountable crisscrossing scars of various depths and widths. Nothing natural would make this pattern. Nothing but someone's own hand could inflict this kind of torture.

"Marcus," I gasp. I look up at him from where I'm still sitting. "Tell me," I say.

"I will," he says. "Soon." Then he dives into the water and disappears.

I strip down to my underwear and bra and leave my tank top on so he won't see my portacath. I am not nervous as I follow him into the water. I am not embarrassed. For once, I am with someone who hurts, someone who's damaged like me, someone who's broken. Maybe I don't have a place anymore with people like Kasey and Will, people who aspire to perfection, who are foolish enough to believe it exists, who want nothing more out of life than to avoid complications. For people like Marcus and me, complications are all we have. We have scars. He has shown me his, and I want to show him mine, too.

We meet each other in a deep part of the lake next to the fallen log. Our feet cannot find the bottom. The lake could go to the center of the earth and we wouldn't know the difference. We wrap ourselves around each other, held up by only a few fingers laid on the slippery wood. We float, entwined, our foreheads together, the tips of our noses almost touching, our lips half a breath away from each other. I close my eyes and feel his breath tickle my upper lip. We float like this for a long time, listening to the water lap against us, breathing each other in.

"I can't believe you exist," I say.

"I could stay here forever," he says.

"Tell me," I whisper. "About your scars." Maybe if we tell our secrets in the water, it will make them buoyant. They will float away like leaves, like flower petals. They will leave us and we will be unburdened, weightless.

"I've never really talked about it with anyone. Not even the shrink my dad sent me to."

"You're safe with me."

He takes a deep breath. "My mother left two years ago," he says, and I hold him tighter. "Just left. One day, she was gone. Didn't even leave a note. Didn't call or write. Took some clothes and jewelry and withdrew a bunch of cash from the family checking account and we never heard from her again."

I run my hand across the scars on his shoulder, textured like the bark of the fallen tree that is keeping us afloat.

I want to ask about DL. I want to give him my secrets. I want to give him everything. But the sound of a boat motor interrupts our solitude. The magic of the moment leaves us. Our secrets sink to the bottom of the lake.

"You two," says the garbled voice of a bullhorn. Birds chirp in protest of the interruption. It seems impossible that such a loud, unpleasant noise could be possible here now. "No swimming allowed. Get out of the water right now and leave the park immediately or you will receive a citation."

Several yards away is the khakied form of a park ranger in a small boat.

"Yes, sir," Marcus says. "We were just leaving."

We swim to shore and collect our things. Our tiny beach has been consumed by shade and is suddenly chilly with the arrival of the evening coastal breeze. The ranger motors away on his quest to ruin more perfect moments. I am wet and cold and covered in pine needles. I want to swim out to that ranger's boat and pull him under.

"Lame," Marcus says.

"I'm freezing."

"Let's get out of here."

We walk to the car quickly, in silence, holding hands. The sunny glow of earlier has been replaced by muted shadows as the sun gets ready to set. My leg hurts from climbing the hill back up to the trail, but I say nothing. I don't want him to worry. I don't want his pity. I don't want to ruin the moment any more than it already has been.

"School tomorrow," Marcus says when we get into the car.

"Ugh."

"I still have homework to do."

"Yeah," I say, even though I stopped trying to do my homework a long time ago.

"Can I drive you home? Or do you still want me to drop you off on Telegraph?"

"Drive me home, I guess," I say, doing nothing to hide my disappointment.

"Hey," he says, reaching out his hand and turning my face gently toward him. "We'll do this again soon."

I nod.

The music he plays on our drive down the hill is beautiful and sad. Just a guy and a guitar and his sweet, mournful voice.

"I like this," I say.

"Yeah, my brother turned me on to this guy," Marcus tells me. "One of the best songwriters ever, until he stabbed himself in the chest."

"That's morbid."

"And such a cliché. Troubled genius and all that. He was a drug addict and an alcoholic, too, of course."

"He must have been in a lot of pain."

"We're all in pain. But that doesn't give us a fucking right to waste life like that." There is a storm across his face. He is talking about something else, someone else. His mother, maybe. Or DL.

There is so much more to say, but we will talk about it later. We are driving back into the real world now. The moment for secrets has passed. Why do I feel like time is running out?

I tell Marcus how to get to my house and he drops me off in front and kisses me good-bye. A part of me thinks I should keep him hidden, as if some magic will be lost if my two worlds collide. But I am tired from the sun and wine and weed and walking. I am too tired for sneaking around.

I walk in the house and straight into my room, not even bothering to say hi to Jenica, who is studying in the living room. I lie in bed and look at the ceiling, making up stories to fill in the holes of Marcus's secrets, until my thoughts become thinner, until they become air, until I fall into a dreamless sleep and they become nothing at all.

if.

Stella,

I'm screwed. I'm seriously fucking screwed. Not only am I out of pills, but my parents and Dr. Jacobs and the whole fucking world knows I was stealing them and now everyone thinks I'm a drug addict and a criminal. I don't know if Mom forgot about Dr. Jacobs's speech about tapering off the pills, but she tried to refill my prescription even though the bottle said no more refills. Some red bells probably went off on the pharmacist's computer that said "Warning! Warning! Drug addict alert!" Then Dr. Jacobs called and the shit hit the fan.

You would never have let things get this far. You would know how to keep things cool and under control. But everything I do seems to run away from me and get bigger and bigger, way bigger than me. I'm no match for it. All I ever wanted was to be free and brave like you, but it's like I traded in one prison for another.

The worst part is, Mom isn't even mad. She just sat on the couch crying like I broke her heart. "You were stealing them, Evie? You were sneaking into our room and stealing?" she kept saying, as if it did not compute, as if wires got crossed and she was getting an error message. She was practically comatose when she told me Dr. Jacobs wants me to come in and see him. She got real small and practically whispered, "He thinks maybe he should refer you to an addiction specialist," as if saying it quietly enough would make it less true.

I wish she would scream. I wish she would get angry and cruel so I could be mad at her. This is so much worse. "I don't know how to help you," she whimpered. "What did I do wrong?" And then I started comforting her. "You didn't do anything wrong, Mom," I kept saying. "It's all my fault. I screwed up."

Then that's when Dad chimed in, "Damn right you screwed up," which made Mom cry harder as he yelled, "What the hell is wrong with you?" at me. And I kept saying I don't know, I don't know, which is the only true answer I can think of. I don't know what's wrong with me. I don't know why I have to keep taking these pills. I don't know why I had to steal. I don't know why I turned into this twisted version of the girl I used to be. I don't know why I have to keep smoking pot and not telling them where I'm going and not doing my homework and not studying for tests. I don't know why I do anything anymore. Stella, if you were here, I don't know if you'd even like me anymore.

"How can we help you?" Mom said, which really made Dad lose it. "Help her?" he screamed. "Are you insane? Are you a fucking idiot? First, you don't even notice her stealing from you, now you're treating her like she's still sick? She's manipulating you, Pam. Are you really that stupid?" Jenica ran in from where she was hiding in the kitchen and started yelling at Dad to stop yelling at Mom, and Mom was hyperventilating, and Jenica started screaming how I'm destroying the family, how Mom and Dad never fought until now, and then Dad started crying, and he started apologizing to Jenica, and to Mom, and then they were all crying, a big, wet heap of sadness on the couch, and me by myself facing them, everyone crying except for me.

I felt nothing but shame, and shame doesn't make me cry; it just makes me want to roll into a ball and eat myself alive until I'm gone, destroyed, nothing. But I was still there, still in the living room, watching the people I love unravel because of me. All I could say was "I'm sorry." I said it over and over until they were quiet, until my voice was the only sound in the room. I couldn't face them, couldn't look any of them in the eye. But I could say those words and mean them. I managed a few others—I'm having a hard time; I feel like no one understands me; I'm going through a lot; I never meant to hurt anyone. I said I'd try harder. I said I promise. I said I'm sorry, I'm sorry, I'm sorry.

My family's breaths returned to normal; their eyes dried up. I don't know exactly what I promised them, but I know it means quitting the pills. Maybe this was meant to happen. Maybe this is a sign. It's my chance to make good on my promise to Marcus, to quit the drug I promised him I'd never even try, to really be the person he can trust. If it weren't for him, I don't know if I would have enough reason to quit. Even without my prescription, there are always other ways to get things.

I will try to be good. I will try to be nicer to Jenica and join my family's conversations at dinner. I will try to start doing my homework again, will take my teachers up on all their offers for after-school help. Maybe I will find my way back to become someone resembling the perfect daughter I once was.

But I am not hopeful. That girl is gone. Maybe I can pretend just enough to keep them happy. Maybe I can work harder at my secrets. Maybe I can show them who they want to see, someone they love, and they can keep that mask, they can hold her and love her and she can take my place at the dinner table and fill up my space in the family, and no one will notice that I'm really gone, that I've become someone they cannot recognize at all.

I don't know what's going to happen now that the

pills are gone for good. I've always managed to get enough just in time, before the want turns into need turns into pain. I'm scared, Stella. I'm scared this is going to hurt. I'm scared of needing something I'll never get. I'm scared of opening the hole where pain lives. I'm scared that once it is open, it can never close again, and it will always be empty, I will always be empty, and the absence will just grow and grow until it takes over everything and I am really, truly gone.

I am going to quit. I am going to get off the pills. This is not who I am. I am not someone who steals from her mother. I am not a drug addict. I will not let these pills own me like Marcus warned. I am done. I am done. I am done. If I say it enough it has to be true.

God, I wish you were here. You would know exactly what to say to me right now. You would know how to zip me back up and stuff myself full of confidence. You could convince me I deserve to exist.

Come back, Stella. I need you. I need you really bad.

Love,

Evie

twenty-four.

THE WORLD IS AS SMALL AS MY MOTHER'S LAP. ALL I FEEL are her fingers in my hair, their mindless back and forth. All I hear is the faint echo of her heartbeat, the mysterious gurgles of her stomach. I am a child, home with the flu. I am taking a sick day. She will make me soup and I will try to eat it and I will let her think she's making me feel better; she's loving me back to wellness like she used to, when sickness was something far more simple, when it was a little virus you caught like everybody else.

Never mind the throwing up, the sweating, the cramping, the diarrhea. Never mind that a virus has nothing to do with this. Never mind that I brought this on myself, that this is purgatory, that I deserve none of my mother's kindness.

Is it normal to forget how to breathe? To have anxiety tie me up from the inside until I'm gasping for air?

My legs threaten to walk away without me. My hip is engulfed in a white cold fire. I am burning up from the inside, but instead of flame, I am made out of ice. My bones are brittle with icicles. I will never be warm again. You could crack me open and see the frozen rivers inside me.

I have come too close to pressing send on the wrong texts to Marcus, words written by desperation: *Are you sure you don't want to try a few Norcos with me? Are you sure you can't get me any Oxy? Just a little? Just immediately? Just RIGHT THIS VERY MINUTE BEFORE I TEAR MY FUCKING HAIR OUT? Are you sure? Are you sure? ARE YOU SURE?* All erased, just in time. All of it, other words for *Help me.*

But he is not the one to help me. Not with this. Marcus knows the other me, the one who is fearless, the one who glides through water. He cannot know this puking, shivering girl. He must never see her.

He is the reason I'm doing this. He is the only reason strong enough for me to endure this. Because I made a promise. Because he's taking a chance on trusting me.

I want I want I want

I need something to take this pain away.

"This is a bad flu," Mom says, her voice far too chipper for the end of the world. "I really hope the rest of us don't catch it." She knits the angora of my hair with her fingers.

Mom is happy. She has something to do now. She has her sick daughter back. She knows how to do this. There are things mothers do that no one else can do. Her fingers in my hair. Her directionless humming. But she cannot help me. No one can help me but a pharmacist or a drug dealer.

She leaves to get me some Advil from the kitchen and I make plans to jump out the window and rob the nearest drugstore.

I have the flu, I text Marcus. *I feel like I'm dying.* I want to tell him to bring me drugs. I want to tell him I'll take anything. Why hasn't he written me back yet?

How is this even possible? How is it possible to want something this bad?

I should be back in the hospital. This could be the cancer come back for revenge. Except now it's in my heart. Now it has broken my soul and thrown it around the room and I can't get it back, I can never get it back.

I'm dying. I'm dead. I'd rather die than feel like this.

This is the definition of hell.

Last night I dreamed of Stella. She was running through the Oakland streets, dodging the honking, screeching cars, her middle finger raised in salute, her big black boots shaking the earth with their stomps. She was dancing with danger. She was so fast, so graceful; she was practically flying. I called her name but she couldn't hear me. We went up and up until we were on top of the world, until all of our problems were tiny specs far, far away. And I thought, *This is it! This is what we've been waiting for.* But she kept going, she kept flying up, even though there was no land left, even though I couldn't follow, and she was singing, she was so happy she didn't even notice I wasn't coming with her, and I called for her but she couldn't hear me, and she kept flying up until she was only a spec, as tiny as everything else, and then even farther, until she was nothing.

I was on the ground, full of rocks, so heavy I couldn't move, I would never move, I would be stuck in that place forever as my punishment. I have stolen something that wasn't mine to have, something that should have been Stella's. It was me who was supposed to be the disappeared one. It was me who was supposed to be taken. I was the one who stopped treatment. I was the one who had already given up. Stella never stopped fighting. She should still be on the ground, dancing, singing, running through traffic. It should be me flying away, becoming invisible. I am the one who was supposed to die.

I woke up screaming, drowning in a pool of sweat. "Oh, Evie," my dad's voice said in the dark, then I felt his arms around me, and I let myself soften into a seven-year-old version of myself, a tiny girl my dad could still love, a girl who hadn't yet done anything to terrify him, hadn't yet pulled on his hope and terror and disappointment, a girl who was still innocent. He held on to that girl and I almost believed I could stay as her. "Daddy," I said, and for a second I believed I was worthy of his forgiveness.

But then I remembered why I was sick. I remembered I am not innocent and never will be again.

"Stella!" I cry now. It is day, but it is still so dark inside me.

"Oh, honey," Mom says. "Oh, my love."

Stella, we are sitting side by side getting chemo again. It is your hand in my hair. You are telling me a joke and I laugh even through the sickness.

"Do you want me to call Will?" Mom says. "Do you want him to come over?"

I say yes. I need someone who knows how to love me when I'm sick.

Help me help me help me

"Will," I say, and let him wrap me in his arms.

It is months ago. It is before everything changed. It is back when I was dying, back when everything still made sense. Death is simple. Death makes everything clear. It uncomplicates love.

"I missed you," I say, and it doesn't feel like lying.

I am someone who still loves Will. I am someone his embrace makes safe. I am someone who says "I'm sorry" until he kisses my wet forehead. We make sense like this. When I am dying and weak and he is healthy and strong, and he is in love enough for both of us.

The worst of it is over now. It's been five days and my stomach is starting to feel normal again. I'm finally able to eat a little. I'm finally getting over that "flu." It should be obvious what it really was to anyone who's ever watched a TV cop show or seen a PG-13 movie. My parents aren't stupid, but they choose what they want to see, and no one wants to see their kid going through opiate withdrawals.

One second I'm a cancer survivor, the next I'm a drug addict. How did I ever let this happen?

Most of the physical symptoms are gone, but I'm exhausted and the cravings still knock me over with their power. They come out of nowhere, a tidal wave of sadness and desperation and need and every bad feeling imaginable, tons and tons of it, headed straight for me.

I feel emptied. I am hollow. I am only half here. The other half is in some different dimension I can't even imagine, let alone find. But I have to get used to this. I have to if I'm going to be good again.

I want to. I want to be good. At least I think I do.

The house is the calmest it's been in a long time. Even Jenica felt sorry for me while I was sick. Kasey came to visit, and seeing me sweaty and pale and weak made her forgive me. Will resumed his place at my bedside and was everything solid I came to rely on during my year of cancer. I let him hold my hand. I let him rub my back. I don't want to get back together, but maybe there's room for something else, something like friendship. Maybe there's room to let him love me just a little.

He asked me to go to prom with him and I said yes. I made it clear that we would be going as friends, and he said he understood, but I'm not sure he really believed me.

Being sick has made me salvageable. Like cancer, the flu only has victims. It is not controversial, not a matter of will or moral character. No one ever deserves it. So I get to resume my familiar role as victim and give everyone a chance to love me again. I don't deserve their sympathy, but I'll take it. I'm getting another second chance.

Marcus calls but I don't know what to say to him. I hear his voice and I want to taste it. I want to run away into the night and light the sky with him. But I am still too sick. I don't want him to see me like this. And I don't trust myself yet to not beg him to find me more pills. I have to wait. I have to be patient. But I crave him almost as much as the pills.

I still want them. God, I still really want them.

I'm going to try to be good now. I really am. Maybe there's an Evie I haven't tried yet, one who can be two people at once. Maybe there's a way to make everyone happy. There's the girl who still wants to find a comfortable little place somewhere inside my old, clean world. Then there's this girl I'm just starting to get to know, the one who wants to live on the edge, the one who belongs with Marcus. Maybe they can share a body. Maybe they can share a soul.

Maybe.

twenty-five.

I'VE CREATED A MONSTER. WILL IS TELLING EVERYONE WE'RE back together again. He was at my locker this morning with a dozen of his red roses, and I realized what a perfect example they are of everything that's wrong with our relationship—raised in a hothouse to look pretty and perfect, so far removed from nature and anything that's real.

I tried studying last night but everything I read looked like a different language and I had to give up after ten minutes. I tried to hide my fidgeting while we all watched TV, a tentative step back toward family togetherness. Then everyone went to bed, and I spent the night smoking pot and staring out the window, waiting for my pulse to slow down and trying to breathe like a normal person. Without the pills, I'm finding it impossible to sleep. My body forgot how.

It's only a couple of hours into my first day back and already I'm questioning my plan to be normal. There's too much in my way. I've gone so far in the other direction, I don't know if I can find my way back. A life isn't something you can just slip back into after leaving it.

My history teacher asks to see me after class. "I'm worried about you," she says, but her old teariness is gone. I've worn out my Cancer Girl sympathy, even with her. Now I'm just bad. I'm not turning in homework, she says. Not participating in class. I only answered three questions on the last quiz and I didn't even get them right. All I can say is I'm sorry. That's all I can ever say. I walk out of the room without even waiting for a response. What can she say that will change anything? School's over in three weeks and there's no way I can catch up.

I catch Kasey throwing up in the bathroom. Her excuse is that she needs to fit into her prom dress. She tells me this casually as she rinses her mouth out, as if it's a perfectly reasonable explanation for deciding to have a deadly eating disorder. I don't say anything about how I struggled to keep food down for most of last year. I don't remind her about my wasting away, about needing to be fed through tubes. Another thing that's not worth it.

Then I get this text from Caleb: *Hi Evie. Are you mad at me? Why haven't you returned my texts?* Ten minutes later: *I really want to talk to you.* Delete, delete.

It's lunch now and Kasey's not eating and all anyone can talk about is prom. The freshman girl who sits at our table is wearing a hat identical to Stella's. Next she's going to start walking around with a limp and chemo hair.

Will has his arm around me all during lunch, even though

I keep trying to wiggle out of it, even though I keep making excuses to get up. But every time I sit back down, his arm is there again, like he's my keeper, like he's afraid of me running off. All my subtle hints are wasted, so eventually I stop trying to escape, and I shrivel under the weight of his arm.

I'm trying to be nice now, right? I'm trying not to make a scene. Is this what nice is? Letting people think things that aren't true just to avoid hurting their feelings? Letting them get away with things you don't want them to do? Being nice is dishonest. Being nice makes me a liar. What if, deep down, I'm just not a nice person? I'm pretty sure nice people don't ignore the texts of friends with brain cancer.

I squirm and Will whispers in my ear, "I'm not going to let you push me away this time," and it makes me sick, like actually physically nauseous, like I am trapped in the trunk of a car and being driven over speed bumps and potholes for miles and miles and miles, and no matter how hard I push and kick and scream, I can't get out.

I want to push and kick and scream. I want to run out of this lunchroom and this school and this life and never look back.

I want to take back what I promised, when I was sick and half out of my mind and thought maybe this could be my world again.

"Do you have your dress yet?" someone asks me.

"No," I hear myself say. "Do you?"

"Well, yeah. Obviously," she says, like I'm an idiot.

"Evie," Kasey says, her face crumpled in concern. "Prom is

this weekend." The whole table looks at me like I've told them I have cancer again.

I don't give a shit about prom. I wish I'd never told Will I'd go with him. I wish I'd never let him rub my back while I was sick. I wish I wasn't still sitting at this table with these people. Why did I ever think I could find a way to fit back into their world?

I was wrong about there being room for two Evies. The old one has to go. The new one is stronger, bigger, and she does not want to share space with that silly, pathetic girl any longer.

I text Marcus and tell him to pick me up on Telegraph when he gets out of school. I skip the rest of the day, just walk out the front door and spend the next couple of hours wandering around downtown Berkeley. I walk by People's Park four times, each time barely talking myself out of approaching the group of seedy-looking kids to ask about getting some pills. It is scary how close I get. I feel giant magnets pulling me in their direction. I feel the hole in my heart threatening to swallow me. The kids don't notice me, but their dogs do. The dirty pit bulls stare me down with their beady eyes, taunting me. They say, "We know what you want, girl. Just say it."

But I don't. It's a miracle, but I don't. I keep reminding myself of the promise I made Marcus. Not my parents, not Dr. Jacobs. I don't care about getting caught or in trouble. I don't care about being a loser or an outcast. Marcus and his trust in me, that's what keeps me strong.

As soon as he pulls up in Bubbles, the world instantly makes more sense. I get in the car and must kiss him right away, a long, desperate, gasping kiss that only ends because the car behind us honks.

"I guess you're happy to see me," he says.

"You have no idea."

"I'm glad you're feeling better. I missed you."

"What's that?" I say, noticing a pile of clothes at my feet.

"Oh, that's my uniform. Feel free to step on it all you want."

"I forgot you wear a suit to school," I say, inspecting the black slacks and jacket, the white button-down shirt, the striped tie. "That's hilarious."

"Yeah, real funny."

I relax more as we drive to César Chávez Park by the Berkeley Marina, as we set up his blanket in a secluded spot on the hill, as we smoke weed and lie in the sun. We watch people flying fancy kites. We laugh at the white boys with dreadlocks doing bad capoeira. We make up stories about the private lives of the fat squirrels climbing in and out of holes. I don't ask about the secrets Marcus left untold last time we were together, and he doesn't ask me about mine. I'm not in the mood for anything heavy today.

So instead, we pick dandelions. We make tiny bouquets of grass and weeds. I think of Will's expensive roses stuffed in my locker at school, how they must be infusing everything with their sticky, sweet perfume. I think of how much more beautiful

Marcus's and my little arrangements are.

"Who decided a dandelion is a weed and not a flower?" I say.

"Probably some old, straight white guy," Marcus says, sticking one behind my ear.

Being stoned makes me philosophical. "The only difference between a weed and a flower is that a weed is strong and can take care of itself, and a flower is weak and fragile and needs someone's help."

Marcus smiles. "So which one are you?"

"What do you think?"

"I think you're even stronger than a dandelion. And way more beautiful than any flower."

I laugh and we kiss, and for a moment I feel good enough to forget about the hole inside me where the pills no longer are. I forget about how good it felt when Will held me when I was sick. I forget about my pledge to be good, to stop getting in trouble, to try to fit back into my old world. It seems so long ago, so distant, like it was a different person entirely who made those empty promises.

Not even a day back and I've already given up.

I guess I know who I really am now.

twenty-six.

IT'S THURSDAY NIGHT, PROM IS ON SATURDAY, AND I DON'T have a dress. This is quite possibly the stupidest problem a person could have. And yet, it is mine. Of all the problems I've ever had, this is the one I have to deal with at this moment. I don't know which is worse, having to scrounge at Jenica's door for help, or having to go to prom at all.

I wish I could tell Will I'm not going. I've picked up the phone to call him, but it never happens. I've even thought of texting—the ultimate coward move—but I can't bring myself to do that. At least I'm not that much of an asshole. Not yet, anyway,

I swallow what little pride I have left and knock on Jenica's door.

"Yeah?" she says.

"Can I come in?"

It takes her a while to decide to answer yes.

She is sitting on her bed studying when I walk in. "What do

you want?" she says, visibly tensing, getting ready for a fight.

"I was wondering if you still have your prom dress from last year." I can't look her in the eye as I ask this. I don't want to see the hatred I know is there.

"Um, yeah." Her voice is softer. I can hear her surprise.

"Do you think I could maybe borrow it? I don't have a dress and I know money's tight so I don't want to ask Mom and Dad. It's okay if you don't want to. I'd understand. It's just—"

"Yes. Of course," she says. "Of course you can borrow my dress." I look up and am surprised to not see the angry, irritated face I'm so used to. There's an imposter in my sister's place—someone kind, someone sympathetic. "I'll go get it," she says.

I sit on Jenica's bed while she rummages around in the closet. Her room is so tidy, so sparse and clean, not at all like a normal teenager's. She's always been like this, even as a kid. It's like she was meant to skip childhood and go straight to being a forty-year-old woman with a great career and a solid marriage, like her entire youth, all of its silliness and manic uncertainty, is just a nuisance until her real life starts. I've always secretly admired her for this, for her inexhaustible confidence. She's always seemed to know exactly who she is and exactly what she wants. She never seems confused about anything.

"Here you go," she says, handing me the dress in a plastic dry-cleaning bag. As I take it out, I remember the night she wore it, standing in the living room while her junior year boyfriend slipped a corsage on her wrist. She was wearing makeup, her hair was in a fancy updo, and she looked so beautiful, so glamorous compared to her usual, plain bookworm self, and I was jealous. I couldn't wait until this year, until I could finally go to prom too. I had just received my first diagnosis at that point, and it seemed like such an extravagant wish, but one I was determined to get.

And now, that wish is coming true, but it seems like a chore. In a year, everything can change. The world can turn upside down. A wish can turn into a curse. But back then, going to prom with Will was enough of a reason to want to survive.

Jenica zips me up and I stand in front of her full-length mirror. I have gained some weight, but the dress still sags in too many places, most noticeably the bust. The spaghetti straps are hopelessly loose. The tiny blue sequins I thought so magical when Jenica wore it now seem dull and misplaced. But the dress is good enough, I guess. It has to be.

I can see Jenica standing behind me in our reflection. She tries to smooth my patchy hair with her hand. She licks her finger and tries to style the front into some sort of side bang.

"Did you really just rub your spit in my hair?"

"Shh," she says. "I'm working." She fusses a little more, but I don't see much of a difference. She stands back and says, "There. Pretty good."

"Do you think this'll look good with tennis shoes?"

"It's going to have to," she says. Then, after not even a beat, "Are you and Will getting back together?" Jenica can always be counted on to be direct.

"No," I say.

"I didn't think so." She fluffs the back of my hair with her fingers. I fight the urge to close my eyes and lean into her hand. "He thinks you are, though."

"I know."

"For some reason that guy is crazy about you."

"I have no idea why."

She shrugs, neither agreeing nor disagreeing. She steps out of the reflection. "The dress fits well enough," she says.

That should be my cue to go, but strangely, I don't want to be done here. "I've kind of been seeing someone," I say, and I realize this is the first I've ever spoken of Marcus to anyone out loud.

"Really? Who?" Jenica sits down on the edge of her bed. I could sit next to her. We could talk about boys like real sisters. But I stay standing.

"He goes to Templeton."

"Wow, you got yourself a Templeton man?" She looks genuinely impressed. "You may not be as hopeless as I thought."

"Yeah," I say, trying not to show how much that stings. "Maybe."

"I was kidding," she says. "I don't think you're hopeless."

"It's okay."

The silence that follows is bigger than us. Bigger than this room and this house and this family and our history together.

"Evie," Jenica says, and we lock eyes. "Are you okay? I mean, really?"

I feel so awkward standing in the middle of the room in a formal gown and bare feet. Jenica's eyes burn holes in me. I feel naked, exposed. I am a specimen on display, being poked at, prodded. She is too close. She sees too much. I have let her in too far, and now I need to push her back out before she sees anything more.

"Yeah," I say, grabbing my clothes from the floor. "I'm fine."

"I don't believe you."

"Thanks for the dress." I move toward the door.

"We can talk, you know." No, Jenica. No, we can't.

"Yeah," I say, and I walk out of the room, closing the door behind me.

I have just enough of Stella's weed left for one joint. I will be able to smoke away this mistake, just barely. I will inhale stillness. I will inhale clouds. I will exhale this fog of sadness and regret that follows me out of Jenica's room.

I wish my parents drank. I wish they had a liquor cabinet I could raid for reinforcements. I wish I had some sort of promise that I'll be able to sleep until tomorrow, that I'll be able to get through the school day, that I'll survive until I get to see Marcus again, until the brief relief of the clock finally ticking hours I don't want to forget.

if.

Dear Stella,

I get through the day in one-minute increments. Fifty-five of them add up to one class, during which I have to sit still and not fall asleep. Five minutes adds up to the time in between classes, when I limp through the hall quickly and pretend to be in a hurry to avoid having to stop and talk to anyone I know.

The forty-five minutes of lunch are the worst. I am supposed to do something besides sit, walk, and be silent. I am supposed to speak and engage and act interested and not show how much I wish I were somewhere else.

My life has been reduced this—a collection of tiny fragments to endure and survive, a countdown of sorts. Everyone else is looking forward to prom tomorrow night, and the end of school two weeks from now, then summer, then senior year, then the rest of their lives unfolding in front of them like flowers, everything getting better and better and bigger and longer until they reach out into forever and become massive, infinite. My world is so small in comparison. I busy myself with seconds. I survive these series of unendurable minutes, these miniscule fragments of forgettable life, until the end of the day when I get to see Marcus. And then the world opens up and becomes infinite again.

I wonder if you would have gone to prom. Would you have taken Cole? Or would you have planned some kind of amazing anti-prom night?

Tonight is going to be special, Stella. Something's going to happen. Something big. Marcus says he has a surprise for me.

I'm ready to ask him about DL. I'm ready to ask him about his scars and I'm ready to tell him about mine. And then maybe we won't have to creep around in shadows. Maybe our secrets will be released and they'll float away into the night and be replaced with light, and I won't feel the need to lie all the time, I won't feel the need to hide, and I won't feel so lost, and everything will become clear. Everything.

Love,
Evie

twenty-seven.

I TRY TO GET OUT OF THE HOUSE WITHOUT ANYONE NOTICING me, but Mom pounces as I'm reaching for the door.

"Evie," she says. "Before you go. We need to talk about making your appointment with Dr. Jacobs next week."

"We can talk tomorrow," I say, the doorknob already in my hand. "I don't want to be late."

"No," she says, unsurely, the word so foreign in her mouth. "I've been trying to pin you down for days. You're due for blood tests again."

"I don't understand why I can't get blood drawn in the outpatient clinic."

"Dr. Jacobs wants to see how you're doing. You know that. And he still wants to talk to you. You never went in after that whole thing with the—" But she stops. She can't say it. She can't say "pills." She can't say "drugs" or "addiction." So she starts over:

"I don't understand. What are you scared of? They're just going to take a little blood."

How can she be so blind? *No, Mom, I'm not scared of blood.* I'm scared of everything else. I'm scared of seeing a sweet, confused boy with a brain tumor who refuses to give up on me even though all I do is treat him like shit. I'm scared of Moskowitz reminding me that I'm responsible for the outing that got Stella sick. I'm scared of seeing Dan and his big brown eyes full of sympathy I don't deserve. I'm scared of all the kids who believed I was some sort of miracle, of the little girl who couldn't catch it, who's probably not there anymore, who's probably not anywhere anymore.

Shit. Tonight was supposed to be fun, and now I feel like I'm on the verge of crying.

"I'm going now," I say.

"But what about the appointment?"

"What about it?"

"When is a good time?"

"I don't know. Whenever." I turn the doorknob.

"So I should just make the appointment for any time? You'll be free? Are you sure?"

"Yeah, Mom. Whatever." I walk out the door and down the street three blocks to the corner where I told Marcus to pick me up.

It feels weird being inside Marcus's house. It's weird being somewhere that isn't just ours, a place where he exists separate from me, where he inhabits a life that has nothing to do with us.

But the house itself is nothing of Marcus. It's one of those Victorian mansions in the rich enclave of Piedmont, but the inside is decorated in the starkest, most modern style possible. Almost everything is white or black, sharp angles, and shiny leather. The furniture is hard and uncomfortable-looking, like you could hurt yourself trying to sit on it. There's nothing that says real people live here. There is nothing that says family, no awkward school photos, no vacations or holidays, no pictures of Marcus as a baby.

"Pretty ridiculous, isn't it?" he says as I stare at the spiral staircase that goes to the second floor.

"It's beautiful."

"I guess," he says. "If you're into the minimalist thing."

"Do you actually, like, hang out in here?"

"Honestly, I can't remember the last time someone sat on that couch. My dad and I don't really spend time anywhere besides our own rooms. Sometimes we accidentally meet in the kitchen while we're grabbing food to take back to our lairs. We don't eat meals together or anything. The oven hasn't been used in like two years. Living here is like sleeping in a museum."

"Is your dad here?"

"No, he's at some kind of fund-raising gala with his new girlfriend of the week who's probably barely older than me."

"Gross."

"Yeah, tell me about it."

We climb the staircase to the second floor where the house

separates into two distinct wings. I follow Marcus to the left, down a long hall to the very last door.

"Dad lives on the other side," he says. "As far away from me as possible."

"Where's your brother's room?" I say, looking down the hall at so many doors to so many rooms.

Marcus looks at me like I've caught him off-guard, like there was something strange about my question.

"That one," he says flatly, pointing down the hall. "Third door on the right." He turns around and opens the door to his room.

Marcus's bedroom is a relief from the coldness of the rest of the house. His walls are covered with posters of bands I've never heard of. The hardwood floor is softened by a huge blue rug. A big, soft couch sits against one wall, his unmade bed against another, a desk and shelves stuffed with books next to that. Everything colorful and cozy and funky, as if in direct retaliation to his father's stark aesthetic. There are plants everywhere, green leafy things of various sizes in colorful pots on the floor, on shelves and tables, hanging from the ceiling. There is life all over the place.

"It's a jungle in here," I say.

"All of these were my brother's. One of his many special talents."

"I'm impressed."

Marcus shrugs. "Someone had to take care of them after he moved out."

"I don't know. Most people I know can't take care of anything besides themselves."

Marcus opens a desk drawer and pulls out a small bag of weed, far less than Stella left me, but enough to last me for a week at least.

"Here," he says, handing it to me. "As you ordered. Though I have to say it feels kind of sucky to be selling drugs to my girlfriend."

"You're not really selling them; you're just helping me procure them. It's not like you're making a profit."

"So I'm the middle man, then?" he says. "And I'm not even getting anything out of it? Yeah, that makes me feel a lot better."

"Who said you weren't getting anything out of it?" I put my arms around him, pull him close, and find his lips with mine.

"Are you going to pay me in kisses?" he says when we come up for air.

"Maybe," I say. "Maybe other things." I could stay here all night. I could stay here forever.

"Do you want your surprise?" he says.

I nod my head, not believing this moment could get any better. He pulls away, opens the same desk drawer as before, and takes out another small plastic bag. He sits on his unmade bed and pats the spot next to him. I sit as he opens the clear plastic, revealing a tangle of what looks like dry, shriveled sticks.

"What's that?"

"Mushrooms. You ever tried them?"

"Not yet."

"You want to?"

"What do they do?"

"They make you see God."

I'm not sure if I want to see God. I'm certain I don't want God to see me.

"Do you trust me?" he says.

"Yes," I say. "I trust you more than anyone."

"Good," he says. "I'll take care of you, you know."

"I know."

"I won't let you get hurt."

"Okay," I say.

"Are you sure? We don't have to."

I put my hand out, palm up, ready.

We chew the dirty stems in candlelight. In silence. The houseplants send intricate patterns of shadow across the room, dancing as the flame flickers.

"Let's go to the cemetery," Marcus says. "We can climb the fence."

I am scared but I say yes. I want to be brave. I want to be the tough girl Marcus thinks I am.

We walk through the streets of Piedmont, passing the stately mansions and perfectly manicured front yards. We're holding hands, like we could be any normal couple, anywhere. A woman walking a poodle smiles at us. She has no idea we just ate mushrooms and are about to sneak into a graveyard.

"When do they kick in?" I say.

"About an hour after you eat them."

"How will I know?"

"You'll know," he says, and squeezes my hand.

The night is warm and smells like flowers. It's so perfect, I can forget about my other life, my false life, the one that threatens to consume me, the one that keeps holding on no matter how hard I try to shake it off. This is the only one that matters. This is the only one that's real. This place Marcus and I make exist by our being together.

It's nearly ten o'clock, only two more hours until my curfew, but I don't care. My parents can't find me here. I am untouchable. And if I get grounded, I'll have a perfect excuse to not go to prom tomorrow night.

When we reach the gate, the perfection of the night is tarnished just a little. "I'm supposed to climb that?" I say. Streetlamps illuminate the fully exposed gate. Anyone driving by could see us. But what worries me more is how high it is, how it requires a far more nimble body than mine to climb it.

"I know you can do it," Marcus says. "I wouldn't have brought you here if I wasn't sure."

His belief in me, however foolish, has to be enough. What's the worst thing that could happen? I could fall and break my leg again? I could get caught? None of those threats seem reason enough to quit this adventure right as it's getting started.

"Here," he says, making a cradle out of his hands. "Let me give you a boost."

I lift the foot of my good leg and push myself up, my hands clutched on the metal fence. His hands support the back of my legs as I scramble the rest of the way up, kicking and clawing as ungracefully as possible, until I've somehow made it to the top and he can't reach me anymore, until all I have are the fence and gravity and myself.

"You made it," he says.

"I still have to get down the other side."

"Just swing your hip over."

Easier said than done. My hip doesn't want to obey. I send it the command, but it's like the message doesn't compute. Somehow "swing over" is something it lost the ability to do after so many surgeries, after so much bone was removed and replaced with metal.

"I can't," I say. "My leg is stuck." I am starting to panic. I feel the world swirling around me, the metal grating of the gate turning to string. This net can't hold me for much longer. It will collapse and I will go down with it, and I will smash to the ground, which suddenly looks so far away—fifty feet, a hundred, a thousand. "I'm scared," I say. Marcus is so far away and there is no way he can help me.

"It's okay," Marcus says, his voice so smooth and strong and calm that it turns the string fence back to solid metal. "I'm coming over," he says. He climbs up quickly, gracefully, like he is made for the air. He kisses me when he gets to the top, then climbs down the other side.

"Now what?" I say.

"I'm going to catch you."

"No," I say. "It won't work." He is a thousand feet down. Gravity would catch me and together we would crush him.

"Look at me," he says. The world is swirling and dark, but

I find his eyes so far below, blinking up at me from the depths. They are the only stable thing I see. They are the only light.

"Trust me," they say. "I promise I won't let you fall."

What choice do I have? Either he saves me or I am unsaveable.

I close my eyes and let go.

I don't know how long I'm flying, how long I float through the nowhere space between here and there. I am neither dead nor alive. In those brief moments, I become light. I am a wave and a particle. I am nothing and everything and I am nowhere and everywhere. There is no up and no down, no past and no future, no grief and no joy. I am all movement. I am plummeting through space and I am perfect.

And then Marcus catches me. Everything is solid. Marcus is solid. I am solid.

"Are you okay?" he says somewhere beneath me. Are we on the ground? Am I on top of him?

"I think so," I say. "Nothing hurts." My eyes focus and for a moment I think I am looking in a mirror. *Whose eyes are those? Why are they so close?*

I start laughing. "I tackled you." The eyes smile. Marcus's body is the sturdy ground beneath me. His arms and legs are tree roots. "Marcus," I say. "I am definitely not sober."

Then two white eyes in the distant dark, headlight beams, searching for the live people among the dead.

"Oh shit," Marcus says, but he is not scared. This is a game and we are winning. "Let's hide."

A flurry of movement and we are running in the stars. I don't know how it happens, or when, but I suddenly know that this place is the sky and we are angels; these are not gravestones, they're clouds. This is not a hard place, not a place of stone and sadness. It is trees and grass and sky and stars. It is a place where Marcus's hand is fused in mine and we are one body, and we are climbing, up and up the hill we go, and the shadows are pillows, just here to soften the edges of the things with spikes and points and thorns and corners. We bend in and out of darkness and light. The ghosts help us find the best hiding places. There is nothing here to be scared of. We run and dodge and dart until the lights of the security guard's truck are a distant memory at the bottom of the hill.

"This way," Marcus says. "We're almost at my favorite spot."

He takes me to a giant, round stone tomb the size of a small cottage. It is covered in moss and ivy, like something out of medieval times, like something out of Narnia. It is surrounded by a ring of grass, then bordered by a stone wall that opens to a perfect view of the sparkling Bay Area skyline. We are hidden from everything except the sky.

"Oh wow," I say. The lights of the city are a million stars, so close I can touch them. They pulse with my heartbeat. We are connected, all of us—me and Marcus and all the little ant-people down there, doing their jobs in service to some fat queen they never even see, all because of some vague promise programmed inside them, a blind faith that their hard work and suffering will be worth it. But what if it's not? What if the queen doesn't even exist? What if they're making themselves miserable for nothing?

"They should come up here," I say.

"Who should?" Marcus says.

"The ant-people. All of them down there. They don't know what they're missing."

"What if they don't even know up here exists?"

"That is so sad."

I am leaning in to Marcus. His fingers are in my hair. He smells like man and sky and grass.

"I wasn't in a car accident," I say.

"Me neither."

"No, I mean my leg. That's not why I had the cane. That's not why I limp."

The sky is pulsing. I feel the pressure change in my ears. It goes *whomp, whomp, whomp.*

"I had cancer. Like, really bad cancer. Like, I almost died. Like, I had two weeks to live. Like, my parents had already started making funeral arrangements."

He doesn't say anything. I feel his body warm behind me, but he is silent.

"Hello?"

He squeezes me and the universe melts into my blood.

"I was supposed to die. The cancer was everywhere. They did radiation and chemo treatments until I lost all my hair and had no immune system. I lived in the hospital."

"Are you an angel?" he says, with no surprise and no fear in his voice. "Maybe you died and came back and you're an angel."

"Everyone said I was a miracle." I turn around to face him.

Without the sky and lights in front of me, we are suddenly enclosed. There is no opening to the night. We are bound to this place. It is solid and it is ours.

"You are." His eyes light up and I see the moon.

"But not a good miracle."

"Yes, Evie," he says, cupping my face in his hands. "The best miracle."

"But I think my friend died for me. I think she died so I could live. I think I took her life and I'm wasting it."

And then the sky opens up and takes us in it, hands like cherry blossoms, and all the statues nod their blessing, all the skeletons in the ground dance for us, and the earth shakes, and the grass shivers, and Marcus's breath is the world, and his arms are its bones, and his lips are the kiss of God that makes me exist, that make my life worth something.

"Was that an earthquake?" I say.

"That was you."

The ground settles. It is his body, my body, moving. It is our limbs taking root. It is our clothes drifting away and becoming clouds. It is all the passion and truth it is possible to feel, burning through my skin and into his.

"I didn't want to tell you. I didn't want you to think I was sick. I didn't want you to think I was weak."

He stops kissing the valley between my ribs and touches my nose with his. "Evie. Are you crazy? You're the strongest person I've ever met. I had a feeling. I knew it before I knew. "

"You had a feeling I had cancer?"

"I had a feeling you survived something. I knew you were like me. We have dark places to climb out of."

"Sometimes I'm so tired. Sometimes I want to stop climbing."

"You have to climb. It's the only way to get out."

He returns to my ribs. He kisses each one of them. He kisses the place between my breasts that is bursting with warmth. He kisses my shoulder, my throat, my ears, my face. His skin glides across my body and I wrap myself around him until there is nothing between us.

"I want you," I say.

"I want you, too."

"Do you have a condom?"

He nods. He says, "Are you sure?"

I say, "Yes." I say. "Absolutely."

"Are you sure you want our first time to be in a graveyard?"

"I have never been more sure of anything in my life."

Our bodies merge and our histories swirl around us. One of us is crying but I don't know who. I see scars but I can't tell if they are mine or his. Our love patches up the mysteries. Our breath paints healing across our bodies. His hands are gentle, confident; they are mending me; they are putting me back together.

The dead dance around us, but they are not scary. Not sad. They tell us, *Stay where you are.* They say, *We're not ready for you to join us yet.*

And the night explodes in every color. The lights from the city march a parade around us. I laugh at their production, at the showiness of it all. The particles and waves weave us a cocoon of light. We are wrapped in it. We are held.

"I died too," Marcus says in the stillness that follows. "We're the same." We lay in each other's arms in the grass. The city has taken a break from its pyrotechnics. It is as spent as we are. I look up and see nothing but the blackness of the sky, like a thick blanket over us.

"Who is DL?" I say. I am not scared of her. Whoever she is, she cannot find us here.

"My brother," he says. "David. David Lyon. My brother," he says again, as if to practice the sound of a forbidden word. I turn my head to look into his eyes. They are as deep as the sky above us.

"Tell me about him," I say. "Tell me everything."

"He was the greatest," Marcus says. "For a long time. Then he wasn't."

"Why?"

"He always liked to party. But I guess he got hooked. It was coke and Ecstasy at first. He stole a little money from Dad, but never got in any real trouble. But then he got in a bike accident and got prescribed Oxy, and it stopped being a party. He started going to different doctors to get new prescriptions, and filling them at different pharmacies. He got caught and Dad kicked him out of the house. He was supposed to go to Harvard. He had already been accepted early decision. But instead he started living with his girlfriend and got hooked on heroin when he couldn't afford the street price of pills anymore."

"I'm so sorry," I say. I think back to all the times Marcus has mentioned his brother. I'd thought the past tense was because he was away at college or something, off to start a grown-up life.

"My dad was pissed when he found out Mom was secretly meeting with him. She'd take him out for lunch sometimes, buy him groceries. They were really close. When she left, he fell apart. If you can imagine falling farther than becoming a heroin addict."

"Did he OD?" I say.

"No. Suicide. Even heroin didn't numb his pain enough."

I know I'm still tripping hard, but I feel almost ultra-sober, as if all this truth has taken me into a new realm where it is impossible for fear and hiding and lies to exist. I cuddle into Marcus and collect our discarded clothes to lay on top of us. The moist earth contours to our bodies; the grass sends up its feathery tendrils and secures us in place.

Marcus curls his body around mine. "I used to think my mom left because she didn't care about us," he says. "But now I think maybe the problem was she cared too much. And she didn't want to. Because it hurt too much to care. Maybe she thought running away would help her stop caring."

"Do you believe that?" I say.

"I haven't decided yet. Maybe it makes it better. Out of sight, out of mind." He pauses and the whole world inhales. "Or maybe it makes it worse."

He squeezes me from behind and runs his fingers from my stomach to my breast, then traces a circle around the bump of the portacath implant in my chest. "It connects to my superior vena cava," I say. "Easy access to my blood for tests and chemo and everything else so I don't have to get stuck every single time. Plus, chemo's too harsh to go through the little veins in the hand, which is where normal IVs go. It would burn them up."

"Does it hurt?"

"Not at all. At first it did. Right after it got put in. It was really swollen and bruised and I remember being so embarrassed. I was pissed because I couldn't wear tank tops or anything low-cut because it would show. It seems so stupid now. Everything does. All the dumb shit I used to worry about. Like how I looked and what I was wearing. Being home before curfew."

"Which you're not going to do tonight, by the way."

"I'm totally okay with that."

"I figured."

"Tell me more about David."

After a moment, Marcus says, "He was a genius. Like, certifiable. He was the one who was supposed to make my dad proud." He pauses. "Now I'm all he's left with."

I pull his hand to my mouth and kiss his fingers one by one. "My sister's the smart one too," I say. "She's the one who's supposed to grow up and have a great career. I was supposed to *marry* someone with a great career."

"'Was'? Not anymore?"

"I don't know. I used to be the pretty one. Then I was the sick one. Now nobody knows what I am."

Marcus squeezes me tight. "I know what you are."

I turn around to face him. The moon paints his face silver. "What am I?"

"You're everything."

We fill the next few minutes with slow, lazy kisses. But I want more. More secrets. More truth. "How did your brother kill himself?"

I feel him pull away. He is no longer in this world with me. "My dad has a gun," he says from somewhere distant. "Even now. He kept it. The motherfucker kept it."

"Marcus" is all I can think of to say. I pull him closer.

"You don't recover from finding the person you love most in the world with his brains all over the wall."

There is no breeze behind our little stone wall. The night has stopped its forward momentum. It is so still it almost goes backward.

I run my fingers over the crisscross of cuts on his arm. "So you did this," I say. "To make it stop hurting."

"Those were for my mom," he says. "When David died, I stopped. Here, on my leg"—he points to the messy initials and date on his shin—"that was my last act of self-mutilation. The night of his funeral, I carved it into my skin as a reminder. As a promise."

"A promise to what?"

"To not waste my life like he did. To not throw it away." He looks at me so hard it makes the universe wobble. "And to never trust anyone. To never let anyone get close enough that they could hurt me. But—"

"But?"

"But then I met you. And I broke my promise. I let you in."

I wrap myself around him. "You're safe," I say with all the air in my lungs, with every cell in my body. "I won't hurt you. I'm not leaving."

"Evie Whinsett," he whispers. "I think I'm in love with you."

"I love you too," I whisper back.

"It's just us," Marcus says. "Just you and me. It's just you and me against the world."

There is something to live for. There is finally a reason for my miracle.

I don't know what time it is when Marcus drops me off at home. The clock in his car is broken and both of our phones are dead. The sun hasn't come up, but I can tell it's closer to morning than to night. I kiss him good night and leave the warmth of his car. I must fight the magnetic urge to stay with him, to stay in the timeless space we created.

The world has stopped its swirling, but there's still a trail of electricity following me. My body glows where Marcus and I touched. Outside, the neighborhood is so quiet, unmoving. Everyone and everything sleeps. I'm exhausted and I want to sleep too, but my mind is racing, not ready to say good night.

Mom is in the living room waiting for me, as I expected. She is lying on the couch with a blanket over her. She sits up groggily when I turn on the light.

"Evie," she says with a sleepy voice, not yet registering my crime. "What time is it?"

"I don't know."

She blinks herself awake, and I watch her face turn from

sleep to confusion to fear. "Where were you?" she says. "Are you okay?"

"I'm fine, Mom. I'm great."

"Your father's going to be furious."

"I know. I'm sorry."

She studies me, and I know my serenity must shock her. I can feel the peaceful smile on my lips. Her fear, my father's anger—neither of these things seems important anymore. Their feelings do not touch me. I am too happy to be bothered.

"Go to bed," she says, and sighs. "We'll talk in the morning."

"Okay," I say. "Good night."

She looks at me like I'm a stranger and she can't quite figure out how I got into her house.

"Good night," she finally says, almost as a question, and I walk to my room and close the door.

It takes me a while to fall asleep because I can't stop thinking. The night is on replay inside my head. I close my eyes and let myself drift through it. My skin tingles with the memory of Marcus. I run my finger over my lips, still soft with his kiss. When sleep finally takes me, I am in Marcus's arms again.

twenty-eight.

IT'S AFTERNOON WHEN I WAKE UP. MY HEAD IS FUZZY AND my stomach is empty and acidic. I can hear my parents talking with low voices in the kitchen as I brush my teeth. I take a deep breath and prepare myself for what I know is going to be an unpleasant conversation.

I walk into the kitchen and say, "Good morning." Neither of my parents says anything. They look at each other as if wondering who this person is in their kitchen pouring herself a bowl of cereal.

"Are you ready to talk?" Dad says in his low, this-is-going-to-be-a-serious-discussion voice.

"Sure," I say, inspecting the half banana I find in the fridge.

"Will you sit down, please?" Mom says.

I take a seat across from them at the breakfast table. I wonder if they've been sitting here all day, waiting for me, like this—hands folded in front of them, cups of hours-old cold coffee on the table as props. I look my mother in the eye, then my father. I take a big bite of cereal and chew for a few moments as they stare at me. I swallow and say, "So am I grounded? Should I call Will and tell him I can't go to prom tonight?" I take another bite of cereal. They look to each other for help. They have already lost. I am running this show.

"Where were you last night?" Dad finally says.

"Hanging out with a friend."

"A friend we know?" says Mom.

"No."

"We'd like to know who you're spending time with, Evie." As usual, Mom is the good cop, her voice soft with concern.

"What the hell are you doing with a friend at three o'clock in the morning?" Dad growls with his bad-cop voice.

"We were just walking around and talking. I guess we lost track of time. Sorry if you were worried."

"You should have called," Mom says.

"My phone died."

"You lost track of time for three hours after your curfew?" Dad says, his agitation rising. "I find it hard to believe that was a mistake." He's leaning forward in his seat. His hands are fists.

His energy is threatening to overpower mine, so I match it. I lean forward too. I show him I'm not scared. "So maybe it wasn't a mistake," I say. "Maybe I wanted to stay out that late." Mom's mouth opens in shock at my brazenness. "So am I grounded or what? I should tell Will."

Mom shrinks into herself, shutting down. She does not know

how to be a part of this conversation anymore. She does not know how to talk to this version of her daughter. For a brief moment, I feel sorry to be putting her through this, but then I look at Dad, at the sliver of saliva on the side of his mouth, and I am all anger once again.

"No, you're still going to prom with Will," Dad says. "Don't think I can't tell when you're trying to get out of something. You're not going to make that poor boy suffer more than he already has. Maybe if you spend more time with him and Kasey and your old friends, you'll remember who you really are."

"Oh really?" I say with a tightening throat, the acid in my stomach rising. "That's what you think is going to happen? Who am I, Dad? Who exactly do you think I am?" My fists are as hard as his.

"You're definitely not this girl who stays out all night doing god knows what with people we don't even know."

"This isn't you, Evie," Mom says from her shrunken place. "You're a good girl. We know that. That's why we're so worried."

"So I'm not grounded?" I say, slouching back in my chair. They will not get me worked up. I am beyond this. I am beyond caring.

"Damn it, Evie. Are you even listening?" Dad says.

"Yes, Dad, I heard you. My punishment is I have to hang out with Will and my old friends."

"How the hell is that a punishment?" Dad says.

"We want to know exactly what you're doing, where you're going, and who you're doing it with," Mom says, trying valiantly to add some firmness to her voice.

"You're getting off easy," Dad says. "Your mother and I are not exactly in agreement about this."

"So I can't hang out with new friends?" I say.

"Not unless we meet them first," Mom says. "We want to get to know them." Dad looks at her like if it was up to him I'd be locked in my room for a year.

"What about Caleb?" I say. "Can I go see Caleb at the hospital?" Somewhere deep inside, a part of me cringes. How dare I bring him into this? How dare I use him to lie?

"Sure," Mom says, almost smiling. "I think that'd be good. How is Caleb, by the way?"

Dad shakes his head. "No, Pam. We are not here to chat about Caleb. We're here to talk about consequences." He pounds his fist on the table at "consequences," as if that will make up for the fact that they are so terribly ill-prepared to do this part of parenting. They've only ever had two angels as daughters. They've never needed to be strict. They've never needed to come up with a punishment for something this severe.

"Fine," I say. "So I'm allowed to hang out with Will and Kasey and Caleb and the people from my past so I can stay the same old Evie and never change."

"That's not what we mean, honey," Mom says. "Of course you're allowed to change."

"Oh, I'm so glad I have your permission." I stand up. Neither of them says anything, and I don't know if it's from shock at my talking back or because they're actually so dumb they don't hear the sarcasm in my voice.

"I'm going to start getting ready," I say as I put my cereal bowl in the sink. "I'm meeting everyone for dinner at six." Another lie. "I can still use your car, right, Mom?"

"Yes, we already talked about that, didn't we?" She doesn't seem so sure.

"But there is going to be absolutely no drinking," Dad says. "Right, Evie?"

"Right."

"We have your word?"

"Yes, Dad. I promise."

"And you promise to call us for a ride if you do drink?" Mom says.

"Pam," Dad scolds. "Don't give her any ideas. Jesus, it sounds like you're giving her permission."

"But we don't want her driving drunk," she pleads. "I'd rather she be drunk and call us than to drive because she's afraid of getting in trouble."

"Are you done?" I say. "Because I have to take a shower."

They look at me, their mouths slightly open. They blink simultaneously.

"I'm glad we had this chat," I say, and walk out of the kitchen.

Smart parents would do something. They wouldn't let me talk back like that. They'd demand I come back to the table. They'd make sure they had the last word. They wouldn't let me make them look like such fools. But my poor, naive parents don't know these rules. They give up too soon. They just let me go.

And I think that's exactly what I wanted. I want to be free. I want to run wild. But a softly nagging part of me almost wishes they would have tried a little harder, would have been more formidable opponents, would have put up more of a fight.

Maybe I actually want them to hold me closer. Maybe I want them to try to keep me safe.

twenty-nine.

I HAVE NO IDEA WHAT NORMAL LOVE IS SUPPOSED TO FEEL like. Maybe that's what I had with Will—warm but not hot, comfortable but not thrilling. Our love was safe.

What I have with Marcus is something entirely different. It feels almost dangerous. He makes everything else disappear until I am lost and he is the only one who can find me. I crave him like I still crave pills—like a surge of lightning that lights up every part of my body and soul. I want him to fill me up until there's no room left for anything else. I want him to consume me.

It seems such a waste of time to do anything besides be with him. Tonight is the worst waste of all: prom with Will. The worst parts of high school plus the most foolishly loyal part of my past, all dressed up and full of expectations I cannot fulfill.

Jenica's new boyfriend is here to pick her up, corsage and all, and they're in the living room with Mom and Dad taking pictures, everyone doing their happy-family routine without me. Jenica is doing it all right, this daughter performance. The funny thing is I used to do it even better than her. She was always the surly one while I was the cheerful princess, but now we've changed places. I know I should be out there with her; Will should be slipping a gaudy corsage on my wrist and I should be pinning a boutonniere to his suit, and we should be giddy with the spectacle of it all. We should be double-dating with Kasey, going out to dinner before the dance, sneaking a little champagne in the parking lot beforehand, just enough to get tipsy but not enough to get drunk. We should dance and be happy, maybe make out in the car before going to the after-party. This is supposed to be a rite of passage. This is supposed to be fun.

But I am beyond all that. It seems so foolish. I managed to get out of dinner with Will and Kasey and her date, some guy I've never met, by lying about having a physical therapy appointment, even though I haven't had physical therapy in weeks, even though it's six o'clock on a Saturday night and who has physical therapy appointments then? I know Kasey didn't believe me, but she didn't say anything. She wasn't about to break Will's heart even more than it already is. He pouted, but he believed my excuse. He had to. What choice did he have? What else would make it bearable to sit at home, waiting, while everyone else he knows is out having dinner with someone they love or will at least make out with later tonight?

But I can't think about that. If I imagine what he must be doing right now—alone, all dressed up and nowhere to go, still loving me even though all I do is reject him and lie to his face—a tsunami of feelings threatens to drown me. It hurts too much to imagine how I've hurt him. And now that I've quit the pills, I am no longer immune to pain. It is always there, storming around me like a hurricane, threatening to wipe me out entirely.

I pull Jenica's old dress over my head. I lace up my black winter boots, the only things beside tennis shoes I can wear with my bad leg. I run some pomade through my hair and sculpt my baby-bird fluff into a kind of faux hawk. I line my eyes with thick black eyeliner and paint my lips blood-red. I walk through the living room where the rest of my family is acting so normal. I feel the mood sour as soon as I enter.

"Are you leaving now?" Mom says as I take her car keys from the hook by the door.

"Yeah," I say.

"Have a great time, honey."

"Thanks, Mom."

"Don't do anything stupid," Dad says, not ready to pretend everything's okay like Mom is. "I'm serious, Evie. I'm still not okay with you taking your mom's car."

"I'm meeting Kasey and Will for dinner. They're good chaperones. You trust them, don't you?"

"Trusting *them* is not the issue and you know it."

"Oh, come here," Mom interrupts. "Let me take your picture."

"No, it's okay, Mom."

"No really, come on. I want one of you and Jenica together."

Jenica rolls her eyes as I make my way over. Her dopey boyfriend gets out of the way and I take his place next to my sister.

"You look nice," I say.

"Thanks." Her eyes narrow in suspicion at the compliment. She probably thinks I want something.

"Okay," Mom says. "Say cheese."

As hard as Mom tries, her forced cheer can't make up for our lack of enthusiasm. We mutter the most pathetic "Cheese" in history. Dad waits this picture out and sits on the couch with his camera in his lap. He has no desire to remember this moment. He doesn't want the night marred by any photographic evidence that I was here to ruin it.

I'm struck by the sudden urge to cry. For a moment, I wish Will was here with his arm around me. I wish Kasey was here taking way too many selfies with her phone and posting them to every social media outlet in existence. I wish I was wearing heels instead of these big black boots. I wish my hair was long and curled. I wish my makeup was subtle and pretty. I wish Dad was smiling and proud of his two girls, dressed up like princesses, on their way to a magical evening.

"I have to go," I choke. "I'm going to be late." I grab my purse and get out of the house as fast as I can. Only when I shut the front door behind me can I remember who I am now. I am someone who does not want those things. I am someone whose heart is not breaking.

I get in Mom's car, take Stella's mix out of my purse, and turn it up so loud that it drowns out any feelings of sadness I have left.

I text Marcus to see if he wants to get together before I have to meet Will and Kasey, but he texts back that he's out with a friend. A surge of jealousy rips through me—he is having fun without me. He is with someone else. Is it a girl? I know these thoughts are ridiculous, but still I can't imagine him with a life outside of ours together. Maybe because mine is so empty without him.

I drive fast up winding roads into the hills of Berkeley, music blaring, until I find the spot Stella and Cole took me to the night that changed everything. I remember the feeling of being suspended in the back of the van, being completely powerless and at their mercy, and how liberating that seemed. I remember the van doors opening and for a moment feeling like I was flying. I was on top of the world that night. Life opened up in a way I never imagined.

And then, just as quickly, it closed.

It seems perverse that I felt so much hope and possibility in this same spot a handful of weeks ago, that life brightened right as I was ready to say good-bye to it. And now that I've been given another chance at it, the possibilities are suddenly frightening. There is too much space around me, too much distance to cover, too many roads and paths and hills and mountains I have no idea how to navigate. This is not why people survive. No one beats a terminal illness just to be terrified of everything.

I roll a joint and smoke the whole thing while I look over the sparkling bay. I blow my fear out with the smoke into the night. This will never be as good as the pills. Nothing will. But I inhale some stillness. Some relief.

The magic of the night with Stella is gone. This is only a hill with a nice view now. What would happen if I kept going, if I released the parking break and flew into empty space? Would I be weightless? Would I be lifted to somewhere better? Would I touch the freedom of that night, just for a second? Would I find Stella?

I sit for a long time, long enough to listen to most of the CD, long enough to finish an imaginary physical therapy appointment, long enough to finish a nice dinner on a nice date with a nice boyfriend, long enough to use up the time until I said I'd meet Will and Kasey. My head is pleasantly cloudy, but I'm afraid of it wearing off too soon, so I roll another joint to smoke on the drive back down the hill, to fortify me for the inevitable. Even as I'm doing it, I know it's a bad idea. But it's either that or risk sobering up too soon.

There are few streetlights up here and the roads are windy and steep. My vision is blurry and my reflexes are slow. I am finding it hard to stay inside the lines of the road. One wrong turn and I would run right into one of the hillside mansions. I would make a garage out of their living room. I could keep going, straight through, and fly through their million-dollar view.

As I drive around a sharp turn, I barely avoid crashing head-on into another car. The sound of its horn in the quiet night jolts me awake. I am vaguely scared, but not enough to stop driving. I know I'm a menace. I could hurt someone. I could hurt myself. I should care, but I don't. I smoke through my fear and my shame until I make it to the bottom of the hill, still alive. Just barely.

I consider turning around when I see the crowd in front of the rented banquet hall where prom is being held, all the clumps of bare-shouldered girls with tiny purses, all the guys in matching black suits. But the night is just a cloud now, just a puff of smoke. I am not bothered by it. So I park and limp my way to the entrance, only half here. The other half of me is gone, sleeping.

"Evie!" Kasey's voice cuts through the manic chatter of my classmates. There she is near the door, flanked by vague girls I used to call my friends, and their wholesome athlete boyfriends. Will is off to the side, poking at his phone the way people do to avoid looking lonely. He looks up and smiles—hopefully, sadly—and shame tears through my haze of pot smoke.

I realize how stoned I am as I walk toward them. It takes extra concentration to coordinate my legs. I don't know if I should look people in the eye or not. My face feels like it's put on crooked. My stomach growls with hunger and I feel briefly nauseous. I can't remember the last time I ate.

"Hi," Will says, leaning toward me out of habit, either for a kiss or a hug, neither of which he gets. "You look nice."

"Thanks," I say. "So do you." It's true, he does look nice. Will always looks nice. Everything about Will is always nice.

"I like the punk thing you're doing," a girl I used to consider my friend says. "You look cool."

"Oh," I say. Is that what I'm doing? "Thanks."

"Want some?" another someone says, discretely pulling a

flask halfway out of her purse. I grab it and gulp down almost all of it.

"Jesus, Evie," Kasey says, disgusted.

"I'm thirsty."

"Shall we go in?" says Kasey's date, some guy from Skyline High she met at a party a month ago who I know nothing about.

In another life, I would have been squealing with the other girls about how beautiful the place looks. But in my condition, the fake Eiffel Tower and cardboard painted to look like old brick looks gaudy and cheap. The blaring hip-hop doesn't help the attempt at Parisian ambience.

"The lights are so pretty," someone says, but they're nothing more than white Christmas lights.

"Are there snacks here?" I think I say, but no one answers, so I wonder if I actually said it out loud or if I just thought it.

Will's holding on to my waist like he's afraid I'm going to run off, and he's probably smart to do it. I want to find somewhere to hide. I don't want to dance. I don't want to wait in line to take overpriced pictures with multiple cheesy background selections. I don't want to stand around with these people I have nothing to say to.

Not to mention that I don't think I'm capable of standing much longer. My legs are wobbly. Every beat of the too-loud music threatens to tip me over.

"I'm going to sit down," I manage to say out loud.

"Already?" Will says. "Don't you want to dance?"

"My leg hurts." I know he can't argue with that.

So we sit. Will does what he does best and holds court, talking to everyone who comes by in his charming talk-show-host voice. I do my best to smile, but I'm not capable of much more than that.

I watch people dance, mostly badly. The good dancers are too aware that they're good, and are just as comical for taking themselves so seriously. I laugh to myself until Will looks at me weird and I shut up. I watch girls sizing each other up, shooting daggers at each other with their eyes. I watch guys checking out other guys' girlfriends. It's all so predictable, all this posturing. If it weren't for the different dresses, everyone would look exactly the same.

Will's voice chirps next to me but I have no idea what he's saying. I text Marcus *I miss you* and I don't care if Will sees.

"You look great," everyone tells me.

"Are you sure you don't want to dance?" Will keeps asking me in between greeting the visitors to our receiving line.

People offer me their hidden flasks and I drink instead of talking.

My phone buzzes. *I miss you too*, it says, and now everything is all right with the world.

"Let's dance!" I say, suddenly sick of sitting. I stand up too fast and the room swirls around me. The Eiffel Tower turns to rubber and the strings of lights get tangled.

"Uh-oh," Will says, catching me like a true gentleman. His straight white teeth sparkle in the low light. "Did someone have a little too much to drink?"

I choose to ignore his patronizing tone. "Come on," I say, and pull him onto the dance floor next to where Kasey and her date are dancing. I see Jenica across the room and she actually looks happy. It's weird to see her out of the house, in a different context than our family. She actually has a life in the real world. She's someone besides my bitchy sister.

For a moment, I think maybe I can be happy tonight. I am drunk and stoned enough that it may be possible to salvage this night and have a little fun. So I dance as well as I can with a leg that only half works. Will seems satisfied enough with my performance. People dance around us like we're the centerpiece of this strange party, smiling at me like I'm making them proud. Look at Evie, she finally cheered up! She's one of us again! She finally pulled that ungrateful stick out of her ass and is having a little fun!

But then Kasey grabs me by the wrist. "Calm down," she says. "You're making a fool out of yourself."

"What are you talking about?"

"You're acting weird."

"I'm dancing. Isn't that what I'm supposed to be doing?"

"Are you *on* something?"

"God, Kasey. Shut up." I keep dancing. I dance away so I don't have to look at her pouty face.

"Are you okay?" Will says, so I dance away from him, too.

The sound changes. The music stops. Someone is talking and her voice is coming from everywhere. People clap. The room is not pulsing with movement. Everyone is facing the Eiffel Tower. The

Arc de Triomphe has been made into a stage. A giant projection of the smug, eyebrowless *Mona Lisa* stares down at us. A familiar-looking girl has a microphone and is saying something, beaming her college-interview smile. More clapping. More smiling. More talking. I lean on someone for balance, but I don't know who.

The student-body president, that's who she is. But what is her name? I know I should know her name. She says, "Drumroll, please," and people make noises that sound nothing like drumrolls. She takes a piece of paper out of an envelope. She says, "Oh, what a surprise," with a sickly sweet sarcasm and a look on her face the exact opposite of surprise. Then she says my name.

"I am proud to crown our new prom queen and king: Evie Whinsett and Will Johnson."

The room erupts in applause. I feel Will's arm tight around my waist. "Come on," he says, but I can't move.

"Evie and Will, come on up to the stage!"

The crowd starts chanting "Evie, Evie, Evie." The floor vibrates with my name. I think I'm going to be sick.

Will pulls me and my legs manage to work well enough to get me onto the stage. I stare into a sea of faces, all these people I've known for years but who are now strangers. And they're saying my name, like it means so much to them that I'm standing up here, and I wonder, What have I done to deserve this? What have I done to earn their admiration? I survived when I should have died. I'm alive by mistake. I've turned into a monster, and this is what I get? A crown? A standing ovation? What is wrong with these people?

Everyone cheers. Their faces turn into black empty holes. I

look at Will and he's got his big, proud grin, and his arm around my waist is the only thing keeping me up. I don't want to be here. I don't want all these people looking at me, wanting me to be someone different, someone I used to be, wanting me to be someone they can believe in, someone inspiring, someone who deserves to be crowned. But I'm nobody. I'm nothing. They're cheering for an imposter, a thief.

The edges of the room start to blur. All color drains away until the only thing I see is the glow of Christmas lights, and then even they go out, and everything is black, and Will's arm is too loose, and my head is too heavy, and the night is too crowded, and the last thing I think is, How is it possible to be so lonely in a room so full of people?

When I come to, the first thing I notice is the spongy chorus of "Oh my god"s all around me. I am on the operating table, waking up from the anesthesia. The first thing I think is, *I survived.* Then relief. Then disappointment. What did I survive for?

But these are not doctors looking down at me. They are not wearing surgical masks. A hospital would never have this kind of lighting. There's Will. There's Jenica. They would never be allowed in the operating room.

"You're wearing makeup," I say. Jenica looks confused, worried. "You look beautiful," I say. Then a single, mascara-blackened tear falls from her cheek onto mine.

"Evie, are you okay?" Will says. How many times have I heard him say that?

"Should we call 911?" says the student-body president.

Michelle. Michelle Chang. That's her name.

"No," I say. My voice sounds distant. It rattles inside my head. "I'm okay." *I'm okay I'm okay I'm okay.*

I push myself up to sitting. There's Principal Landry rushing toward us, worrying about lawsuits. There's one of the teacher chaperones. The grown-ups have been summoned out of hiding. "I'm fine," I say before they have a chance to ask. "I just got excited, I think. Just a little light-headed. I didn't eat any dinner."

No one bothers to smell my breath. No one asks if I'm on anything. Anyone else passes out at prom, and alcohol and drugs would be the first suspicion. Anyone else falls down on the cardboard Arc de Triomphe, parents would immediately be called, maybe even the police. I'd be arrested and expelled, or at the very least, suspended. But cancer makes me untouchable. I can get away with anything.

"Do we need to call your parents?" Principal Landry says. Then, in a quieter voice, leaning in, "Do you need a doctor?"

I can't help but laugh. I look around and people have their hands clasped in front of their mouths, their eyes wide with worry. All for a girl who smoked too much weed and drank too much booze on an empty stomach. What a waste of sympathy. It might make me sad if I could stop laughing.

"I don't understand," Principal Landry says, the poor woman. "Why is Evie laughing?"

"I'll drive her home, Ms. Landry," Will says, taking my arm. He and Jenica help me to stand. Then the dance floor erupts in applause.

"Are you fucking serious?" I say. "What is wrong with you people?"

"Thank god they can't hear you," Jenica says.

"Where's the microphone? Get me the microphone." I want to tell them. I want them to know how foolish they are.

"Come on, Evie," says Will, and they whisk me off the stage.

I wave good-bye like a good prom queen. "So long, suckers!" I say, but they can't hear my insult over their applause.

Kasey is waiting by the front door, her arms crossed, her face angry. "Kasey!" I say, reaching out for her, but she pushes me away.

"Well, that little performance certainly got some attention," she says.

"What's her problem?" I ask my attendants.

"What's *my* problem?" she says. "God, Evie, you're a mess. I don't even know who you are anymore."

"Let's get you home," Jenica says softly, so unlike her, and I could kiss her for her kindness.

"Maybe you guys can talk in the morning when Evie's feeling better," Will says. My savior. My knight in shining armor.

"No," Kasey says. "I have things I want to say right now."

"You're jealous you're not prom queen," I say. "You try so hard to be popular, but you'll never be able to compete with cancer." I think I mean it as a joke, but then I see the wave of sorrow wash across her face, and I realize that's what I wanted; I meant to hurt her.

"Evie, stop," Jenica says. "Kasey, she's drunk. She doesn't know what she's saying."

"You're not the same person anymore," Kasey says. She is trying to sound strong but I can see her bottom lip trembling. "You used to be so positive. It felt good to be around you. But now you're so, I don't know, *angry* or something. You're mean. You're someone I don't think I even like anymore."

I feel nothing but the syrupy disorientation of my body. I will focus on the nausea of my empty stomach so I don't have to really hear what she's saying. "Will, are you going to take me home or what?" I break free from his and Jenica's grasp and start stumbling in the direction of the parking lot. "Where's your car?" I shout into the night. "Where's my car?" I can feel eyes on me, students who came outside for a breath of fresh air who didn't know they were going to get such a show.

I can hear Kasey crying. I know the sound of her cry. I have heard it so many times during our quiet nights together—when her dog died, when she found out her parents were getting divorced, so many times during the cancer. But now it's different. I am not the comforter. I am the reason for her tears.

"Will, come on!" If I yell loud enough, I will not cry.

As soon as I feel him next to me, before he even gets a chance to open his mouth, I tell him I don't want to talk.

"Fine," he says with a tired voice.

I fall asleep on the drive home and wake up in Will's arms as he carries me to the front door. For a moment, I feel so cozy and safe, but then I'm filled with a surge of anger. How dare he just pick me up? How dare he carry me around without my permission?

"Put me down," I say. But he doesn't. I try to wriggle free, but that makes him hold on tighter.

Mom and Dad are standing in the open doorway before we get there. "Jenica called," Mom says. "She said you were coming."

"What happened?" Dad says.

I am so tired. I am too tired to be angry. "Will you put me down now?" I say with as polite a voice I can.

Will is so gentle. Part of me doesn't want him to let me go. It is cold outside of his arms. My feet touch the cement of the front steps and I want to be in the air again, held by someone strong.

I do not look up. I do not want to see my parents' faces. I can imagine their disappointment, and that is all I can take right now. Actually seeing it is more than I can deal with. I blindly make my way to the bathroom without bothering to speak for myself. I will let Will report the events of the evening. I am too tired to lie. All I want is a toilet to lean on. That is all I deserve. I may not even deserve that.

I throw up the measly contents of my stomach. I listen to myself retch and dry heave so I don't have to hear Will tell my parents how worried he is about me. I feel the sting of stomach acid, taste the poison of so many kinds of liquor. I smell the toilet's faint trace of urine and toxic cleansers mix with the sour contents of my stomach.

There is something so satisfying about this kind of vomiting, something so cathartic. There's a feeling of getting something done. Not like chemo, where the vomiting accomplished nothing. It didn't get any of the poison out. It never made me feel any better. It was just a sign of my body destroying itself.

But I do feel a little better now. Empty. Purged. The cool, hard porcelain of the toilet base is comforting in my arms.

I hear the door squeak open. "You ripped Jenica's dress." It is Will's voice, with a hard edge I've never heard. "There's a huge rip down the side."

"Arghmmn" is what I think I manage to say.

I feel a blanket draped across my shoulders. He throws a pillow on the floor next to me. "Here," he says. "Your mom gave me these. She was too mad to come in here herself."

Mom, mad? What is he talking about? Mom doesn't get mad.

I lift my head and open my eyes enough to see the blurred outline of him in the doorway. "Can you turn off the lights?"

"Anything else?" he says after the room goes dark.

"Will you rub my back?"

"Jesus, Evie," he hisses. "How did you get so horrible?"

Nothing so mean has ever come out of his mouth. Nothing has ever been said with so much anger and disgust.

I hear the door close behind him. I hear his footsteps as he walks away, back into his own life. I hear the murmuring of his and my parents' voices. And I am glued to the floor of the bathroom, shivering under the blanket that is far more kindness than I deserve.

if.

Dear Stella,

I'm done with school and I'm done with this family. I'm done with Will and Kasey and lunch-table friends. I'm done with concerned teachers and homework and tests and thinking about my future. I'm done with caring if I fail junior year. I'm done with giving a shit what anyone thinks about me. I'm done with giving a shit about anything.

I don't care if I get in trouble, if I get grounded, if Dad looks at me like I'm the biggest disappointment of his life, if he slaps me across the face in front of Mom and Jenica, and Mom is finally so sick of me she doesn't even say anything, doesn't even defend me, the one ally in this family I thought I had left, and the sting of it goes from my skin to my bones to my blood to my heart and freezes up any of the love I still had left, so cold that it shatters into a million pieces, but there are no screws, no titanium rods, no smart doctors to sew up this fracture; there is just me and my fury and the ice in my veins, just the people I used to love screaming at each other about the best way to punish me, my family turned into monsters because of what I have become, their sweetness turned sinister, their love turned rancid.

I am the kind of girl who deserves to get slapped by her father. I am the kind of girl who deserves to sleep on the bathroom floor, to be kicked awake by Jenica's slipper, even though it should have been a stick or a sword or a knife or a gun; I should have woken up to real pain, real punishment, something worse than being grounded for eternity, something worse than a hangover, something worse than spending a Sunday in the comfort of my room. I deserve something harder, harsher. I deserve something cruel, something that leaves a mark, something irrevocable. Because the damage I've done can never be taken back. The bridges I've burned cannot be rebuilt. The love I've chewed up and spit out and ground into the mud cannot be cleaned up and made whole again.

I feel sick. God, I feel sick. But I know I deserve to feel even sicker for all the disease I have spread. I am contagious. I make everyone around me sick. I've made my family sick. And you, Stella. I made you sickest of all.

I'm not going back to school. I can't face those people

again after what happened last night. I'm never going to visit poor Caleb in the hospital; I'm not going to let him think I'm someone worthy of his devotion. I'm doing Will and Kasey a favor by not begging for their forgiveness, not begging for them to give me another chance. I'm doing everyone a favor and getting out of their lives.

They are my history. They are before, yesterday, behind me, gone. The future is a vague "maybe"; it will only happen by accident. It is nothing I can count on.

There is only now, only this moment. There is only me and there is only Marcus. He is all I have left. He is the only person who matters. Without him, there's nothing. I'm nothing. I'm just scars and history. Without him, I evaporate. I turn into dust.

This prison of a room cannot contain me. The window is open and the ground is not too far down. It is night and I am an outlaw and Marcus is waiting for me down the street with his car running and he has no idea what I'm leaving behind.

Love,
Evie

thirty.

JUMPING INTO MARCUS'S CAR LIGHTENS MY GLOOM immediately, but even his kiss can't get rid of my headache and hangover. I need something stronger.

My jaw still stings where Dad hit me, but I can forget about that now. I can leave it in that house to fester with all the other family drama. I don't have to take it with me. I don't need to bring it into my world with Marcus. He doesn't need to know. It does not need to spoil our perfection.

"Are you okay?" Marcus says as he pulls away from the curb.

"Yeah, I'm great," I say, trying to make my voice sound as cheerful as possible. "Why do you ask?"

"You look kind of tired."

"Didn't anyone tell you you're never supposed to say that to a woman?"

"Oh, sorry," he laughs. "But you do. Look tired."

"I'm fine. Just a little hungover."

"What'd you do last night?" he asks, and I know there's nothing behind his curiosity, but still I feel exposed, embarrassed, like somehow he already knows what a fool I made of myself last night.

"Just hung out with some old friends," I say. "Nothing special. I wish I had been with you instead."

"Yeah," he says, smiling, his eyes locking on mine. "Me too."

"Hey, watch the road!" I say as we swerve slightly and barely miss sideswiping a parked car.

"You're just so beautiful I couldn't take my eyes away."

"Yeah, sure. Where are we going, by the way?"

"You'll see," he says. "You want to know what I did last night?"

Strangely, I don't. As much as I don't want the rest of my life infecting our world, I don't want his, either.

"I got stoned and ate Taco Bell and watched my friends Dan and Edwin play video games."

"Wow. Sounds thrilling."

"Yep. We sure know how to party."

"I can't believe that's what you did instead of hanging out with me."

"I know. It's pathetic. But I was thinking about you the whole time. I couldn't shut up about you."

"Oh yeah? What did you tell them?"

"I told them how smart and funny and beautiful you are. How I've never met anyone like you. How I feel more alive when we're together. How when you look at me I know you really see me."

My chest flutters and I'm so happy, I don't mind that we're driving through a part of Oakland where boarded-up houses are covered with graffiti and dark, shrouded figures are hunched in doorways. "You told them all that?" I say.

"Well maybe not in those exact words. I had to translate it into dude language they'd understand. But they know I'm crazy about you."

"Well, good. Because I'm crazy about you, too."

"I'm glad we're in agreement on this issue," he says, grinning.

I look out the window and finally realize where we are—in West Oakland, by the bridge. We drive past liquor stores and the BART station and into the part of town where no people live, where the streets are empty except for a few parked semi-truck cabs without trailers. We pass a busted RV that looks like it's being held together with duct tape, light peeking through the cardboard covering the windows, hinting at life inside. Besides that, there are no people anywhere.

"God, it's creepy down here at night," I say.

"I like it," Marcus says. "It's peaceful."

"It's scary," I say. "Wait, why are you slowing down?"

"We're here," he says. We're the only car parked on the street except for a burned-out metal skeleton without wheels several yards away.

"Where? This is nowhere."

"It doesn't look familiar?"

"Well, yeah, it looks familiar. We're by the bridge."

"Exactly."

"I'm confused."

"Just trust me." He pecks me on the cheek, then gets out and pulls a big hiking backpack out of the back of the car. He opens my door and offers me his hand. "Madam?"

"Are we going hiking?"

"Yep," he says, and starts walking. I lock my door and follow him toward the bridge.

After a few minutes, we turn left down the road that goes to the parking lot for the Bay Bridge Trail. A gate has been lowered to keep cars from entering, but we walk around it.

"Look familiar now?" Marcus says. He takes my hand and we walk in silence to the tunnel where we first met.

Luckily, the lights inside the tunnel are working now. Otherwise, I don't think I'd be brave enough to follow Marcus down the stairs, even with the big swig I take from the bottle of vodka he shares with me. The tunnel is illuminated with the sickly blue glow of fluorescent bulbs; I can hear them buzzing in the concrete silence.

"It's weird there's no homeless people here," I say, hoping the sound of my own voice will make me less scared. "This would be a perfect place to sleep."

"There are cameras everywhere," Marcus says. "And cops come through here several times a night. If anyone tried to stay here, they'd get kicked out right away."

"What's keeping us from getting caught?"

He turns to me and smiles. "Luck."

After a few hundred yards, a set of stairs leads up to the administration building that sits on its own little island between the east- and westbound lanes of the freeway. We walk around the building as the late-night traffic buzzes by us. On the other side is another set of stairs that go down under the other half of the freeway. We enter another long white tunnel, but this one has a much lower ceiling and is lined by several small staircases going up. "That's how the toll booth workers get to work," Marcus says. The first staircase is labeled with a stenciled sign: LANES 1 & 2; the next is LANES 3 & 4, and so on. The sound of the freeway is much louder here than in the other tunnel. I hear the boom of a car stereo playing something in Spanish. It's so weird to think people have to walk through here to get to work, then climb a set of stairs to pop out of the ground in the middle of a freeway and sit in a box breathing traffic fumes all day. But how different is any other life, really? Most people's lives are spent in some kind of box. Most people's lives are some kind of toxic.

I don't know why, but it seems appropriate to stay silent, as if this is someplace worthy of reverence. It is so empty, so still. Unlike the rest of Oakland, which seems perpetually covered in a layer of crumpled brown paper bags and cigarette butts, it is strangely clean down here. It's as if we discovered it, as if no other eyes have seen it but ours.

We pass several sets of stairs until we get to the end of the tunnel and the very last staircase. The sign says BUS STOP. We climb the stairs to a tiny isolated platform on the edge of the freeway, overlooking all the tollbooths and lanes of traffic. An OUT OF SERVICE sticker covers a faded AC TRANSIT sign.

"This is so weird," I say. "Who would catch a bus here?"

"No one, apparently."

"Now what?" I say. A short metal fence separates us from a darkness that I'm guessing is the Emeryville salt marsh. Radio or cell towers blink in the near distance. Unless we climb the fence, there's nowhere to go but back.

"You know what to do," Marcus says with a grin, setting his backpack down.

"What are you talking about?" But just as I say it, I know the answer. "Oh, hell no," I say. "Are you crazy?"

"It's a little fence. You don't even have to climb. Just throw your leg over."

"Yeah, but then it's, like, eight feet to the ground."

"That's nothing. Aren't you dying to know what's on the other side?"

Whatever it is, it's probably better than turning around and admitting defeat. It's definitely better than going home.

"What is it with you and fences?" I say as my hand wraps around cold metal.

"I like to go places I'm not allowed." He throws his backpack over the fence, then leaps after it, landing perfectly on two feet on the ground beneath me.

I take a deep breath and jump. I feel the foot of my good leg hit the ground, and for a second I think I made it, as gracefully as Marcus, but my other foot gets the timing wrong and I stumble. I lose my balance and fall to my hands and knees.

"Oh, shit!" Marcus yells. "Are you okay?"

I think for a second. I don't know yet. There is something like pain, but I can't quite locate it. It could be a scrape. It could be something worse.

Marcus's hands are on me, checking, searching. "Evie," he says, his voice thick with worry. "Oh, Evie."

"Ow," I say, then I roll onto my ass and start laughing.

"Can you move your legs?" Marcus says.

I do a few slow kicks and nothing terrible happens, though my knees are sore from the landing and I will have bruises tomorrow for sure. My palms are coated in blood and gravel, but it looks way worse than it really is.

"Fuck," Marcus says, holding my hands in his. "I'm such an idiot. I'm so sorry."

"It's not that bad," I say. "Nothing a little vodka can't fix." I wipe my hands off on my pants and stand up. Marcus pulls the bottle out of his bag and hands it to me. I take a big swig, then pour a little on my hands to disinfect, and the sting tells me I'm going to be okay.

"Will you ever forgive me?" Marcus says as he brushes me off. I pull him close and kiss him as my answer.

"I didn't break you?" he says softly when we come up for air.

"Do I look broken to you?"

"You look beautiful."

"So now what?"

"We're almost there." He hoists the backpack onto his

shoulders and takes my hand. “Can you walk?” The ground feels stable; paved, even.

“Is this a road?” I say.

“Something like that, yeah.”

We start walking, the freeway raised on our left side. Then Marcus leads me to the right, and the road is replaced by a mixture of sand and rocks. The farther we get from the freeway, the more my eyes adjust to the darkness and I see the murky shapes of water lapping against a sandy beach, a border of driftwood and beach grass, then darkness over the marshlands for probably a mile until it reaches the solid ground of the city.

“What is this place?” I say.

“It’s our own private beach.”

He leads me to a spot at the other end of the beach, past where the light from the freeway ends. I turn around and see it sparkling in the distance, the fast lights of traffic and the majestic span of the Bay Bridge leading to the famous San Francisco skyline.

Marcus opens his backpack, takes out some blankets, and lays them over the rocky sand. He pulls some snacks out of a crumpled grocery bag.

“Have a seat, my love.” He hands me the vodka bottle. “Want to go camping with me?”

“What else did you bring?” is what comes out of my mouth. Not “Thank you.” Not “Wow.” Because the first thing I think is, *What if the vodka is not enough?*

“What do you mean?”

"Never mind," I say. "This is wonderful. This is so romantic." Then, "Did you bring your pipe? Want to smoke a bowl?"

"Sure," he says, and I think I hear some sadness in his voice.

"Did you bring any of those mushrooms?"

"You shouldn't do them too often. It can make you crazy."

"But do you have any left?"

"No. We ate them all the other night."

"We should do them again soon," I say. "Hey, can you get some Ecstasy? I really want to try that." What is wrong with me?

We sit in silence for a while. From here, the brightly lit bridge looks almost festive, like a carnival. A digital billboard switches advertisements every ten seconds. Our eyes are glued to it, like we're in a living room, sitting on a couch and watching TV.

This night should be magical, but I haven't let it.

Marcus hands me the pipe and lighter, and I take a huge toke. I hand it to him and make a silent promise to myself to be nicer. We pass the pipe back and forth a couple more times, then I take Marcus's hand. We sit there like that for a while, watching the traffic on the bridge. Where are these people going so late on a Sunday night?

I wonder what my family is doing right now. They must have realized I'm gone by now. I could check my phone for messages. I could at least text them to let them know I'm okay. But I won't. Let them worry. Let them know what it feels like to have me gone.

"Why don't you ever talk about your life?" Marcus says, slicing the thick silence between us. "Tell me more about the cancer."

"No," I say. I hear the sharpness in my voice and I know he did too. I grab the vodka bottle and take a huge gulp, feel it burn down my throat and into my chest, erasing my fear of his question.

"But the other night. In the graveyard. I know it was a big deal for you to tell me. I want to understand what you went through."

I don't want to talk. I don't want Marcus to understand. I don't want to bring him into that history. He is supposed to only exist *now*, here, in my present. He is supposed to take up so much space that it crowds the past out.

"I don't know anything about your friends or school or family," he says.

"They're not interesting."

"They're interesting to me."

"My parents are boring. My sister's annoying. School is boring and annoying."

"Come on," he pleads. "Tell me something real."

There's something in his voice that melts me, that makes me let down my guard. Something real. He wants something real. Isn't that what I want too? Isn't that one of the reasons I love him, because I don't have to hide, because I can let him see me? He's the one I'm supposed to be letting in. He's the only one.

"Okay," I say. "You're the only person left in the world who doesn't hate me. I'm letting everyone down. That's what's real."

"Why do you think you're letting everyone down?"

"I'm not who they want me to be. Ever since I got home from the hospital, all I seem to do is screw up." I notice the slur in my voice. The vodka is doing its work. "But that's the thing," I say. "That's what happens when you love people, right? You find out they're not who you thought they were. Either that, or they leave you. Same difference."

"That's what people have done to you?"

"I guess."

"So that's what you're doing to them?"

"I don't have a choice. I'm not the person they love anymore." The sadness snuck back in. I feel on the verge of tears. The vodka didn't fix anything.

"But why can't they love who you are now?"

"I don't know." If anything, the vodka is making the sadness worse.

"Well, I know you. I know you're amazing. And I'm pretty sure they'd think so too if you gave them a chance."

"But what if they don't?" And this is when I start crying. Big, fat, pathetic tears stream down my face. What happened to tough Evie? What happened to the Evie who didn't care what anyone thought? "What if they get to know me and they still hate me?" I cry.

"Why would they hate you?" The kindness in Marcus's eyes makes me cry even harder.

"I hate me," I say, and I am full of so much disgust, I don't understand why Marcus is wrapping his arms around me, I don't know how he can stand to be near me, how he can stand to touch me.

"You have to let people love you," he says. "You have to at least give them a chance."

This was supposed to be romantic. But I ruined it by bringing this shit up and turning into this crying, whiny drunk.

"That's the past," I say, smiling big enough to wipe the slate clean. I will my tears to stop. "I want to focus on right now. Right here, with you."

I lean into him so his face is all I can see. I kiss him until I am sure he no longer wants to talk, until his body takes over and we have avoided the conversation. Our kisses make the past go away. I put my hand on his belt and we both forget.

I keep my eyes open as we make love. I look into the night sky, saturated and dull with all the lights of the city. There is a smattering of bright stars, but not many; only the strongest and brightest shine through. I know there are so many more up there, infinite, but we can't see them. They're light-years away, burning their hearts out, but we're so crowded down here, too busy to notice. I almost feel sad about this, but then Marcus moves against me in a way that makes me close my eyes and forget the sky. Finally, I am truly here, truly with him, and my mind stops wandering, stops wanting other things, and I only want him, I only want now, and my body finally feels everything it wants to feel.

When we are done, wrapped up and warm in Marcus's blankets, I say, "Let's run away together."

"Okay," he says sleepily. He doesn't know I'm serious.

The white noise of traffic lulls us to sleep. We are tangled in each other's arms, cradled in this sea-smelling womb we have created.

Maybe this is what freedom feels like: making a bed between two pieces of driftwood, being hidden from every direction except up. The sky is the only one who can see us and no one knows where we are. We can forget. We can be forgotten. Maybe this is what it feels like to win a tiny battle against the world.

thirty-one.

I WAKE UP WITH A DOG'S NOSE IN MY FACE. I SWAT HIM away, and he sniffs around us and pees just a few inches from my feet. My head is cloudy after a night of shallow, troubled sleep brought on by too much alcohol and sleeping on the ground.

Whatever magic we managed last night is most definitely gone.

The sun is too bright. The air is thick with the salty decay of a dirty beach. I look at the sand around us and it is filthy with rotting seaweed, flies, cigarette butts, beer cans, plastic bottles, broken glass, and unidentifiable other trash, none of which I noticed in the darkness of last night. I hear voices and look up to see a group of men in wet suits just a few yards away, getting kiteboards ready. The dog runs up and down the beach, barking, rattling my fragile head in its second consecutive day of hangover. The stillness of last night has been replaced by howling wind.

This isn't a romantic private beach. This is the kind of place gangsters dump dead bodies.

"Hi," Marcus says as he sits up next to me.

"We have visitors," I say.

"Oops," he says, and leans over to kiss me. His morning breath makes my stomach turn.

The beach ends at a road that goes alongside the freeway. I see two trucks parked near the abandoned bus stop where we climbed over the fence and I skinned my hands.

"We could have driven here," I say. My body burns with the surprise of feeling so furious so soon after waking. "We could have slept in Bubbles. Why didn't we do that?"

"A car parked overnight would have given us away. We would have been caught." He puts his arm around me. "Plus, wasn't it way more fun to go the way we did? Wasn't it cool to go back to where we first met?"

"It was stupid, Marcus. You made me sleep on the ground like a fucking homeless person."

Marcus pulls away, as if I hit him. The hurt shock on his face makes me want to eat glass. "Shit, I'm sorry. I'm so sorry. That was really mean. I'm just really hungover. It's making me an asshole."

"You're right," he says, looking away. "It is."

"Hey," I say, pulling him close. "I'm sorry. Last night was wonderful. Thank you. And sorry I got so emo. Alcohol seems to have a pretty unpredictable effect on me."

He meets my eye and smiles with one side of his mouth, as if he is only thinking about forgiving me. "Should I drop you off at school?" he says. "It's a little after nine. I hope you didn't miss too much."

"Ha-ha," I say, because I assume he's joking. But when I look at him, there's no humor on his face.

"I need to go home and take a shower so I can make it to school in time for my afternoon classes," he says, completely serious.

"You're going to school today?"

"My morning classes on Monday are throwaways, but I have calculus and AP American History later and I can't miss those."

AP American History? Who is this guy?

"Hello?" he says, staring at me. "Evie? Is anybody there?"

"Yeah. I mean, no. Don't drop me off at school."

"At home, then?"

Those are my only two options, aren't they? Where else am I going to go? I'm sick and exhausted and I need to sleep and the only place that's free and mine is my bed in my room in the house of my parents. I can't be done with them yet. As much as they hate me, as much as I'm sick of them, I'm still theirs. They still own me.

"Fine," I say. "Take me home."

"Hey. Are you okay? Why do you seem so mad?"

"Sorry. I just don't want to deal with my parents right now."

It's after ten when Marcus drops me off in front of my house. We managed to patch things up so that I'm pretty sure he's not mad at me, but I can tell he's worried now, like everyone else. He was supposed to be the one person I could count on, the one person I could be free with. But now he's turning out to have some of the same fears and expectations as everyone else. I don't know what to think about this. I don't know what to feel. All I know is I need to sleep for a very long time, and as soon as possible.

Mom storms out of the kitchen as soon as I walk through the door. "What the hell were you thinking?" she says.

"I'm tired, Mom. Can I sleep for a few hours and then we can talk about this when I wake up?"

"Not until you tell me where you've been."

"I spent the night at a friend's house. You don't know her." I can't look her in the eye. "I was upset."

"So you climbed out your bedroom window? You didn't answer your phone all night? You didn't even leave a note? Do you have any idea how worried we were?"

"I'm sorry."

"And you missed your appointment with Dr. Jacobs this morning."

"I forgot."

"Damn it, this isn't a game. You can't just play with your life like this."

"Where's Dad?"

"He's at work. After not sleeping all night."

I look at the floor. I have nothing to say. He hit me. It's hard to feel bad about making him worry.

Mom sighs, taking a few steps toward me. "He made a mistake. He's sorry. He was so angry. He was so scared."

"Scared? Of what?"

"We almost lost you once," she says softly. "We don't want to lose you again."

I feel unsteady, like someone could blow on me and I would crumble to the ground. I think about what Marcus and I talked about last night, about letting my parents in, letting them know who I am now. Maybe they could love her. But maybe they can't. I've made such a mess, I don't even know where to start cleaning up. I don't even know if it's possible.

"Go to bed," Mom says. I fight the urge to fall into her, to wrap myself in her arms and tell her everything.

"We'll talk when your dad gets home," she says. "There are going to be consequences this time, Evie."

"Okay," I say. I walk into my room, shut the door, and crash into my bed and a leaden, lonely sleep.

thirty-two.

THE CLOCK SAYS 5:12. AFTERNOON LIGHT LEAKS UNDER THE curtains and draws a beam across my hand. I pull it away, back into the safety of shadow.

I can't lie here forever. I'm going to have to face my dad eventually. I might as well get it over with.

I pull some clean clothes out of the pile of laundry on my floor. As I splash water on my face and brush my teeth, I repeat the mantra inside my head: *Don't feel don't feel don't feel. Just endure the speeches. Just nod and say yes. Don't fight back. Just get this over as quickly as possible.*

I almost feel brave as I walk into the kitchen where I can hear my parents talking.

As soon as I enter, Dad says, "Are you ready to talk?"

"Can I get some water first?" He nods.

I sit across from them and wait.

"We got a call from the school while you were sleeping off

whatever you did last night," Dad snarls, ready to fight.

"James," Mom says. "Let's try to keep things civil."

He turns to her. "How am I supposed to keep things civil when she has absolutely no respect for us or herself?"

Mom sighs. She must be so exhausted from trying to keep this family from falling apart. "Principal Landry is worried about you, Evie. After what happened at prom. And your grades."

"And apparently you've been skipping class," Dad adds.

"We have an appointment with her tomorrow morning at eight thirty," Mom says. "All of us."

"I have to take off work for this, Evie."

I say nothing. I take a sip of water.

"Do you have anything to say?" Dad asks.

"No." I don't look up. I don't want to see the way he's looking at me.

"Who are you?" Dad says. "It's like you're not even our daughter anymore. We didn't raise you like this."

"I'm sorry," I say.

"My Evie wouldn't stay out all night doing god knows what and come home reeking of booze."

Maybe I'm not your Evie anymore. Maybe I'm nobody's Evie anymore. Maybe that Evie is dead and gone and buried like she should have been all along.

"Say something, damn it!" Dad pounds his fist on the table and the water sloshes inside my glass. I look up and see Mom shrunken inside herself. I don't meet Dad's eyes, but I can feel them burning holes into me.

"I'm sorry," I say again, but it means nothing.

"We think you need to see someone," Mom says. "We think it would be good for you to talk to someone about what you're going through."

"Since you obviously won't talk to us," Dad says.

"What, like a shrink?"

"Yes, a therapist," Mom says. "I talked to Dr. Jacobs and he recommended someone who specializes in PTSD and—"

"And addiction," Dad barks when Mom can't say it. "Because of what you pulled with the pills. And who knows what else you're doing when you're out all night."

"PTSD?" I say. "Why PTSD?"

"Because of what you went through with the cancer," Mom says. "It was traumatic."

"I guess."

"You *guess*?" Dad hisses.

"James, you don't need to have that tone," Mom says.

"Oh, don't I? And you think your approach is really working? This gentle, understanding bullshit that lets Evie walk all over us?"

"Evie, I think you should go to your room now," Mom says. So I can let them fight in peace.

"And you won't be joining us for dinner," Dad adds. "You have to earn that right back through your behavior."

"She has to eat," Mom pleads.

"Then make her a plate, for Christ's sake," he snaps. "She can eat alone in her room."

"Okay," I say. I nod my head, as if the movement will keep

me from crying. "Okay," I say again, because what else is there to say when your father hates you and there's no chance of him ever loving you again?

I get up and walk to my room. I turn on my favorite of Stella's songs, the one that makes me feel tough and invincible. I turn it up as loud as possible, but it's not working. I still feel like the world's biggest piece of shit.

My door flies open and Dad storms into my room. He tears the CD out of my stereo and breaks it in half. "I am sick of this noise!" he yells. He grabs Stella's hat from my desk and slams the door behind him. Silence follows. Emptiness. A great gaping hole that can never be filled.

I text Marcus: *Meet me at the graveyard in an hour.*

I grab my bag and climb out the window again.

I can't get high enough. No amount of weed will make the memory of the way my dad looked at me go away.

And no amount of weed will make the voice mail Caleb just left go away either. I keep hearing it over and over again: "Hi, Evie, it's me, Caleb. I don't know why you haven't texted me back yet, but don't worry, I'm not mad at you. You're probably the nicest person I ever met, so I know you must have a good reason. Anyway, I really want to talk to you. So could you call me back soon? Thanks. Oh, this is Caleb. Okay, bye."

I smoke and smoke and smoke but the sound of his voice will not leave my head.

"Take it easy, killer," Marcus says.

I exhale a huge cloud of smoke.

"Want to talk about it?" he says.

"My parents are assholes."

"What'd they do?"

"All they do is try to control me. They're mad because I'm doing bad in school and they don't know where I am and who I'm with at every moment."

"That seems pretty normal, don't you think?"

"Whose side are you on?"

Marcus smiles and puts his arm around me. "Yours." He kisses me. "Always. You know that."

We're sitting in the grass in front of the tomb where we did mushrooms and made love for the first time. I wish I felt like I did that night, full of magic. I wish the rest of the world would disappear. But the weed is just making me feel heavy and slow. I keep thinking someone's behind us, hiding, watching. All the creepy cemetery statues seem to be facing us, staring.

"When are we going to run away?" I say.

"Right now," Marcus says. "Let's join the circus."

"I'm serious."

"What's your hurry?"

"I need to get away from my parents."

"I'd like to meet them sometime, you know. See what all the fuss is about."

I don't say anything. We are not having the same conversation. He does not understand the severity of the situation.

I feel antsy. I need to move. I stand up and look around at the acres of green grass, the old gravestones and oak trees. The inside of my head makes the *whomp, whomp, whomp* sound that tells me I am higher than I realized.

I wonder how many of these graves are for people who died of cancer, how many were children. Marble cherubs stand as sentries, naked and pure, wings unfolded, ready to fly. But to where? They are made of stone. They are fused to pillars stuck in the earth. They are babies who are doomed to spend eternity watching over death.

"Evie, what's wrong?" Marcus says. "Why are you crying?"

My face is wet. I am breathless with deep, violent sobs. I don't know how I let myself start crying again.

I shake my head. I can't speak.

Marcus wraps me in his arms and I feel safe for a moment, like maybe he is strong enough to guard me from this world of pain. But then I open my eyes and it all comes flooding back. Even Marcus, even love, isn't that strong.

The cherubs mock me. They laugh. They flap their wings. They say, *You should be in the ground too.*

I need something to drive them away. I need to feel something besides this, something bigger, stronger, anything. I feel Marcus's arms, but they are not enough. I need all of him. I need to feel all of him.

I grab his face with my hands and kiss him with everything I have. My tongue finds his tongue. My teeth smash against his teeth. I push him back down behind the stone wall of the tomb, where no one can see us.

"Wait," he says. I grab for his belt buckle. "Stop." He grabs my hand. He pulls away.

"What's wrong?" I say.

"You're crying. It doesn't feel right."

"It feels right to me." I reach for his belt again, but he takes my hand in his and doesn't let go.

"What's going on with you? Tell me."

"I don't want to talk."

"Hey," he says, guiding my cheek with his hand so I can't help but look at him. "We don't always have to get high, you know. We don't always have to have sex. We can do something normal like have dinner or go to a movie. We could do things normal couples do."

I can't help but laugh. How did Marcus suddenly turn into Will? "Why would I want to be a normal couple?" I say. "What's the fun in that?"

Marcus looks stung. I've hurt him. I've hurt everyone now. The others didn't matter, but he does. I've gone and broken the only relationship I have left that matters.

"I'm sorry," I say. "I really am. I'm a mess right now."

"Maybe you need some sleep," he says, not unkindly. But not kindly, either.

"Yeah, that'd probably help."

We sit in silence. The sun is going to set soon. The cemetery will be closed. The cherub statues will do whatever it is they do when no one's looking.

"It's a school night," Marcus says. "I can't miss class two

days in a row." *Was it just this morning we woke up on the beach?* "Maybe I should take you home now."

I want to say no. I want to say, *Take me with you.* His house is huge, full of unused rooms and a father who's not paying attention; surely he could hide me for a while. But the look on his face tells me that's not a good idea. His jaw is set and his eyes are hard and I can tell he's getting sick of me.

"I meant it about wanting to meet your parents sometime," he says when we pull up in front of my house after a silent car ride. "I may even be able to swing a dinner with you and me and the judge if I book him a couple of weeks in advance."

"First I have to get them to stop hating me."

"I really doubt that they hate you."

"I probably would if I were them."

He kisses me good-bye and says "I love you, Evie," and that gives me the strength to return home.

Dad, Mom, and Jenica are on the couch watching TV. Mom turns around when I walk through the front door, a look of sadness and fear on her face, but Dad and Jenica don't move.

"In your room, now," Dad says, still facing the TV. "I don't even want to look at you."

I walk straight to my room and close the door behind me. A cold plate of food is sitting on my desk where Stella's hat used to be. My window is covered with boards, nailed on the outside, so now it's impossible for me to escape.

thirty-three.

I WAKE UP TO MOM SHAKING ME AND DAD YELLING FROM the hallway, "Just pour some water on her head." It's already eight fifteen, only fifteen minutes before we're supposed to be at school to meet with Principal Landry.

"I've been trying to wake you up for an hour," Mom says, her face surreal, hovering above mine. "You keep saying you're getting up, but then I come in here and you're asleep again." I don't remember any of that. I don't remember falling asleep. I don't remember sleeping. The last thing I remember is thinking about the stone cherubs at the cemetery, wondering how they got their wings, wondering how they got stuck with their crappy job of watching dead people sleep.

I'm in a daze as I search for something clean to wear. I haven't taken a shower in four days. My vision is hazy; everything is a step behind where it should be. I feel naked without Stella's hat. I am too exposed. I have nothing to hide behind.

When I step into the living room, Mom and Dad grab their things and we walk out to the car without speaking. Dad turns on the radio to fill up the silence, and it's all bad news as usual.

Luckily, classes are already in session when we get to school so I don't have to run into anyone. I can't face them after what happened at prom, after I'm sure Kasey spread the word that my performance was due to my being drunk, not something innocent like being sick or tired or cancer-y as everyone probably wanted to believe.

Principal Landry has her best serious face on as she sits us down in her office and explains that with only two weeks left until the end of the school year, I'm not passing any of my classes, not even art anymore, and it's practically impossible to fail art. My attendance record is dismal. I haven't been paying attention in class. I haven't taken advantage of any of my teachers' generous offers of extra help. I haven't coordinated with tutors.

"We expected her to work harder," she says.

"So did we," say my parents.

"Frankly, we expected her to be a little more grateful," she says.

"So did we," say my parents.

But I didn't ask for anyone's help. I didn't ask for any of this. Why should I be grateful for something I never even wanted?

Principal Landry folds her hands together and leans forward like she's about to make us a great deal on a used car, such a great deal she has to whisper so her boss won't hear. She's going to pull some strings, she says. The teachers and administration remain sympathetic, she says. (*Cancer! Cancer!* she doesn't say.) "We don't want Evie to be held back while all her friends move on. We want Evie to succeed."

I have to laugh at that one. If only it were that easy. Everyone looks at me like I'm crazy. "What's so funny?" Dad says, and I say, "Nothing," and they continue their conversation without me.

I look out the window while they work out a plan where my teachers will put together coursework for me to do over the summer, and if I complete it all, have perfect attendance for the remaining days of school, and pinkie-swear-promise to shape up, I can start senior year with all my "friends." Yippee!

"Oh, isn't that generous," Mom says, and beams, still foolish enough to hold on to hope after all this time.

"It'll only work if Evie's on board," Principal Landry says.

Dad looks at me like he already knows I'm going to let them down and all their generosity is going to be wasted.

"One more thing," Landry says. "We want Evie to attend regular counseling sessions. Either with the school counselor or a therapist of your choice."

"We already thought of that," Mom says almost proudly, like she's kissing up to the teacher, like she wants a gold star. "Evie's doctor recommended someone. I was planning on contacting her today."

"Excellent," Principal Landry says. She and Mom are so proud of themselves for figuring out such a great plan for me. But Dad just sits there, scowling, checking his emails from work.

Unlike them, he gave up on me a long time ago.

"So what do you think, sweetheart?" Mom says, her face so fragile with expectation. It hurts to see her still believing in me, to know she's going to get her hopes up and be disappointed yet again. The only honest thing I can do is to crush those hopes now, before they get any more out of control. If she won't do it on her own, I'll have to do it for her.

"I think you can all fuck off," I say, and I stand up and storm out of the office.

I hear a scuffle of chairs as I walk away.

I hear Principal Landry say, "Should I call security?"

I hear my dad say, "No."

Mom: "James, we have to get her."

Dad: "Let her go. It's not up to us anymore. She has to decide to want help."

No one follows me. No one threatens or begs me to stay. They just let me go.

Now I sit in People's Park, waiting for Marcus to pick me up. I told him it was an emergency. I told him it was worth skipping classes for.

I have Mom's credit card and eighty dollars in my pocket. She should know better by now than to leave her purse on the kitchen counter. I had a hundred, but some of that went to a bottle of vodka, plus the five-dollar service charge I gave to a homeless guy to buy it for me.

The regular crew of drug dealers that hangs out at the park is nowhere to be seen. Maybe there was a raid recently. Maybe they're in hiding. I know that's probably a good thing, but my disappointment burns. If the dealers were here, there'd be nothing stopping me from talking to them this time. There'd be nothing stopping me from buying what I need.

I'm already drunk by the time we get to the beach by the Bay Bridge. Marcus wasn't too excited about me opening the bottle in the car, but I did it anyway and he didn't stop me.

This time we drive straight to the beach instead of that bullshit with the tunnel. I get out of the car and start walking without waiting for Marcus. He has to jog to keep up as I head to the end of the beach. I nearly step on a decaying, fly-covered seagull carcass. I cannot drink the vodka fast enough.

"Are you going to tell me what's wrong now?" Marcus says as I plop down on a piece of driftwood. I refused to tell him before we got here because I was afraid he'd turn around and drive me home and force me to talk to my parents. But now that we're here, I'll tell him everything. Between swigs of vodka, I tell him about the visit with the principal, about failing school, about Will and Kasey turning on me, about my pathetic mom and cruel dad, about Dad slapping me and boarding up my windows. I talk so fast and furious, I almost forget he's there. My rage swirls around us until I'm dizzy and the smell of the beach reaches the back of my throat and makes me gag.

I close my eyes and swallow. Small waves lap against the

shore and I have to remind myself this water is not stuck here like I am; it will soon touch the ocean and be released.

"Are you done?" Marcus says. His voice surprises me. It seems so long since I've heard it.

I pass him the half-empty vodka bottle. He shakes his head.

"This is the emergency?" he says. "This is why I skipped school?"

There is anger in his voice. Anger. At *me*.

"Marcus," I say. I have done something to upset him, but my brain can't catch up fast enough to figure out what it is. I take his hand in mine. For a second, the world feels a little more solid.

"Evie," he says. "Look at me." His eyes are sad, serious. I am in trouble. "Promise you won't get mad at me for what I'm about to say."

"I can't promise that." Something catches in my throat. This is going to be bad. I can feel it.

He sighs. Looks down. Looks back up at me. "Maybe they're a little bit right," he says. "I'm worried about you too."

"About what?" I pull my hand away from his. "What is there to be worried about?"

"I don't think your partying is about having fun anymore."

"I'm having fun."

"Really? You're having fun right now?"

I don't answer. I can't answer.

"Evie," he says, his voice cracking. There are tears running down his face. "You keep acting like you're invincible, but your life is falling apart. I can't stand watching you self-destruct. I love you too much. Nobody's invincible, not even you."

I can't even hear the waves anymore. Anger fills my head with static until all I hear is electricity.

"Say something," he says.

"I can't believe you're on their side."

"You know that's not true. I'm on your side. I've only ever been on your side."

"I can't believe you're sitting here giving me a drug speech when it was you who got me into them in the first place."

"What are you talking about? That's not what happened."

I don't know what I'm saying. I don't know what words to attach to everything I'm feeling right now. All I know is I've never felt more alone or betrayed than I do right now. Marcus was the one person I thought I could trust, after everyone else abandoned me. He was the one person who never worried about me or judged me, who never tried to protect or baby me. Now he's as bad as everyone else—worse, because I truly believed he understood me, *really* understood me. I thought we were going to take on the world together. But now he's just as much a part of that world, and this is a war I'm going to have to fight on my own.

"Fuck you," I say. But I stand up too quickly and fall right back down, my bony ass hitting the hard edge of the driftwood. Marcus catches me. He holds on too tight. "Let go!" I shout, pushing him off of me. I stand up again, and this time I'm sturdy enough to start walking. "I don't need your protection," I say as I head toward the road.

Marcus follows me. "I'm not trying to protect you," he argues. Why won't he let me go like everybody else? "I'm trying to protect myself. I can't handle watching this happen again to the person I love most."

I go cold. "Don't worry," I say. "I'm gone. Now you won't have to watch." I keep walking. "Stop following me!" I scream at him. "It's over. I don't need you."

"I'm driving you home," he says behind me, his voice almost unrecognizable, from either anger or hurt or both.

"I can walk."

"It's, like, ten miles to your house from here."

"Oh, you're so kind."

"Jesus, Evie. Since when is that a bad thing? When did caring about someone become such a crime?"

I slam the door as I get into his car. I can't believe I used to find this piece-of-shit Mercedes charming. With all the money his dad has, Marcus could afford a much nicer car, but he drives this one around, wearing his thrift-store clothes and listening to his sensitive indie music, pretending to be someone he's not. He's a rich kid who goes to the most prestigious prep school in the Bay Area. That's who he is. The lie is what I fell in love with, not this guy who wants to control me like everyone else.

I turn as far away from him as possible during the excruciatingly long ride home. The mix of anger, vodka, and bad Oakland roads makes my stomach churn. I close my eyes so the world will stop moving, but even in the darkness it goes by too fast; I cannot stop it, I am out of control, I am shuttling through madness, and everything is happening without me.

I don't want to look at Marcus because I'm afraid of what will happen if I do. I'm afraid a flood of feelings will drown me. I'm afraid of what anger can turn into when sadness is allowed to defile it. I will not let myself be weak. I will not let myself hear his sniffles beside me. I will not acknowledge that I have made him cry. I have finally lost the last piece of my old self. I am fully cruel. There is nothing of nice Evie left in me.

I finish the bottle of vodka and throw it out the window. I want the satisfaction of hearing the glass breaking; I want to hear it smash, but we are going too fast, and it gets lost in the sound of moving.

I get out of the car without saying anything. I am grateful for my drunkenness, grateful that it takes so much concentration just to walk; there is nothing to spare for feeling. For fear. For regret.

Just walk without falling down. Just make it to the front door. Just open it and get through the living room without anyone stopping me. Just get to my room and peace and quiet. They will be mad. They will want to talk. They will follow me. But if I just keep moving, they'll eventually have to give up. That is my plan. That is what will happen. I am in control now.

But that is not what happens.

When I get inside, no one jumps up to scream at me. No one asks me where I've been. No one asks who I was with or what I was doing. Mom and Dad are sitting on the couch, waiting for me as I expected, but it is not anger I sense.

"Evie," Dad says. "Sit down. We have something to tell you."

What, I'm grounded again? They put actual bars on my windows this time? They've fixed my door so it can be locked from the outside? Oh fuck, is this an intervention?

But something is off. Their eyes are puffy and red with tears, even Dad's. This is not how it should be. The room spins and I stumble over to the chair across from them. I do sit down, but not because they told me to.

"Sweetie," Mom says, leaning forward to take my hands in hers, not even caring that I'm obviously drunk. "I'm so sorry to have to tell you this."

Somehow, I'm able to focus long enough to look in her eyes, and that's when I know. This isn't about me at all.

"No," I say, shaking my head, suddenly way too sober.

"It's Caleb," Mom says. "His parents just called."

"No, no, no."

"He went into emergency surgery last night," Dad says. "He didn't make it."

I hear a sob that must be mine, like all the air being sucked out of me, but it sounds far away, as if I am somewhere outside this room, listening through the heating vents. Who are these people? What are they saying? Who is that girl who looks like me? Why is her heart so broken?

"I wish you'd told us he was doing so poorly," Mom says. "We had no idea. He seemed so healthy the last time we saw him."

"I have to go," I say, standing up. I must get away from this news and this house and these sad faces. Anger, I would know what to do with. Anger, I can deflect with my own. But sadness and loss, how am I supposed to fight with that?

"Sweetheart, wait," Mom says. "Let's call a truce for now, okay? We're here to support you through this."

She doesn't get it. I don't deserve their support. I don't deserve their comfort. I don't deserve anybody's comfort. It's my fault I was such a lousy friend to Caleb, that I wasn't there for him at the end. Stella never would have done that. She never would have abandoned him. I've failed her. I've failed them both.

"I need to be alone," I say. They don't try to stop me as I walk out the door.

if.

Dear Stella,

I'm sitting in a cab I'm going to pay for with my mom's stolen credit card and I just bought $80 worth of pills from a drug dealer at People's Park, so I guess I'm a real outlaw now. It seems like it should feel at least a little fun being bad, but all it feels like is necessary, a chore, like homework or washing the dishes. Except there's no shame in dishes. The dishes aren't dangerous.

I walked up to the seediest-looking guy I could find, complete with multiple face piercings and neck tattoos, and said, "I'm looking for Norcos." No "Hello." No "How are you?" It was so easy. Too easy. He only had Oxy, so I figured, what the hell? If I'm going to be a fuck-up I might as well go all the way, right? I took one pill just to see how strong it is because I have no idea what my tolerance is anymore, but I have an envelope with a bunch more burning a hole in my pocket. It should only be a few minutes until it kicks in.

I'm not really sure what I'm waiting for. Why don't I just take them all and get it over with? Go out in style. I'm sure you're rolling your eyes right now. I can hear you saying, "Come on, Evie. Suicide is so cliché." But really, Stella, what's more cliché than cancer?

The thing is, everything that matters is gone. You're gone. Caleb's gone. Will and Kasey are gone, in their way. The Marcus I thought I loved is gone. What else is there for me to do? Finish a bunch of homework over the summer so I can do senior year with a bunch of people I don't like? Barely graduate, then go to a crappy college my parents can't even afford, major in something I don't even care about, start a career I hate? Marry some guy I don't love, have some kids I don't want?

Do you think this cab driver is happy? He spends all day and night in this car that smells like puke and air freshener, driving around drunk people like me. He was probably a neurosurgeon where he comes from, but he had to flee his country because people are all ultimately assholes and will always find ways to start wars and kill each other and run innocent people away.

No matter what I do, I'm going to die alone. Even surrounded by people, everyone dies alone. Then what? Then nothing. Then life is over and it wasn't worth anything.

I think I'm going to take a few more of these pills.

Stella, I miss you so much it makes me sick. Remember when you said everything cool has happened already? I know you were just talking about music, but it feels like everything good in my life has happened already too. The best I can wish for is to spend the rest of my life thinking about the past. And what kind of a life is that, wishing the whole time it could go backward?

But maybe it doesn't have to be that way. Maybe I don't have to waste all that time. Maybe I can be with you sooner. Maybe I can be with you now.

Love,

Evie

thirty-four.

I GUESS THIS IS WHAT PEOPLE WOULD CALL A BEAUTIFUL day. The sun is shining and the air is warm. But this beach is still covered in dog shit and garbage. There's the dead seagull from—When was I here last? Yesterday? This morning? I can't even keep track of my own life anymore. The bird is slightly more decayed. Flies have picked it apart a little more. Soon it will be just brittle bones that will sink into the sand.

I wish it was night. I wish it was dark. All this sun and cheerful blue sky and puffy white clouds feel like an insult. I sit on a piece of driftwood and take my boots off. I bury my feet in the sand, feel it cool between my toes. The sensation sends a shiver up my legs, into the parts of me that are broken, the sick bone removed and replaced with something stronger, indestructible. I wiggle my toes and feel this texture created by time, by years of water lapping against stone, softening it, breaking it down to tiny, crystalline pieces. Even the hardest things are porous. Even the sharpest rock can be smoothed by wind and waves. Fire makes rock, but it is the other elements that shape it.

The world shifts and I realize the pills I took a half hour ago have finally kicked in. Relief spreads through me and I am suddenly warm. Suddenly, life doesn't feel like such a huge disaster. I missed this. God, how I missed this. My despair fizzles into nothingness and evaporates into thin air. I am free. I am boundless.

I look at my toes and wonder how they're even moving, how the signal from my brain can make it all the way down my body. How is this even possible, when that seagull is decaying, eaten by tiny bacteria; when Caleb and Stella were so big, so strong, yet lost their wars against microscopic viruses? How is it possible that I am here and they are not?

All of this time, all of these days of self-destruction since I've been out of the hospital, I don't even know what I've been fighting. God, fate, science—whatever I choose to call it doesn't change the fact that I survived and they didn't. No one chose for that to happen. No person decided whose life was worth saving and whose life was expendable. I don't know who I'm angry with. I don't know who to blame. I don't know who to rage against for this injustice.

The answer is nobody. It is not for me to know why certain people are taken and some survive, and my destroying myself is never going to answer that question. My being gone will never bring them back. I can let myself be consumed by fury, by loss, but the waves will keep dancing against the rocks and turning them into sand, life will keep changing forms, and I am powerless to stop any of it.

And I don't want to. The world is complicated and painful, but it is still a place where toes can wiggle in sand, where people can love each other enough to tell them hard things, where people can be forgiven. The only thing that can ever be counted on is change, transformation. I have been transformed. I can be transformed again.

I miss them. I miss them so much. Stella, Caleb, you are being turned into sand. The world is rubbing against you and turning you into something new and small and precious. It's a miracle, all of it. My feet, my legs, my lungs, my heart. My memories of you. The love inside me, lapping against my ribs.

I know I am high, but this feels like clarity.

I don't want to be that girl, that tragedy, that statistic. My life is worth more than that. I lived through cancer and I'll live through this, whatever this is. I will stop burying my fear in the sand. I will say I was wrong. I will tell everyone I love them—Marcus, Mom, Dad, Jenica, Kasey, Will, everyone. I will stop pushing them away. I will accept help. I will stop fighting. I will be still. I will let myself be transformed again.

I text Marcus: *I'm sorry. Meet me at the beach. I love you.*

I walk to the edge of the water and throw the rest of my pills in.

My feet are alive with the pain of sharp rocks digging in. But this pain will make my skin strong. I will build calluses.

Someday I will be able to run across the beach.

I take off my shirt and throw it behind me. I pull off my pants. I look at the scars on my hip, my leg. I will have them for the rest of my life. They will always be there as a reminder of what I survived, of how hard I fought. Every time I look at them I will remember to be grateful. I should not have survived, but I did anyway. And I cannot waste that. I cannot take it for granted. It would be an insult to Stella and Caleb. It would be an insult to their fight.

I step into the water and gasp at how cold it is. I know it's dirty, tainted with agricultural runoff, city storm drains, and industrial junk, but still, I feel cleansed as I walk farther in. The cold water makes my thoughts and senses sharp. It washes away my pain and all the stupid things I've done, all the hurt I've caused the people I love. It washes me and makes me new so I can start over. I wade in deeper and my body shudders. Is this what it feels like to be reborn? I lay on my back and let the water hold me. It can break apart rocks, but it can also cradle me like this. We can be so many things at once.

I am suspended and full of peace. I look at the sky, at the great blue-and-white blanket, and I feel safe. There is a place for me under this sky, a place for me in this world. And as soon as I'm finished floating, I will start figuring out where I belong. But the floating feels so good. The clouds are down pillows, falling, falling, lighting upon my body, my face, my nose, my—

No, this is not what peace feels like. Why can't my feet touch the ground? Why can't I breathe? Why does my body feel so numb? Why is it not doing what my brain wants it to? Why are the clouds that are supposed to be in the sky in my head now?

The pills. In the cab. I took so many pills.

I try to swim. I kick and flap my arms. I am such a good swimmer. Sandy the physical therapist said I am such a good swimmer. But I am not moving. The shore is no closer. Why does it feel like something's pulling me down? My lungs are full of cold. Which way is the shore? Which way is the sky and the earth and the water and all of the things that are supposed to hold me?

I hear someone, a voice. A sound like birds, like angels. Stella, is that you?

Marcus, where are you?

I see the sky through moving glass. I am slipping. I'm falling in slow motion. I'm a feather on the wind.

The world is so beautiful; I didn't see it until now. All of my friends and family, both here and gone, all of them, beautiful.

Everyone, I'm sorry. I'm going to make it up to you. I'm going to make my life worth something.

Stella, keep singing. Stella, I'm listening.

Marcus, I'm waiting for you. Let's start a new kind of adventure.

Are these your arms around me? Why are you screaming?

I love you. I love you. I love you. I love

Evie's and Marcus's stories continue in book two,

UNFORGIVABLE

Coming in Summer 2016

Acknowledgments

Thank you, as always, to my fearless agent and tireless cheerleader, Amy Tipton.

Anica Rissi, my brilliant editor and collaborator, who gets me like no other. Thank you for believing in me all these years, and for taking me with you on this new adventure. It is an honor to have been chosen.

My husband, Brian, who keeps me sane throughout this crazy business. Thank you for keeping me grounded, and for helping me keep an eye on the forest when all I want to do is inspect every little tree. Thank you for holding my hand during the part where I thrash around and want to give up.

My daughter, Elouise, who gives me a reason to do everything.

Very special thanks to the following:

Cheri Gillies, friend and nurse, for sharing your knowledge of pediatric oncology, prescription painkillers, cancer treatment, hospital jargon, and all things medical.

Melinda Krigel, Media Relations Manager, Children's Hospital & Research Center Oakland, for your generosity and enthusiasm in helping me with this book.

Suzanne Berks, Child Life Oncology Specialist, Children's Hospital & Research Center Oakland, for taking the time to meet with me and discuss the amazing work you do.

And a big thank-you to everyone who dedicates their life to healing children. The depth of your hearts astounds me.